Seraph of the End

Guren Ichinose: Catastrophe at Sixteen

1

Story by Takaya Kagami
Art by Yamato Yamamoto

Translated by James Balzer

VERTICAL.

First published in Japan in 2013 by Kodansha, Ltd., Tokyo
Publication for this English edition arranged through Kodansha, Ltd., Tokyo
English language version produced by Vertical, Inc.

Art by Yamato Yamamoto.

Originally published in Japanese as
Owari no Serafu - Ichinose Guren, 16-sai no Hametsu 1 and *2.*

This is a work of fiction.

ISBN: 978-1-941220-98-6

Manufactured in the United States of America

First Edition

Third Printing

Vertical, Inc.
451 Park Avenue South
7th Floor
New York, NY 10016
www.vertical-inc.com

Book One

When I was young, I was sure all of my dreams would come true.

I could be with the person I love. I could have the things I wanted.

I could live happy.

It all seemed so easy.

It really did.

"Guren?"

" ... "

"Hey Guren? Guren Ichinose?"

"Yeah?"

"When we get older..."

" ... "

"...do you think the two of us could get married?"

" ... "

"We could be together, forever, just like we are now."

She held my hand as she spoke. We were sitting on a fresh, green lawn. The sky above us was perfectly clear, without a cloud in sight.

She was sitting so close I could hear her breathe. I liked the sound. I liked her voice. I liked listening to her heart beating next to mine. I liked everything about her.

Which is why I didn't look at her when I answered.

"That can't happen."

"But why not?" she said. Her voice trembled when she spoke.

"You know why," I said.

"Is it…because of my family?

"I belong to a minor clan. You belong to the head clan. You might even lead it someday. We're from two different stations."

"But…why does that matter—"

"Because it does," I said, cutting her off.

She was quiet after that. I think she might have been crying. She knew it was the truth. She knew it deep down. The sound of her breathing grew ragged, and she gripped my hand tight. As tight as she could.

That's when we heard someone, shouting in the distance.

"She's over here!"

"Lady Mahiru!"

"She's with that brat from the Ichinose Clan again! He must have tricked her into coming out with him!"

"Ichinose brat! Learn your place!"

I lifted my head up as they approached.

"They came to get you," I said.

Her ashen hair fell around her face. I was right, she had been crying.

"I… I want to stay with Guren," she told them, still holding my hand tight.

"…"

"I… I…"

I don't know what she said after that. She was still speaking, but I couldn't hear her anymore.

I had been punched.

The adults who had come to get her began pummeling me with their fists.

"Stop! Please, stop it!!" screamed Mahiru.

But they didn't stop.

They just kept shouting and hitting me.

"It's time to teach you a lesson, you little mutt!"

"We're gonna flatten you! You Ichinose scum aren't fit to kiss our shoes!"

"We'll kill you, you punk!"

Mahiru. I stared at my friend through swollen eyes as the blows continued to rain down on me. I belonged to a lowly branch clan. But from my place, down in the dirt, Mahiru shone like the sun.

"Stop it! Please, leave him alone!"

For a moment, everything went black.

They must have hit me so hard I lost consciousness.

I remember the tangy copper smell of blood.

Above me, the sky was broad and blue and clear.

And the grass was so soft.

When I was young, I was sure all of my dreams would come true...

That I could be with the person I love...

That I could have the things I wanted...

That I could live happy...

It had all seemed so easy...

It really had...

"...power," I muttered, as I fell to the grass, my hands clenched in fists. "I'll never get the things I want in life...unless I have power..."

When I was finally able to lift my head again, they were already dragging Mahiru away. She cried as they left with her, and stared back at me as they went.

She was begging me to forgive her. Over and over she cried that she was sorry.

I'm sorry.

It's all my fault, I'm sorry.

But Mahiru had done nothing wrong.

It was my fault. For not having more power. For being born into such a lowly clan.

"..."

I stretched my hand out as I watched her go.

Up toward the sky.

Up toward the sun.

Up toward Mahiru.

And I began to think. About how much farther I would need to reach, before my arms were long enough to latch onto my dreams...

◆

But almost before I knew it, a whole decade of tomorrows had passed.

Chapter One

Welcome to High School, Jerk

"Master Guren, high school starts today. You're going to be a freshman. Do you think you're ready?"

"..."

"T-T-To be honest...I'm feeling kinda nervous. I mean, I'm supposed to be your bodyguard so I know that sounds silly. But...But...I can't help it! We're your followers, we live to serve the Ichinose clan... But we're going to be attending First Shibuya High School. It's hard not to get a little freaked out!"

The girl continued speaking, but Guren Ichinose ignored her. He was staring up at the sky.

Cherry blossom petals were dancing in the air.

It was spring.

The first day of the new school year.

Guren wore a school uniform with a stiff, high collar. He thrust both his hands into his pockets as he walked beneath the trees. They were on the long road leading to First Shibuya High School, where Guren was about to become a student.

Guren had black hair, with a slight wave. There was just a hint of coldness to his eyes. Those eyes were now directed toward the girl next to him. She was still chattering away.

The girl was fifteen—the same age as Guren—and about 5'3" tall. She was wearing a sailor-suit school uniform, and had wheat-colored hair. In contrast to her awkward babbling, she had a very pretty face.

Her name was Sayuri Hanayori.

Sayuri pressed a hand nervously to her chest. The more she spoke, the more flustered she seemed to become.

"So…you see…I know I'm inexperienced, but I promise I'll try my hardest to be a good bodyguard for you while we're here, Master Guren! If there's anything you need, anything at all—"

"Sayuri?" said Guren, cutting her off.

"Y-Yes…Master Guren!"

"You're babbling again."

"Augh!!" Sayuri threw both her hands into the air. A shocked expression appeared on her face.

"F-F-Forgive me, Master Guren!"

Sayuri fell into line behind Guren. She looked crestfallen. Every few seconds she sniffled loudly. Another girl was already following Guren, faithfully, from behind. Sayuri leaned in close to the girl.

"Sh-Shigure… He just scolded me. He said I was babbling."

The other girl's name was Shigure Yukimi.

Shigure glanced over at Sayuri. Shigure was small—less than five feet tall—and had a tiny frame. Unlike Sayuri she seemed very composed. She wore a stone-faced expression.

Shigure was also fifteen. She had been training under the Ichinose Clan for years, as one of Guren's bodyguards.

"That's because you *were* babbling," she said. Her expression didn't change.

"What?!"

"If you don't start acting calmer it will reflect poorly on the Ichinose Clan. And not just the clan, either. Remember, Master Guren is next in line to be head of the clan. Pull yourself together, before you make him look bad."

"Oh no, Shigure! Don't you team up on me, too!" cried Sayuri.

Together, the two were even louder than Sayuri had been on her own.

Guren glanced back at his two servants, who were both the same age as he was.

"Ahh…"

Guren sighed in exasperation before turning his eyes forward again.

The road to First Shibuya stretched out before him. Overhead, cherry blossoms drifted playfully in the air.

There were other students walking in small groups, chatting and laughing boisterously with one another.

At first glance it looked like a typical high school scene. However…

I can't blame Sayuri, thought Guren. *Walking along this road would be enough to freak almost anyone out.*

The truth was, it was no ordinary high school they were headed toward.

It was a foul and dangerous place, where demons and dark magic held sway.

It was First Shibuya High School.

First Shibuya High School was a special school, run by a religious sect known as the Order of the Imperial Demons. The school specialized in training magic users.

Of course, none of this was public knowledge. On the surface, First Shibuya High School appeared for all intents and purposes to be an ordinary school. The truth was that nearly every student at the school was the son or daughter of a clan that belonged to the order and believed in its teachings.

It wasn't enough to simply be a member of the order, however. First Shibuya was also a school for the elite. It was only open to the best and brightest of students, chosen from adherents throughout Japan.

That was First Shibuya High School's dark secret. In other words…

"…anyone here could be a threat."

Guren stared at the other students. They all seemed excited over the start of school. Shigure stepped forward and began walking next to Guren. She scanned the crowd once and then laughed condescendingly.

"I doubt any of these pint-sized Imperial Demon brats have as

much power in their whole body as you have in one little finger, Master Guren."

"Th-That's right!" chimed in Sayuri. "Those Hiragis think they're so high and mighty. We should show them what the future head of the Ichinose Clan can do. Why don't you give them all a good walloping, Master Guren?"

The Hiragi Clan were the leaders of the Order of the Imperial Demons. They had ruled over the order ever since it was first established, 1,200 years ago.

The Ichinose Clan had split off from the Hiragi Clan around 500 years ago, forming the Order of the Imperial Moon. The relationship between the two sects had been strained ever since.

Unfortunately, the Hiragi Clan dwarfed the Ichinose Clan, both in terms of size and power. As a result, the Ichinose Clan dared not defy the Hiragi Clan. At least, not openly.

"The only reason we're coming to this school is because they want to get the next leader of the Ichinose Clan on their turf, while he's still young. They just want you under their thumb," said Shigure.

Shigure was a faithful servant of the Ichinose Clan.

"It shows how weak they really are," she went on. "The Hiragis are on their way out, and they know it."

"Exactly!" said Sayuri. "I was thinking the exact same thing. Don't worry, Master Guren. I bet we could mop the floor with anyone else here!"

"I'm not the one who's worried," said Guren, turning his head toward Sayuri. "You're the one making all the fuss."

"Augh!"

"As for you, Shigure…" said Guren, staring down at the top of her head.

"Yes, sir?"

"You just referred to the Hiragis as pint-sized brats a moment ago…"

"Oh…forgive me, Master Guren. I spoke out of turn. Sometimes the Hiragi Clan makes me so mad that I get carried away…"

"It's not your manners I'm complaining about."

"Then what is it?" asked Shigure, tilting her head.

"If we're judging by appearance," said Guren, still staring down at her, "you're the only one here who looks pint-sized to me."

"Ah!"

Although she was usually so stone-faced, Shigure blushed slightly and bit down on her lower lip.

"I think you just said that because you know how upset I get about my size."

"Haha. Actually, I said it because you two are underestimating the Hiragi Clan. I'm gonna repeat this one more time. Don't get reckless. Not even for a second. We have to be on our guard at all times. Apart from us three, no one at this school is loyal to the Imperial Moon. They're all enemies. Every single one."

What Guren said was true. They were deep in enemy territory. In contrast, the other students all had the powerful support of the Hiragi Clan behind them.

That was a given, though. Because they were on their way to First Shibuya High School.

It was their first day at a school completely controlled by their enemies.

Shigure and Sayuri clenched their jaws in apprehension.

Maybe they had finally noticed how many pairs of eyes were directed their way. Or how many students were whispering about them behind their backs.

—What are they doing here…

—Look at the pins on their uniforms. Those aren't Imperial Demon pins…

—It's those filthy Ichinoses. Remember? They're letting charity cases into our school this year…

The whispers spread like wildfire among the other students.

Guren raised his head warily.

He could feel them staring. There were at least a hundred pairs of eyes on him. Those eyes were cold, full of mockery and undisguised contempt.

"They're all laughing at us," said Shigure.

"You'll get used to it," said Guren. "Don't react."

"But…"

"I said don't react. As long as we're here, we keep our heads low and hide how powerful we are. There's no reason to get carried away and act like children. We don't want to tip our hands."

Guren turned toward his two followers, raised his eyebrows, and flashed them a private grin.

Neither of the two seemed very happy with the idea. But it had been Guren's plan all along.

They were going to keep their strength hidden so long as they were students at the school.

In particular, there were magical techniques that had been developed in secret by the Ichinose Clan and which only they could use. Guren wasn't going to let the Hiragi Clan get a glimpse at those.

"…"

THWACK.

Something suddenly hit Guren in the head, while he was still facing Sayuri and Shigure.

It was a plastic soda bottle. Someone had thrown it at his head. The cap had been left open. Guren turned around. His head and shoulders were soaked in sticky soda.

"Master Guren!" shouted Sayuri.

"Those snakes," hissed Shigure, tensing up in preparation to attack.

Guren placed a hand on her shoulder to hold her back.

"Leave this to me," he said. He couldn't see the look on her face. Instead, he raised a hand to his own head, grinning sheepishly so that all the other students could see.

"Geez, that hurt, guys."

The other students burst into huge guffaws of laughter. They were all allies of the Hiragi Clan.

—You gotta be kidding me!

—What a weakling! Do you think he'll cry?

—What did you expect from an Ichinose?

Guren wasn't sure who had thrown the bottle. He didn't really care. After all, they were all his enemies. Every single one.

For now, Guren let them laugh and jeer.

"Sayuri? Shigure?" he said, calling his two followers to his side.

"Yes?"

"What is it, sir?"

Their voices were shaky as they answered. It did seem unfair. They were there to protect Guren. Instead, he was being ridiculed. It was hard for them not to feel sad.

Guren blamed himself for their sadness. If only he was more powerful they wouldn't have to feel that way.

If Guren had possessed enough strength to crush the Hiragi Clan in one blow—if the Ichinose Clan had enough power to defy the Hiragi Clan—they wouldn't need to put themselves through this charade.

He turned back toward Sayuri and Shigure once more.

"I'm sorry. I know this will be hard. But it's only for three years. Do you think you can stick it out with me until then?"

Sayuri and Shigure both looked ready to cry. *Don't give them the satisfaction…* thought Guren. Luckily, they both lifted their chins up and bravely took a step forward toward Guren.

"O-O-Of course, Master Guren. I only live to serve!" cried Sayuri.

Guren planted a palm on her head and pushed her backward.

"Don't get carried away, now," he said.

"B-B-But…"

"…it's true, we live to serve. This isn't fair," Shigure chimed in. "If you could use your magic you'd show them all. Everyone says you're the most powerful Ichinose to be born in a thousand years."

"A thousand years, huh? Who's been saying that?"

"My…my father said it."

"Samidare?"

"Yes, sir. All the other clan leaders in the Imperial Moon, too. They say you've got the kind of gift that only comes once in a millennium, and that they'd risk their lives to protect you—"

Guren interrupted her.

"I didn't know everyone thought so highly of me."

"They do, sir."

"But next time you see those old geezers?"

"Sir?"

"Tell them they're off their rockers. How can I be the most powerful Ichinose in a thousand years when the Ichinose Clan has only existed for five hundred? They're probably so senile they forgot how to count."

"H-Haha, I guess you've got a point," said Shigure. Her face twisted up into a smirk.

"If I'm not mistaken, Shigure, I think you just smiled for a change," Sayuri said, laughing.

At the very least, both girls seemed to have calmed down. Guren gave them one last meaningful look before turning around. Most of the other students had already dispersed. School would be starting soon.

They must have figured they'd wasted enough time picking on some Ichinose weakling.

The only ones left behind were Guren—who was now soaked in cola from the bottle that had been thrown at him—and his two followers.

"C'mon, let's go," he said.

"Master Guren…" said Shigure.

"Yeah?"

"We're your bodyguards. We're supposed to protect you. But in the end, you're the one who protected us. I'm sorry…"

"Don't be stupid. It's a leader's duty to protect his followers."

"S-Sir!" said Shigure, pursing her lips and growing quiet.

Sayuri suddenly interrupted the moment by screaming at the top of her lungs.

"Hey, Shigure? Shigure? Your face is all red. Why is your face so red? Are you blushing?"

"Sh-Shut your mouth!"

"Ow, ow! Shigure! Hey! Stop hitting me!"

It's going to be a long three years, thought Guren. He began walking toward the school again, with a grimace on his face.

Guren could see the school ahead. Technically they were already on school grounds. The area was off limits to ordinary people.

The road to the school stretched out before them. It was long and straight, and lined along the way with cherry trees.

It ended at the school's gate. Someone else, however, was already there. A lone boy, about Guren's age.

He had striking, snow-white hair, and was dressed in the same uniform as all the other students.

The corner of his mouth twisted in a wry smile. He was definitely staring at Guren.

The boy raised his hand.

His right hand.

There was a slip of paper between his fingertips. Guren recognized it immediately. It was a *fuda*—a paper charm with a spell inscribed upon it. The spell was Hiragi Clan magic. The *fuda* disappeared suddenly in a burst of flame.

And a tiny spark of lightning appeared in its place.

It was fast. Whoever the boy was, he was skilled. Perhaps he was even a member of the Hiragi Clan, itself…

…but I can dodge it.

Guren sized up the attack in an instant.

I can even counterattack.

The synapses in Guren's brain began firing, making rapid calculations. Which way to move. What stance to take. Once he had factored all the variables…

…Guren made his move.

Immediately, he turned his gaze to the right, away from the flash of lightning. In fact, he turned around almost entirely, toward his two followers. It looked as if he hadn't even seen the spell coming.

The lightning bolt struck him while his back was turned.

Guren heard a tiny sound, like a twig cracking. The next thing he knew his entire body was being thrown through the air.

"Nggh!"

For a moment, the force of the attack caused everything to go black.

When Guren's head finally cleared, he realized he was sprawled on the ground. It took him a moment before he could move again.

Sayuri and Shigure were shouting something. Their voices sounded like they were coming from far away. Guren's eyes fluttered open, and he stared up at them in a daze. They both looked ready to burst into tears.

That was a close call.

It was. Not because he had been hit, but because he had almost dodged the spell without thinking. That would have revealed to the other boy how powerful Guren really was.

But had Guren's act really been convincing enough? Had he fooled his attacker into believing that he was too slow and weak to react?

"…"

More importantly, thought Guren, as he waited for his body to recover, *if this were a real fight would I be able to defeat him?*

Sayuri, meanwhile, was cradling Guren's head in her lap.

"Master Guren! Master Guren!" she called in tears.

"Sayuri? Your breasts are on my face…" said Guren.

"Augh!"

Shigure, meanwhile, was scanning the gate with her eyes. She stood in front of Guren, protectively.

"Master Guren, forgive me. I should have been faster."

"It's not your fault," said Guren. "I let the spell hit me on purpose."

"What?!"

"Do you know where the attack came from? Were you able to react right away? That makes it look like you're stronger than me. That gives me an idea. I want you to pretend that I'm just a useless weakling, and that I need you two to protect me."

"But…"

Guren began to sit up. He held his head gingerly between his hands.

"Geez, what just happened?" he said.

For a moment Shigure look confused, then she pointed stiffly toward the gate.

"An attack, Master Guren. It came from that direction," she said.

She sounded like she was reading from a script.

Guren didn't turn toward the gate until Shigure pointed in its direction.

The boy was still standing there. He was staring directly at Guren, and the smirk was still on his face.

"Crap…" groaned Guren. "I'm not sure he bought it."

However, the boy just shrugged his shoulders and turned around, heading back into the school. Guren watched him walk away.

"We better go, too," he said.

"But you're injured…" said Sayuri.

"Huh?" Guren touched his hand to his face. He seemed to be bleeding. He tentatively licked the blood off his hand.

"Ha. Tastes like cola. Bring me a change of clothes."

"I'll go right away," said Shigure.

"And look into whoever it was who attacked me," added Guren. "I want to know who he is. He seems strong. We'll need to watch him."

"Sir!"

Shigure nodded and began walking in the opposite direction, away from the school.

"All right then, time for class," said Guren.

Sayuri, however, was still staring at him sheepishly.

"I-I-I'm sorry, sir. I wasn't very much help…"

"You're helping plenty just by being here with me."

"…"

"Remember, we're in the heart of enemy territory. I wouldn't have brought you if you weren't one of my most trusted allies. So wipe that frown off your face, okay?"

Sayuri blushed, and then grew flustered.

"A-Ah… M-M-My life is yours, Master Guren!"

"Didn't I just tell you not to get carried away?"

"Augh!"

Guren pushed Sayuri away again. He couldn't help but laugh at her anxious expression. The two began walking toward the school.

"All right, enough fooling around. Let's go. I have a feeling this is going to be an interesting school year."

And so, Guren Ichinose, age fifteen, began his first day as a promising new high school student.

Chapter Two

King of the Classroom

Homeroom.

It was a typical classroom scene.

" ... "

Guren sat silently at his desk. He was in Class 1-9. His desk was at the very back of the room, by the window.

It was morning homeroom, on the first day of school. A woman, who appeared to be their teacher, was telling them about the entrance ceremony that would take place later in the day.

Sayuri and Shigure were not in Guren's class.

Sayuri was in Class 1-1 and Shigure was in Class 1-2. Someone had clearly arranged to have them placed in the two classrooms farthest away from Guren.

"Why am I not surprised?" muttered Guren.

After all, as the future head of the Ichinose Clan, Guren had only been brought to the school so that the Hiragi Clan could show off their power. They were going to try to cow Guren into submission.

They'll try to isolate me, bully me, and make me obedient, thought Guren. *It's the same kind of dirty tricks they've been pulling for the last two hundred years.*

Guren laughed under his breath.

Twenty-five years ago, Guren's father had attended this very same school. The Hiragis had worn him down into total submission. Whether Guren's father liked or disliked the Hiragis no longer entered into the equation. Whenever there were any important decisions to make, he would visit the Hiragi Clan first to get their approval.

The rest of the Order of the Imperial Moon had a very poor opinion of Guren's father.

Guren, however, didn't blame his father for the way he ran things. It was just how things were. Guren still had total respect for the man.

His father knew his own limitations, and was doing the best that he could under the circumstances. He had managed to keep the organization running smoothly and without conflict. That was an achievement, in and of itself.

But Guren still remembered.

"…"

The day he had last seen Mahiru. When Guren had still been a child.

Men from the Hiragi Clan had come and beaten Guren senseless. He had returned home bloody and bruised that day.

Guren remembered the look of sorrow on his father's face.

"Please forgive your old man for being so powerless…" he had said.

Guren was badly injured. With tears in his eyes, Guren's father had held him in his arms. But afterward he went directly to the Hiragi Clan compound to apologize.

They had beaten his own son to a pulp. But he was the one to apologize.

"…"

Guren lifted his head, coming out of his reverie.

He scanned the classroom with his eyes. There were forty students in all.

The class was split, fifty-fifty, between boys and girls.

Looking at the roll sheet, Guren saw that many of the students were from the highest-ranking clans in the order.

The Jujo Clan.

The Goshi Clan.

The Sangu Clan.

They were some of the most prestigious families in the magic-using world.

Once upon a time the Ichinose Clan had been foremost among the clans serving the Hiragis. Now the opposite was true. The Ichinose Clan occupied the very lowest rung of power.

The clans operated on a strict caste system. Most of the other students glared at Guren out of the corner of their eyes. They clearly resented him for being placed in their class. Their hostility was palpable.

"Attention, everyone," said the teacher. "As of today you are students at First Shibuya High School, the most prestigious of all magical academies. As the very best of the best, I expect great things from each of you during your time here."

The teacher paused mid-speech. She glanced at Guren with a mischievous gleam in her eyes.

"Of course, a certain mangy dog has also managed to sneak its way into this room of upstanding young men and women. But don't let that bother you. This class is for the elite, and as the most capable and accomplished students at this school, it is your responsibility to teach such mongrels their place."

The "mongrel," of course, was Guren.

The students laughed. Not all of them, but nearly so.

Guren grinned along with them like a fool.

As he did so, however, he sized up the teacher. She was quick to ridicule Guren. But was she more powerful?

Guren didn't mind being ridiculed.

He was already prepared for that.

But one thing he couldn't accept was being bested, in terms of strength and spellcasting ability.

In the end, Guren's goals in life were different from his father's.

Guren's father had focused on keeping the organization peaceful and safe. Guren had other aspirations.

" . . . "

The foolish grin remained plastered on Guren's face as his eyes roamed over the other students.

He spotted the girl from the Jujo Clan.

The boy from the Goshi Clan.

Even a girl from the Sangu Clan.

But there was one student in the class who occupied a higher position than all of them combined. Guren had recognized the name the moment he saw the roll sheet.

That student's name...

...was Shinya Hiragi.

A Hiragi. A member of the Hiragi Clan.

The Hiragi name held special power for members of the Order of the Imperial Demons. It was an object of reverence. To the Imperial Demons, a Hiragi was a god among men.

To the Order of the Imperial Demons, the Hiragi name was as important as the Ichinose name was to the Order of the Imperial Moon. They looked up to the Hiragis in the same way Shigure and Sayuri looked up to Guren.

Shinya Hiragi's seat, however, was still empty.

Shinya's desk had been placed as far away from Guren's—as far away from the filthy mongrel's—as possible.

In other words, in the front row next to the entrance.

"As you're probably all aware," said the teacher, "Lord Shinya will also be a student in this class. We are truly fortunate to be graced with his presence..."

The teacher continued to gush about how amazing Shinya Hiragi was and how lucky they were to be in the same class as him.

The other students nodded, listening with dreamy expressions on their faces as the teacher talked about Shinya. It was hard to believe that only moments ago those same faces had been twisted up in contempt as they laughed at the "mongrel."

The change was so obvious that Guren couldn't help but snicker.

He turned his eyes back toward the window. He could see the rows of cherry trees which grew outside the gates.

"I hope Shigure and Sayuri are okay," he muttered, staring at the trees.

Just then, the classroom door opened. A hush fell over the students. They all seemed to sit up straighter.

"It's so quiet in here. What is this, a funeral?"

The voice came from the back entrance of the room, not the front. It was a male voice.

The teacher seemed nervous as she answered.

"Ah, L-Lord Shinya, good morning. Welcome to my classroom... We've prepared a seat for you, up here by the front—"

"No way," interrupted Shinya, "I don't wanna be stuck up front."

"B-But..."

"I'd rather sit over there. You, there. You don't mind switching seats with me, do you?"

"But that...that's..."

The way they were all acting, you would think the king of England had just made an appearance. Apparently the great Hiragi had finally shown up. Guren lifted his head and turned his eyes back toward the class.

He was a little surprised by what he saw.

It was the same boy who had attacked him with a *fuda* outside the gate that morning.

He had white hair, and was dressed in a school uniform with a high collar just like Guren's. Despite the friendly grin on his face, there was a sharp glint to his eyes. His smile was full of confidence.

Apparently, Guren's attacker had been Shinya Hiragi.

I guess I didn't need to have Shigure go to the trouble of looking into him, after all.

Shinya walked toward Guren's seat. He flashed his confident grin at the girl sitting at the desk next to Guren's.

"I'd rather sit here. You don't mind switching, do you?"

The girl was so shocked that Shinya spoke to her that for a moment she froze.

"O-O-Of course! It would be my pleasure!" she stuttered, leaping up from her seat.

"But Lord Shinya," said the teacher, "surely you don't want to sit next to that...that mongrel—"

Shinya cut her off.

"Do you really think it's appropriate for a teacher to refer to her own students as mongrels?" he said, staring at her from under hooded eyes.

"I..."

"This is one of our classmates. Part of your job is to promote class spirit."

"But..."

The girl who had been sitting at the desk quickly moved out of the way. Shinya thanked her and sat down in the now vacant seat. He was all smiles.

"Please, I didn't mean to interrupt," he said. "Continue with what you were saying."

Flustered, the teacher returned to her podium and resumed speaking. She was explaining the entrance ceremony, what they would be learning, and the school's lesson structure. She was acting more like a scolded child than their teacher.

Shinya listened attentively. His smile was beaming.

Guren turned his gaze out the window once more.

"Hey, you..." whispered Shinya, suddenly. "You're Guren Ichinose, right? Mind if I just call you Guren?"

Guren turned back around. Shinya was leaning in close, smiling.

"I'm sorry, were you speaking just now?" asked Guren.

"You're so polite," laughed Shinya.

"The Ichinose Clan has been very strict in teaching me the importance of obeying the Hiragi Clan," said Guren.

"Is that so?"

"It is."

"Well, that's no fun."

"A thousand apologies," said Guren, bowing his head. It didn't seem like Shinya had anything more to say, so Guren turned his head to look out the window once more. A moment later, however, Shinya spoke up again.

"By the way," he said, "this morning, you didn't by any chance let my attack hit you on purpose, did you?"

"…"

"For instance, in order to hide your true strength?"

"…"

"Because that would seem pretty disobedient. Wouldn't it? Insubordinate, even…"

Dammit. Shinya had seen through his act, after all.

"I apologize," said Guren, turning toward Shinya.

"You admit it, then?"

"I wasn't trying to be insubordinate. It's just that my family told me to always obey the Hiragis, and not to make anyone angry. The truth is I let the attack hit me to avoid any trouble. I wasn't trying to hide anything."

"Hmm, is that so?"

"It is."

"I see…" Shinya replied with a perfunctory smile. Then he suddenly leaned in, uncomfortably close, and whispered into Guren's ear, "Hey, Guren. Drop the act already, huh?"

"What act?" said Guren, peering into Shinya's face innocently.

"Fine, fine," said Shinya, pulling back. "But it seems a shame. I was looking forward to meeting you. I was hoping the two of us could be friends."

"…"

"I hate the Hiragis just as much as you do, Guren. I figured the two of us might be able to stir up some trouble together."

"…"

"Speaking of which, did you know that I'm not even really a Hiragi? I was adopted. They've been grooming me ever since I was a kid to become a Hiragi. It's why I hate them. So you see, the two of us actually have a lot in common."

Guren had heard similar stories before. Supposedly, in order to create offspring with strong magic in their blood, the Hiragi Clan searched for gifted children and then forced them to undergo difficult training. Those who survived the selection process were later adopted by the clan.

The adopted children were then forced to marry and have children with members from the Hiragi bloodline.

Those stories had been around for as long as Guren could remember.

But even if they were true, there was no way for Guren to know whether Shinya was really one of those children. And even if he was, there was still no reason for Guren to reveal himself. Guren considered his answer carefully.

"I think there's been a mistake. I'm not the kind of person you think I am…"

…was what Guren was going to say. Before he could, however, Shinya spoke again.

"Did you know, the person they're planning to marry me to is Mahiru. Mahiru Hiragi. They've been grooming me to be her fiancé ever since I was born."

Guren reacted without meaning to, glancing sharply at Shinya. Shinya noticed immediately.

"Ohh, I think I just got a peek at the real Guren," he said, laughing.

"I don't know what you're talking about."

"Don't you? Fine, fine, whatever you say. After all, I didn't expect us to be best buddies from day one."

"…"

"By the way, you know that Mahiru is a freshman here too, don't you? Top of the class. She's our class representative. Apparently she's going to give a speech later. Impressive, isn't it? After all, she's your ex-girlfriend…"

"I don't know what you mean," said Guren, careful not to show any emotion. "There's nothing between me and Mahiru."

"Not anymore, I suppose. After all, she's my fiancée."

Guren clenched his jaw involuntarily, and glared straight ahead. The expression wasn't lost on Shinya. He laughed again, flashing his handsome smile.

"Does it make you jealous?" he asked, trying to provoke Guren.

"Of course not."

"Haha! You should see the look on your face. If you don't want people to suspect you, you're gonna have to try a little harder to hide that ambition. But see? You and me are on the same side. And don't worry about Mahiru. The truth is we aren't that close. Even with the Hiragi name, I'm still just one of their adopted urchins. They treat me like I'm something they stepped in. Basically, the way you get treated at this school is how I get treated at home. It really pisses me off. But someday I'll bring the whole clan falling down on their heads."

It was a dangerous thing to say out loud. If anyone overheard them, Shinya could be executed on the spot.

Was it all a trap? Or did Shinya really want to overthrow the Hiragi Clan? There was no way for Guren to know.

Whether Shinya was speaking the truth or not, it didn't seem wise to get involved with him. Guren decided to change tactics.

"You sure do like the sound of your own voice," he said with a sneer, turning his head away. "Whatever you're after, it's got nothing to do with me. I don't know what you're planning, but how about you leave me the hell out of it?"

"Such language! What happened to being polite?"

"Get lost."

"But we're friends, right? Come on, you and me!"

"I said get lost."

"Ha! All right, have it your way for now," said Shinya, his eyes twinkling. "You'll come around, though. After all, I'm probably your only ally in this whole place."

Guren glanced at Shinya and groaned inwardly. It was only day one—too early to have to deal with so much hassle.

"All right, students," the teacher said just then, "it's almost time for the entrance ceremony to begin. Let's head to the auditorium."

The students stood.

"Here we go," said Shinya. "Time to hear our goddess give her speech."

Goddess? Guren assumed he was referring to Mahiru.

It had been ten years since Guren had last seen Mahiru. The last time he had seen her was that day those adults from the Hiragi Clan had dragged them apart. After hearing her name again, after all these years, Guren wasn't sure how to feel.

But regardless of his feelings, they were about to be in the same hall.

Mahiru was giving a speech as the freshman class representative. Guren had never imagined his next meeting with Mahiru would be under such circumstances.

"All right, partner," said Shinya, reaching his hand out to help up Guren. "Let's go hear that speech."

Guren stared at Shinya's outstretched hand, and then smacked it away with a scowl.

"Just stay away from me, understand?"

"Ha!"

Guren lined up with the other students, and they all headed toward the auditorium.

They were in the auditorium. Every single student from the school was there.

Altogether, there were 1,000 students—600 freshmen, 240 juniors, and 160 seniors.

The reason the number of students decreased each year was because qualifying exams were held several times each term. The exams were actually one-on-one spell duels that pitted student against student. Based on the outcome of the duels students were ranked according to ability. Those deemed too weak to move on to the next grade were expelled.

It was a three-year high school. By the end of freshman year more than half of the students would be cut. Even more students would be let go the following year.

As a result, students at the high school spent nearly all of their time studying or training. First Shibuya's students needed to excel in both spellcraft and martial arts if they wanted to have any chance of surviving elimination.

"I bet there's an exception in my case, though," Guren muttered as he scanned the auditorium full of excited students.

Guren had been required to undergo an exam before being accepted into First Shibuya High School, just like all the other students.

In addition to ordinary subjects such as math, history, and composition, the test also covered magical ability and spellcraft theory.

Guren was careful not to do very well in any subject. None of the questions were very challenging—he could have aced the whole exam in his sleep. The real challenge was figuring out how to answer incorrectly without making it obvious that he was throwing the exam.

He was certain his results were too low to actually qualify for admission.

The people scoring him were probably baffled as to why such a slacker was bothering to apply in the first place. After all, First Shibuya was only for the most elite of the elite.

Despite his test scores, however, Guren had been accepted.

There were other schools where members of the Imperial Demons could study the magical arts. First Shibuya, however, was special. Few students qualified for admission. And yet Guren had been let in.

In other words, his test had been a sham.

It doesn't really matter how bad my grades are, they want me here. I'm just gonna have to put up with being bullied by the other students for the next three years.

Guren stared at the other students, feeling faintly amused. He wondered how long it would be before they all started in on him.

For their own part, the students all seemed to be in high spirits.

They were probably excited over the first day of school. Maybe even anxious about the duels they would be facing. The auditorium buzzed with their conversation.

The principal was standing on the auditorium's stage. He was delivering a longwinded welcome speech. It seemed like it was finally coming to a close.

"...The students I see here today have all been chosen. You have great potential. Those of you who survive the examination process may even be selected for future leadership roles in the Imperial Demons. Remember this, be proud, and enjoy your time here at First Shibuya..."

Waiting for the speech to end, Guren stared up at the principal as the latter spoke.

Suddenly, the girl sitting next to Guren leaned in and brought her mouth to his ear.

"Hey, Ichinose," she said, "I've got a question."

Guren turned his head.

The girl was wearing a sailor-suit school uniform. Since she was sitting next to Guren, he figured she must be in the same class as him.

She had fierce, slanted, almond-shaped eyes and crimson red hair. Her skin was smooth and pale.

"Did you say something?" asked Guren.

The girl sneered haughtily in reply. "Do you see any other filthy Ichinose losers here?"

"Filthy, huh?" said Guren, laughing to himself. He raised his eyebrows in an expression of innocence.

"I'm sorry, who are you?" he said.

The girl gave him an incredulous look.

"I should have expected that from an Ichinose. You're not just rude, you're ignorant too! How can you not know who I am? Look at my hair!"

The girl tossed her red locks over her shoulder.

Obviously, Guren already had a pretty good idea of who the girl was.

She was a member of the Jujo Clan.

Anyone who knew anything about the clans would recognize that red hair.

—Tohito Jujo.

According to legend he had banished a powerful demon single-handedly. In turn, a curse had been placed on his bloodline. Since that time, all Jujo descendants had been born with crimson hair, as red as blood.

The story could be found in every history book of the clans.

One look at the girl's hair was enough to know she belonged to the Jujos. They were one of the oldest and most powerful families supporting the Hiragi Clan. Guren, however, played dumb.

"So what? You're like famous or something? Like a pop star?"

A disgusted look appeared on the girl's face.

"How did someone as stupid as you even get into this school?"

"I must have gotten lucky," said Guren. "I just guessed for most of the questions on the exam."

"It wasn't even a multiple choice exam! Whatever… They probably just let you in because you're going to head the Ichinose Clan. They probably figured it was a chance for you to learn who your betters are."

The girl stared down her nose, contemptuously, at Guren.

"So you're a pop star wannabe," said Guren. "Anyway, did little miss pop princess want something with me?"

"Don't call me that!"

The girl glared at Guren, her face twisted in anger but still pretty, which spoke to her good looks.

"All right, geez, quit shrieking. Just tell me who you are, already."

"It's Mito. Mito Jujo, from the Jujo Clan," she said, staring at Guren with a triumphant smirk. She was probably used to having people grovel at her feet when they heard her name.

"Oh," said Guren.

"Feeling embarrassed?"

"Well…"

"It's all right, you can kneel down and bow if you like. Not that a bow from an ignorant Ichinose would actually mean that much to me."

"Actually…"

"What is it? Are you so excited that a Jujo noticed you that you've forgotten how to speak? Don't worry, I get that all the time…"

"…Actually, I don't know who the Jujos are."

"It's fine, I understand. I'm willing to forgive your insolence, just this… I…I… Wait. What did you just say?"

"I have no idea who the Jujos are."

"You can't be serious. The Jujo Clan?! Descendants of the great Jujo, who sealed away the arch-demon Kaede?!"

"Not a clue."

"I…I…I…"

At a loss for words, the girl sputtered, openmouthed. Her jaw clamped shut and she snapped her head away abruptly. Placing a hand on her small chest, she breathed deeply and shook her red hair.

"Calm down, Mito," she said, laughing haughtily. "Remember that he's just a common Ichinose mongrel. You can hardly expect a dog to have human manners. It's beneath a Jujo to take offense at Ichinose buffoonery."

This girl is nuts, thought Guren.

He stared at her with a raised eyebrow before turning his attention back to the rest of the room.

I wonder if everyone here is crazy.

At the very least, all of the students at First Shibuya had been subjected to intense training in the magic arts ever since they were children. On top of that, they lived in a world of strict hierarchy and castes. Expecting them to have good social skills was probably asking for too much.

"I guess I'm not really the most endearing guy either," muttered Guren, chuckling to himself.

Mito turned on him sharply and said, "What are you laughing about?!"

"Huh? Nothing."

"I bet. I don't know why I bothered talking to someone as ignorant as you in the first place."

"Whatever you say, pop princess…"

"I told you, don't call me that!!" shouted Mito.

This time, Mito's anger got the best of her. Her shout was so loud that it echoed throughout the auditorium.

The principal paused mid-speech, and everyone turned around to stare at her.

Mito grimaced and hunched down in her chair. Her cheeks blushed an even deeper red than her hair.

"S-Sorry," she muttered sheepishly. "Please go on."

The principal stared for another moment, then resumed his speech.

The other students also turned around quickly, without laughing. They had probably recognized Mito's red hair. After all, the Jujos were one of the most powerful and respected of all the clans.

Mito hunched down even further, clearly embarrassed.

"Lucky you," said Guren, as if to console her. "Everyone was looking at you, just like at a real pop star…"

"You shut up before I kill you, Ichinose," she said, punching him in the back. The punch wasn't very strong. Which was only natural, considering how tiny she was. Guren figured she probably used magic to power herself up during fights.

According to the history books, the Jujos used sheer physical strength when fighting demons. They were famous as warriors and soldiers. Many of them served as assassins or guards. Despite her appearance, Mito probably possessed a similar level of power.

Guren glanced at her once more, appraisingly.

He was trying to decide if he was powerful enough to kill her, if it ever came down to that.

His face, however, betrayed no signs of what he was thinking.

"Well?" he said, looking down his nose at her.

"Well, what?"

"You never told me what you wanted. Were you just trying to flirt with me?"

"Flirt?! With you?! Not on your life!"

Mito realized she was shouting again. She quickly lowered her voice. She did seem to get riled up easily.

"I wanted to ask you about Shinya Hiragi," she said.

"Hmph."

"I saw the two of you whispering in class. What were you talking about?"

Guren quickly put the pieces together for himself. Members of the Jujo Clan often served as guards for members of the Hiragi Clan.

Naturally, if she saw Shinya in close conversation with an Ichinose she would want to know why.

"Nothing in particular," answered Guren.

"You're lying. It looked like a pretty serious conversation to me."

"What are you, a stalker?"

"Just tell me what it was you were talking about," she said.

Guren sighed.

"I guess it can't be helped. If you really want to know..."

"Spill it."

"It was guy talk... You know what I mean?"

"No, what?"

"Girls."

"Huh?"

"We were talking about which girls in the class are pretty. By the way, Shinya thinks you're pretty hot. He was talking about asking you over to his place tonight..."

Guren wiggled his eyebrows suggestively.

"Wha... What?!" Mito's face turned beet red. "Y-You're making that up. Aren't you? It's not possible. What...what about Mahiru?"

Apparently, Shinya and Mahiru's engagement was already public knowledge. Everybody else seemed to know.

So why hadn't I ever heard about it before? wondered Guren.

Mito had mentioned the engagement without hesitation. The Ichinose Clan had to know as well. Why hadn't anyone told Guren?

"My dad..." muttered Guren.

A pained expression crossed his face. His father had probably issued a gag order, to keep Guren from finding out.

It was possible that even his two guards, Shigure Yukimi and Sayuri Hanayori, had known about the engagement and hadn't told him.

Shigure and Sayuri had probably even known about today's speech. But they hadn't said a word.

Guren smiled bitterly to himself.

What's wrong with everyone? he thought. *We were five year olds in puppy love. Did they think we were going to elope or something?*

Mito, meanwhile, was still flustered. She began babbling.

"B-Besides, we're of a lower rank than the Hiragis. It would be forbidden for someone from my clan to get involved with a Hiragi. You have to tell Shinya it wouldn't be right. You'll tell him, yes?"

"..."

"I have the deepest respect for Lady Mahiru, as well. Let's just pretend this never happened. Tell him—"

"Hm? You know Mahiru?" said Guren, interrupting her.

Mito's expression suddenly changed from flustered to angry.

"It's *Lady* Mahiru!" said Mito, shouting again. "Show some respect, Ichinose dog!"

"Right, right, *Lady* Mahiru," said Guren, hoping to calm her down. "Do you know Lady Mahiru?"

Mito nodded enthusiastically. She seemed to be bragging.

"Lady Mahiru is so beautiful. And she treats the other houses so kindly, almost like equals. She's really like a goddess."

Mito was the second person to refer to Mahiru as a goddess that day. It seemed like everyone loved Mahiru.

"She's smart, too. And strong. I heard she was first in the class in every single subject on the entrance exam. It's truly an honor for those of us in the Imperial Demons to serve her."

Top of the class. So Mahiru had gotten the highest marks on the entrance exam...

That meant that out of all the other freshmen, Mahiru was the most powerful.

If she's that powerful, wondered Guren, almost reflexively, *would I be able to defeat her? I have to have the strength to overthrow the Hiragi Clan, no matter what it takes...*

Guren's thoughts were interrupted by a memory he suddenly recalled.

It was of those days he had spent playing with Mahiru, long ago.

The bright, green grass.

The clear, unbroken sky.

And Mahiru, always beside him. Her innocent and unaffected smile.

It was hard to believe that ten years had passed since then.

Time moved so fast.

"I apologize for taking up so much of your time," said the principal. His speech was finally coming to a close. "I'm going to hand the stage over now to your incoming class representative. The decision on who would be this year's class representative was unanimous. It is our deepest honor to welcome an illustrious daughter of the Hiragi Clan to our school. Lady Mahiru Hiragi, the stage is yours!"

The principal bowed deeply. As he did so, a young woman approached from the side of the stage.

She had long, beautiful ashen hair and clear, piercing eyes. Her face was almost cold in its perfection. But something about her presence seemed warm and welcoming.

There was something gentle, even graceful, about her. The innocence she had as a child seemed to have stayed with her. Guren understood now why so many people referred to her as a goddess.

"…"

The auditorium, which had been loud and boisterous only a moment before, suddenly fell into an admiring hush. There were over a thousand people in the crowd, but it was so quiet you could hear a pin drop.

All eyes were on Mahiru.

Of course, the Hiragi name alone commanded significant respect. Enough to silence everyone in the auditorium.

This hush, however, was something different.

It was as if something inside Mahiru, some bright light, had captivated the students. They were paralyzed with awe.

Mahiru stepped up to the podium.

She bowed lightly, and then flashed a kind smile.

"Thank you for the introduction. My name is Mahiru Hiragi. I will

be the representative for this year's incoming class."

Mahiru's voice rang out through the auditorium, bright and clear. It seemed to cast a spell on the students.

Sitting a few rows ahead, Shinya Hiragi turned in his seat and glanced at Guren.

Mahiru wasn't looking Guren's way. With so many people in the audience, it was probably impossible for her to spot him.

Unless…

Unless maybe she isn't trying to find me, thought Guren. *Maybe she's lost interest by now in a common mongrel, an Ichinose slacker…*

Mahiru's voice was smooth and pure as she spoke, like a song.

Nothing's changed, thought Guren. *The distance between us is as huge as ever.*

Mahiru was a goddess, and Guren was the dog groveling at her feet.

Guren smirked to himself.

In the dark of the auditorium, where no one else could see, he closed his hand into a fist.

◆

Night.

The time was 7:30 p.m.

After the entrance ceremony they had returned to the classroom so that the teachers could explain the curriculum. Next, even though the entrance exams had just been held, they had to take tests in several magical subjects. It wasn't until late in the day that Guren and the other students were allowed to head home.

Guren was staying in an upscale, high-rise condo, located about fifteen minutes' walking distance from the school.

A spacious five-bedroom apartment had been rented specifically for Guren to use during his time at First Shibuya High School.

To prevent enemies from infiltrating the apartment, the entire floor—as well as the floors above and below the apartment—had also been rented. These two floors were filled with magical traps to keep out would-be intruders. The Ichinose Clan had taken every precaution.

That meant that in addition to his own apartment, there were fourteen other empty units at Guren's disposal.

"So why," asked Guren, sitting cross-legged on the living room sofa and staring at the two girls standing before him, "are you two trying to stay in *my* apartment?"

Those two girls were his bodyguards, Shigure Yukimi and Sayuri Hanayori.

The original arrangement was that Shigure and Sayuri would stay in the two apartments on either side of Guren's. For some reason, though, they were now in Guren's apartment, carrying all their things in knapsacks on their backs.

"As your bodyguards, it's important that we never leave your side," said Sayuri.

"I don't want you here," said Guren.

"B-B-But, there's five bedrooms. You'll still have your privacy. I promise, we won't make a peep...."

"That'd be a first for you."

"But..."

"Just get out. I need my peace and quiet."

"But..."

"But nothing. Just get out," said Guren, pointing toward the door. His two faithful servants, however, had plans of their own.

"Don't worry, Sayuri," said Shigure, "just play along for now. We can sneak back in later tonight."

"That's a great idea, Shigure!" said Sayuri, clapping her hands together. "You always know what to do..."

"Enough!" shouted Guren. He closed his eyes and took a deep breath. "You two are supposed to be my followers, aren't you? So why don't you ever do what I say?"

"Our first priority has to be your safety, Master Guren," said Shigure.

"That's right," said Sayuri, nodding in agreement. "We have to be able to throw down our lives for you, at any time necessary."

They still weren't budging. Guren crossed his arms and sighed.

He was thinking about how uncomfortable it would be to have to share an apartment with two girls for the next three years.

It would mean three hormonal teenagers in one place. He'd never be able to relax. They'd need their space to do girl things. It was too much trouble. But it did give Guren an idea.

"Do the two of you even realize what you're saying? You know what you'd have to be prepared for if you lived here?"

"Prepared for?" asked Sayuri, cocking her head.

"It's occurred to you that I'm a guy, right?" said Guren.

"What do you mean?"

Guren pointed to a cardboard box sitting in the corner of the room. It was still unopened.

"Take a guess what's in that box."

"I don't know. What is it?" said Sayuri, turning her head to look at the box.

"It's porn."

"Wha...!!"

Sayuri's face froze in shock.

There wasn't actually any porn in the box. But that wasn't the point. Guren grinned lasciviously.

"Do you get it? If you wanna share a place with a guy, you're gonna have to be prepared to see guy stuff. Are you sure you're ready for that?"

"I-I..."

"It's decided, then. The three of us in one apartment would never work. So grab your things and get moving."

"N-No, it's fine..." Sayuri objected. She was blushing bright red and her eyes were squeezed shut. "My father explained what I might have to do."

"Huh?"

"He told me that you might have to…c-c-come in at night. So I could t-t-take care of you. It's my d-duty, as your servant, Master Guren…"

"Geez!" shouted Guren. "What's wrong with your dad? That's messed up."

"I'm here to serve you, M-Master Guren…so, you don't have to use porn…if you don't want to…"

"What the hell? Just get out already!"

"Sayuri," said Shigure, quietly.

"Yeah?"

"Relax. There's no porn in that box. It's just magic textbooks."

"What?"

"Master Guren wouldn't spend his time looking at something so puerile. You know how serious he is about his training. When would he even have the time?"

Sayuri's expression instantly grew relieved.

"Th-That's right. Master Guren isn't like that. What was I thinking?"

"…"

"B-But, if you ever do need anything like that, don't hesitate to tell me. I…I live to serve!"

"…"

"Now that that's settled, I'll start putting the things away," said Shigure. "What will you do, Sayuri?"

"I'll make dinner! What would you like to eat, Master Guren?"

Even though Guren hadn't agreed to let them stay, the two began to make themselves busy. As far as they were concerned, it had all been decided.

Some followers I've got, thought Guren. *You'd think at the very least they'd do what I say.*

"…Curry and rice," he said, sighing.

"Right away!" cried Sayuri.

As the two scurried about the apartment, they already seemed at home in their new place.

Guren sighed in resignation.

He sat down on the sofa, pulled his phone from his pocket, and dialed home. It rang a few times before anyone picked up.

"Guren?"

The person on the other end of the line was the head of the Ichinose Clan, Guren's father.

"Yeah, it's me," said Guren.

"Is everything okay?"

"Other than Shigure and Sayuri not listening to what I say, yeah, everything's fine."

"Ha. That's my fault. I ordered them not to."

"Well, it wasn't necessary."

"Anyway, how was school?"

Guren turned over the day's events in his head.

Someone had thrown a cola bottle at his head. And then there was the incident with Shinya Hiragi.

And of course, Mahiru had shown up. Guren suspected that his father had been hiding Mahiru's engagement from him all along.

"Nothing much happened," Guren said.

"Nothing much, huh?"

"Nope."

"Well, you're tough. Not like your dad."

"You're the strong one, dad. I'm too short-tempered."

"Ha! If you say so… Just remember, if there's anything you need—"

"I'm fine," said Guren, cutting him off. "If I can't handle something like high school on my own, then how will I ever learn to lead the clan one day? Right?"

"I guess… But you know your father's here for you if you need him. I suppose you've already surpassed your old man, though."

"That's not true, dad. By the way, how are things there?"

"Same ole, same ole. Don't you worry about us."

"Got it. I'll talk to you later, dad."

"Sure thing. And Guren?"

"Yeah?"

"Be careful."

"I will," said Guren, serious. "Later."

"Bye, Guren."

Guren hung up the phone. Shigure approached him when she saw that he had finished his call.

"Master Guren?" she said.

"What is it?"

"Are there any boxes you'd like me to unpack first?"

"Don't worry about my stuff," said Guren. "You guys just take care of your own things."

"But…"

"Fine, fine. There are some things in the room next to the front door that need to be unpacked first. It's the charms and other magical supplies."

"Yes, sir." Shigure bowed and scurried off to the front room.

Guren watched her small back as she hurried away. He called out to Sayuri, who was in the kitchen.

"Hey, Sayuri?"

"What is it, Master Guren?"

"How long will dinner be?"

"Let's see…if I don't leave it to simmer, it could be ready in about an hour…"

"That long, huh?"

"Should I try to hurry?"

"No, let it simmer. I'm gonna take a nap in the next room," he said, standing up from the couch. There was a long, black bag in the corner of the room. Guren walked over and picked it up.

The bag held Guren's katana.

The Ichinose Clan fighting style combined spellcraft with swordsmanship, integrating magic directly into melee techniques. When it came to using a blade, the Ichinoses rivaled even the Hiragi Clan, itself.

This also meant that without a sword Guren could not access his full power. His magic relied on having a blade. Guren, however, planned to keep his sword sheathed while at school.

He was hoping to graduate without ever showing how far he—or the Ichinose Clan's magic—had developed.

He would still need to train, though.

Which is why he grabbed the bag with his katana now and slung it over his shoulder. He slipped out quietly, hoping neither Sayuri nor Shigure would notice.

"…"

He was planning on using the floor upstairs.

Supposedly, the Ichinose Clan had converted one whole apartment on the upper floor into a training dojo for Guren to use. That was where he was headed.

Guren walked down the hall to the elevators and pressed the up button.

The condo building had auto-locking double security doors. The elevator was configured so that only residents, and people whom they buzzed up, could board. Also, the elevator would only stop at floors for which the passengers had access.

But when the elevator reached Guren's floor and the doors opened, there was already somebody inside.

In all, the building had twenty-seven floors.

Guren's apartment was on the twenty-fifth. The twenty-sixth floor had also been rented out by the Ichinose Clan. That left only the twenty-seventh floor. That was where the building owner and his family lived.

The man in the elevator was wearing a black suit. He appeared to be in his early twenties.

The only people who should have been able to take the elevator up that high were members of the Ichinose Clan and the building owner's family.

Guren eyed the man, carefully.

The man smiled and bowed his head.

"Good evening," he said. "Are you going up?"

Guren nodded.

"I am. You're headed to the twenty-seventh floor?"

The man flashed a disarming smile.

"Yes, the twenty-seventh floor."

"In that case, you must be the building owner?"

"Yes, the owner."

"Thank you for renting us these apartments. It will really be a big help over the next three years."

"I should thank you. It's a pleasure to have such a distinguished young tenant."

Guren smiled and boarded the elevator. He turned around and faced forward, toward the floor buttons.

The button for the owner's floor—the twenty-seventh floor—wasn't lit. It hadn't been pressed. In fact, none of the buttons were lit.

Which meant, the man in the elevator had been headed for Guren's floor all along. The twenty-fifth floor. He had lied. Whoever he was, he definitely wasn't the building owner.

And he didn't care that his lie would be exposed as soon as Guren stepped onto the elevator.

That could only mean...

Assassin!

Guren crouched down, ripping open the bag on his back and unsheathing his sword in one fluid move. Drawing a sword in the elevator's tight space should have been difficult, but Guren managed it smoothly.

Guren had been training, ever since he was a child, to use his blade effectively in any location and under any circumstances.

The other man had already begun moving in response. It seemed as if he had been waiting for Guren to react before he made his move. He slipped an object from his breast pocket and used it to intercept Guren's strike.

It was a chain.

The chain was covered in magical *fuda*—magical paper charms inscribed with spells. Guren didn't recognize the magic. They didn't look like any *fuda* Guren had ever seen before.

And they definitely weren't Hiragi magic.

The Hiragi *fuda* were based on esoteric Buddhism, but incorporated complicated magical arts culled from around the world. Because of the shared history between the two clans, members of the Ichinose Clan could partially read the spells inscribed on Hiragi *fuda*.

But the *fuda* the man was using weren't like any Guren had ever seen before, Hiragi or Ichinose alike. They looked like they were based on an entirely different system of magic. Guren suspected Western magic.

Kabbalah? Maybe something else entirely…

Some old Japanese magics also seemed to be mixed in for good measure. Guren was unable to decipher the spells.

The man tried to twist the chain, with its strange *fuda*, around Guren's sword.

Guren reacted first. He kicked the man in the stomach and drew back his sword. At the same time, he slipped his left hand into the sleeve of his uniform and pulled out the *fuda* he kept hidden there. His hand opened and closed in a series of complex gestures, tracing a *kuji*—a nine-syllable Buddhist mantra—in the air.

The *fuda* disappeared in a flash and a spark of lightning appeared in its place. It was the same spell that Shinya had used against Guren that morning. But Guren's spell was faster, and slicker. It had enough force behind it to kill a man if he wished.

His opponent opened his eyes wide just as the lightning shot forward. It was aimed at his pupils.

As long as he was an ordinary opponent, the lightning would be enough to blind him.

But Guren was taking no chances. He drew his sword around again, aiming for the man's neck.

This man, however, was no ordinary opponent.

"Haha, impressive!" he said, raising his right hand. "Truly relentless."

Guren ignored him, carrying through with his strike.

He swung with so much force that it should have caved the man's chest in and cleaved his head from his shoulder.

Instead, Guren's blade stopped short with a high-pitched ring, like metal clashing against metal.

It had landed against the bones in the man's arm. However, no human bones would have been enough to stop Guren's strike. Even if the man were wearing armor under his suit, Guren was pretty sure he could have cut through it.

How in the world had he been able to block Guren's strike?

The two made eye contact, and the man smiled.

Guren's spell hadn't blinded him. The flesh on the man's arm, above the bone, had been cut deep, and black smoke began seeping out of the wound. The smoke creeped toward Guren, almost as if it had a life of its own...

"Dammit, I'm closed in here," hissed Guren.

He jumped back quickly, diving between the elevator doors. As soon as he slipped free of the elevator he pulled several more *fuda* from his pockets and tossed them into the air. They hit the corners of the elevator door and stuck there, forming a barrier.

A barrier that would kill anyone who passed through it.

Satisfied, Guren returned his sword to its scabbard and slipped the scabbard onto his belt. His hand remained on the hilt, just in case.

"Come on out," said Guren, smiling at the man. "I'll make sure I get your neck this time."

The man, however, remained in the elevator.

With a bemused expression on his face, he reached out and pressed the button to keep the doors open. Despite his deep wound, the man had no trouble using his mangled arm.

"It seems the future head of the Ichinose Clan is no pushover," he said. "But my, such a temper... A person just happens to board an elevator at the same time as you, and you attack without giving it a second thought..."

Guren glanced at the black smoke creeping from the man's arm.

"You're no person," said Guren.

"Aren't I? You must be so vexed."

"You're not a vampire either. Vampires have no interest in humans."

"..."

"So you're an assassin. But who sent you? Was it the Hiragis?"

Smiling and lifting his hands in a shrug, the man said, "Guess you got me—"

Guren cut him off. "Don't lie to me. The *fuda* on your chain aren't Hiragi magic. And the Hiragis don't respect the Ichinose Clan enough to hire a hitman to take one of us out. No more games. Tell me who you are."

Guren slipped into a crouching stance, ready to draw his sword at a moment's notice. Dark hexes had been worked into the blade's scabbard. Guren tapped the scabbard with the fingers of his left hand, over and over, tracing the incantation that would active its magic. The hexes sprang to life, bathing the sword in a powerful curse that caused the blade to glow, crimson red, in its sheath.

"If you want to live," said Guren, "you'll tell me who you are."

"I guess the jig is up. You certainly don't disappoint..."

Guren leapt forward to attack, drawing and swinging his sword while the man was still mid-sentence.

Guren had no intention of talking. His questions had just been a ruse. The man would never tell him the truth. As soon as he had lied and said that he had been sent by the Hiragis, Guren knew there was no more point in talking.

A surprised look flashed across the man's face.

But only for a moment.

Guren's blade hit him beneath his right arm, immediately striking against the man's ribs. Just like Guren first strike, the blade stopped short with a metallic clang.

But Guren wasn't done yet.

"I'll cut you to pieces!!" he screamed.

The crimson blade began vibrating, and the blade suddenly lurched forward, cracking through the man's ribs and slicing clean through to the left shoulder.

If that cut didn't kill him, then the man truly was some kind of monster.

"Haha!"

The man leveled his gaze at Guren and smiled.

Tendrils of black mist seeped out from the gaping wound in the man's chest, along with the chain covered in strange *fuda*. The mist and the chain shot forward to ensnare Guren.

Guren tried to jump backward to get clear of the elevator again.

Unfortunately his right arm—the one which held his katana—was caught by the chain. Guren looked at his trapped arm and quickly calculated his options. He could dislocate his shoulder. If he did that, though, he would probably lose his grip on his sword. He could also ignore the chain, and come in for another strike instead.

But he didn't know how dangerous his opponent was yet. Would it be wise to keep fighting in the elevator's enclosed space?

Guren's biggest worry was the black mist.

The chain wasn't worrying. Guren already had a fairly good idea of the danger it posed. There was no telling what the mist could do, however. Whatever powers it held, at the very least, inhaling it seemed like a bad idea. Guren took care not to breathe while in the elevator.

"Very impressive, indeed," said the man. "My poisonous mist should have paralyzed you by now… Don't tell me you've been holding your breath this entire time?"

Guren glared at the man. "Save your flattery. I cut you nearly in half and hit you with a spell, and you're standing there like it's nothing."

"Ha. I'm pretty impressive myself, aren't I?" said the man. He smiled and lifted his hands in a shrug. His chain and the black mist continued to writhe in the air, as if guided by minds of their own.

"What are you?" said Guren.

"What do you think I am?"

"A monster," said Guren.

"Haha. Believe it or not I'm human, from my head right down to my toes."

Guren scowled at the man.

"A human experiment, you mean. You're a chimera, aren't you?"

Chimerae were genetically engineered fighters. The man smiled in response.

"That's correct. What about the Ichinose Clan—the Order of the Imperial Moon? Do you experiment on humans as well?"

"Maybe the Hiragi Clan does, but the Ichinose Clan doesn't experiment on people. Why should we? I'm already stronger than you, and no one had to play God with my genes for me to get that way."

"Ha. If you say so."

"This isn't a pissing contest. Tell me who you are. Where did you come from, and why are you here?"

The man finally seemed ready to talk. Both the chain and the black mist recoiled, disappearing inside his body. What's more, the wounds on the man's chest and arm closed up. Even the cuts in his suit fused shut. Guren wondered again what kind of creature he was facing. Was the suit a part of its body? Or was its true form something else entirely?

Guren considered a fire hex for his next attack. It might burn away the black mist. While he was thinking tactics, however, the man decided to introduce himself.

"My name is Makoto Kijima. I belong to the Thousand Nights."

"The Thousand Nights…" muttered Guren.

The Brotherhood of a Thousand Nights was said to be the largest of all the magical syndicates in Japan. It had deep ties to the country's political underbelly.

The Thousand Nights' power was far-reaching. Nearly every major politician relied on their support to stay in power. Though few in the general population knew of them, they ruled the country from the shadows.

The Order of the Imperial Demons was also a powerful syndicate. For many years the two had fought to control the reins of power in the country. But after World War II the Thousand Nights had gained the support of the United States.

They had been the dominant syndicate in the country ever since.

According to rumors, the Thousand Nights would stop at nothing in pursuit of power and influence.

Murder.

Kidnapping.

War.

And of course, human experimentation.

In particular, the orphanages run by the Thousand Nights were infamous for their cruelty.

According to rumor, the Thousand Nights searched for children with special gifts. When they found a suitable subject they would kill the parents and bring the child to one of their orphanages, for grueling experiments.

It was possible that the man in the elevator was one of the monsters created at these orphanages.

Guren stared at Kijima's body and lowered his sword.

"A bunch of power-mad politicians. It figures. Well? What does the Thousand Nights want with me?"

"Actually," said Kijima, still smiling, "we believe our interests may already be aligned. I'm here to offer an alliance."

"Our interests? What are you talking about?"

"Destroying the Imperial Demons, of course. And the Hiragi Clan. We know you despise the Hiragis. We'd like to grant you the power to defeat them. That is, if you're interested—"

"I'm not," said Guren, cutting him off.

"Ha. We both know that's not the truth."

"What is up with everyone today? What is this, some kind of test of loyalty or something?"

First there was Shinya Hiragi, and now this guy. Why was everyone trying to pull him into some plot against the Hiragi Clan? Some first day of school this was panning out to be. Guren smirked and shook his head.

"We've been investigating you," said Kijima.

"You should mind your own business."

"You have a lot to be angry about, Guren Ichinose…"

"And?"

"Believe me when I say you don't have enough power to defeat the Hiragi Clan on your own."

"What's your point?"

"That's where we come in—"

"I told you, I'm not interested," said Guren, interrupting him again. "Even if I was, I wouldn't join with you people."

"And why is that?" said Kijima.

Guren laughed.

"Ever since I was little, I've always liked to come in first. If we joined forces, first prize would go to you guys, wouldn't it?"

" … "

"I'm already the Hiragis' mongrel. Am I supposed to jump at the chance to be the Thousand Nights' monkey? Thanks, but no thanks. How about you get lost instead?"

" … "

"I could make you disappear more permanently, if you prefer," said Guren, placing his hand on his sheathed katana.

Kijima laughed. "You're no match for me…"

"I am. And I won't hold back this time. I'll go for the kill."

" … "

"I decided before today that any opponent who sees my full strength needs to die. I'm giving you five seconds. Go back to your masters and tell them the Ichinoses won't play ball. I'll count: Five…"

" … "

"Four…"

Guren gripped the hilt of his blade tighter.

His crimson blade was named Kujakumaru. It held a powerful curse that could be called out with magic. Guren reached out with his mind to summon the blade's sealed power.

"Three…"

For the first time in their conversation, Kijima began to seem worried.

"Crap. There's something different about you, all of a sudden. Not like a minute ago… You're not bluffing, are you? Fine, I'll go. For now…"

"Two…"

"…"

Kijima shrugged and pressed the elevator button.

"But remember this," he said, as the doors began to close. "You'll regret not having joined us, today…"

"One."

The doors closed just in time and the elevator began to descend, taking Kijima with it.

"Hmph. The Brotherhood of a Thousand Nights, huh? Does this mean a war is coming?"

Guren removed his hand from the hilt of his sword and sighed.

In the back of his mind, Guren couldn't help but think that if a war was coming, it might be a chance to defeat the Hiragis.

After all, the Brotherhood of a Thousand Nights was vast and powerful. It was rumored that their influence even spread to other countries. If the Thousand Nights and the Imperial Demons came to blows, the resulting turmoil might give the Imperial Moon a chance to seize power.

Guren's thoughts were interrupted by a voice coming from the direction of the apartment.

"Master Guren! Master Guren?!"

It was Sayuri. She sounded flustered.

Guren heard the sound of footsteps hurrying in his direction. His follower appeared from around the corner.

"Ah, there you are! You shouldn't disappear like that, Master Guren!"

"Sorry, I was just gonna head up to the dojo…"

Shigure poked her head out from behind Sayuri.

"We haven't finished getting the dojo ready yet. Everything should be set up by tomorrow. Why don't you take today off?"

"Hmph. I guess I am tired. Is dinner ready yet?"

Sayuri gasped.

"I left the stove on!" she shouted, rushing back toward the room.

Shigure watched her go, then turned her attention back toward Guren. She eyed the sword strapped to his waist.

"Did you unsheathe your sword here?"

"Hm? Just for a moment. There's actually plenty of room here in the elevator lobby."

"In that case, maybe I should set up this space for you to practice in instead? That way, you won't have to go up to the top floor every time you want to train."

"That's a good idea."

Guren picked his bag up from the floor and put his katana away. He began walking back toward the apartment.

"Master Guren?" said Shigure, calling after him.

"Yeah?"

"Did something happen?"

Guren turned around to look at her. Her expression was worried.

"Nothing in particular," he said, flashing her a smile.

Before long Guren settled into a routine at school.

Most of his time was spent being bullied by the other kids. And then there were spellcraft exams, and of course sparring.

The other students all prided themselves on being experts in Hiragi spellcraft. Guren was careful to never beat them in any subject.

They were at a school assembly. The entire school had gathered together for practice.

"Ngh!"

Guren fell to the ground after getting punched hard by another boy.

The boy's name was Norito Goshi. He had bleach-blond hair, and mischievous, sleepy eyes.

He was one of the elite, naturally. From the Goshi Clan. He and Guren were in the same class. Norito stared down at Guren with a self-satisfied grin on his face.

"Dude, seriously? It hardly counts as practice when I'm fighting a pushover like you."

The students burst into uncontrolled laughter.

"Hey Norito, I hope none of its stink rubbed off on your fist!"

"Someone should remind the teacher that having this jerk in our class brings everyone's morale down," another student complained.

"Right?" said Norito. "Why'd they stick a weakling like this in with all the real students?"

Guren raised himself into a sitting position and wiped blood from the corner of his mouth. Norito's punch had split his lip.

"How can you just sit there and let him talk to you like that? Aren't you ashamed?"

Guren turned around to find out who had spoken. A girl with crimson red hair was standing there. It was Mito Jujo. She glared at Guren, an angry expression on her face for some reason.

"You're not even trying, are you?! You think just because he's stronger you should give up before you've even started?!"

"It's not like I can win," said Guren, laughing. "After all, he's the eldest son from the Goshi Clan, right?"

This only made Mito angrier. She narrowed her eyes and flared her nose in response. Apparently, however, it was something else that set her off.

"You're telling me you've never heard of the Jujo Clan but you're scared of some second fiddle from the Goshi Clan?! You've got some nerve, Ichinose!"

"Hey, who you calling second fiddle!" interjected Norito.

"Huh?"

"Jujo Clan bigshot. You guys think you're so high and mighty. Just wait until I take over for the Goshis. I'll wipe that smirk right off your face!"

Mito laughed, mockingly, and took a step towards Norito.

"Aww, poor little Goshi," Mito said, thrusting her chin out. "Did I hurt your widdle feelings with the truth?"

"Keep it up and I'll hurt more than your feelings. Don't think I won't, just because you're a girl."

"Bring it on. I'll teach you the difference between a Jujo and a Goshi!"

"Get ready to eat dirt!!"

"Just try it!"

The two began fighting. Their movements were fast. Their spellcasting was even faster. The other students all watched in amazement. Mito and Norito were obviously in the elite class for a reason.

The teacher didn't bother trying to stop them.

In fact, she encouraged the other students to watch their fight so that they could learn from them.

"..."

Guren stared at the fight absently. He stood up and gave a tired sigh. Shinya Hiragi approached him from behind. Shinya had his arms crossed, as if he were just there to watch.

"Another great performance," he said. "And the Oscar for getting punched in the face goes to Guren Ichinose."

"..."

Guren didn't say anything. He glanced at Shinya and then turned back toward the fight.

This was a chance for Guren to see two opponents fully trained in Hiragi spellcraft fight each other. Shinya took a step forward, lining up shoulder to shoulder with Guren.

"I doubt there's anything someone at your level could learn by watching a fight between those two."

"..."

"I've been watching you. You're even good at taking a punch. There's never any real damage, but you make it look really good when you fall down—"

"How about you quit stalking me and go find a hobby?" interrupted Guren.

"Ha. I can't help it. You're my future partner against the Hiragis. I've gotta find out how strong you really are, don't I?"

"I'm not your partner."

"Come on, Guren, drop the act. We should spar. It will give me a chance to see what you can really do."

Shinya uncrossed his arms and raised them in fists.

As Shinya prepared his stance, Guren realized that the other students were all staring at them. Even Mito and Norito broke off, mid-fight, to watch.

Shinya was the real star in their class. None of the other students could compare to him in terms of skill.

During their first sparring assembly, Shinya had defeated Norito without even breaking a sweat.

"I'm not holding anything back this time," said Shinya, brandishing his fists. "I don't care how strong you think you are, Guren. If I hit you with full force you're gonna feel it. Even if you take the punch really well, you're gonna wind up with at least a few broken bones."

Guren stared at Shinya's fists and then raised his eyes, meeting his opponent's gaze with an embarrassed grin.

"Come on, Shinya. You know I'm not strong enough to spar with anyone from the Hiragi Clan…"

"Enough! No more excuses!"

Shinya sprang into action. A maelstrom of energy whirled around his fist. He had clearly used some kind of invocation spell, drawing on a demon to give him strength. Maybe one of the Vidyaraja—wrathful guardian deva kings. Maybe some other demon.

Whatever spell he was using, the attack looked serious. Shinya really wasn't holding back.

If Guren didn't dodge, there was a real chance the blow could kill him.

"Fine," muttered Guren, staring at the incoming fist, "have it your way."

…

"Nggh!"

Guren let the punch hit him square in the chest.

Guren's ribs cracked loudly. He was tossed into the air, so high that you could actually count the seconds before he landed. He hit the ground with a thud.

He lay in a daze. The spell had propelled Shinya's fist with so much force that it had momentarily knocked him senseless.

"What's wrong with you?" said Shinya, standing over him with a shocked look on his face. "Are you that stubborn? Or are you really as

weak as you've been pretending?"

To Guren's surprise, Mito also came rushing over.

"Miss Aiuchi! It's Guren! There's blood coming out of his mouth!"

The teacher made no move to help. Instead, she stared at Guren with a wicked smile on her face.

He could hear the other students murmuring. They all seemed to be talking about how impressive the Hiragi Clan was. Mito stared at them, a disgusted look on her face.

"What's wrong with you people?!" she said.

Norito came rushing over next. Although he had just punched Guren himself, and had even been making fun of him, he seemed genuinely worried.

"Look at all that blood," he said. "I think he's really hurt."

It didn't make sense.

I made sure to take the punch in just the right place. Even if my ribs are broken, my lungs should be fine...

Despite what Guren thought, his grip on consciousness began to fade.

Had he miscalculated? Just by a hair, but still a miscalculation...

"Hey, hey! Hang in there!" shouted Norito. "We have to get him to the nurse's office, quick..."

It was the last thing Guren heard before everything faded to black.

◆

When Guren opened his eyes again he was in what appeared to be a hospital room.

A white ceiling.

White walls.

And in the middle of the room a bed, where Guren lay.

He was naked from the waist up, and wrapped in several layers of bandages. There was a throbbing pain in his chest. Apparently his injuries hadn't been fatal. But if he was still alive, then why had everything gone blank?

"…"

Guren stripped off his bandages and took a peek underneath. Nearly half of his chest had turned a sickly blue. It looked like a large artery had ruptured. Apparently, he had such bad internal bleeding that he'd fainted. There was a scar on his chest where an incision had been made. They'd had to stitch up the artery.

"…Hmph," said Guren, satisfied with the extent of his injuries.

"Is that all you have to say for yourself?" called a voice from outside the door. It was a young woman's voice.

A voice he recognized.

Guren turned toward the sound of the voice. A girl was standing in the open doorway. She had beautiful ashen hair and large, dark-pupiled eyes.

It was Mahiru. Mahiru Hiragi.

She stood in the doorway with a troubled expression on her face. After so much time, she seemed unsure of what to say to her childhood friend.

"You shouldn't have pulled your bandages off like that."

"Mahiru…Lady Hiragi… It's been a long time."

Guren bowed his head. This wasn't how he pictured meeting her again.

Mahiru's eyes flickered, faintly, in response.

"So that's how it is now?" she said.

"I don't know what you mean."

"We used to be good friends."

"Things have changed."

"…"

"I'm not the impertinent child I used to be, Lady Mahiru. I know how things work, now…"

"Enough," said Mahiru, "just be quiet."

There was a touch of anger in her voice. Guren stopped talking.

Mahiru entered the room.

"You shouldn't get too close," Guren said. "Your father would be angry."

Mahiru smiled in response. Her smile had been innocent as a child. Now there was a wisp of sadness about it that made it even more beautiful.

"I've changed too, Guren. I decide who I see now, and what I do. It's a Hiragi's duty to look after the clans under our command."

Strictly speaking, the Ichinose Clan had split off to become a new branch and wasn't under the Hiragi Clan's command. But Mahiru had chosen those words and likely knew what she was saying.

Guren looked up at her face. He was right. She did seem angry.

He didn't respond. He couldn't seem to find the right words to say.

In truth, despite all the time that had passed, nothing had really changed. The relationship between the Hiragi Clan and the Ichinose Clan was exactly the same as it had always been.

Guren found himself remembering the events of the last few days, and what the man from the Brotherhood of a Thousand Nights had said.

Enough power to defeat the Hiragis...

Guren remained silent.

"It really has been a long time," said Mahiru. "I thought you'd have more to say to me."

"There's nothing I *can* say."

" ... "

This time, it was Mahiru who was at a loss for words. An awkward silence descended on the room. Guren noticed the ticking of the clock. *Tock. Tock. Tock.* The second hand seemed unnaturally loud.

"Are you very hurt?" said Mahiru, unable to stand the silence any longer.

"I'm fine," Guren replied.

"You don't have a very good reputation at school. Everyone says you're very weak... Is it true?"

"If that's what people say, then it must be true."

Mahiru stared at Guren. She seemed to want to say something more, but Guren wasn't sure what. Whatever Mahiru expected from him, it was a mystery to Guren.

Even if he'd known what Mahiru wanted, there would have been nothing he could do.

It had been ten years since they had seen each other last. But in practical terms he was just as powerless now as he had been as a child. The relationship between the two clans was still the same, and as long as that remained unchanged, there could be no change in his relationship with Mahiru, either.

Mahiru was just as aware of that as Guren was.

"You've grown up," said Guren, looking up into her face. "You've become strong and beautiful."

A look of surprise flashed across Mahiru's face. She smiled slightly, as if pleased.

"You were more rough-and-tumble as a child. When did you learn to say such flattering things?"

"..."

"I don't care if it's flattery," said Mahiru. "I'm just happy to hear you call me beautiful."

Mahiru bit her lip. She almost seemed embarrassed. Guren stared into her face, but he was careful not to betray any emotions.

"Was there anything else you wanted, Lady Mahiru?"

Mahiru's expression took on a sorrowful cast again.

"No... I just heard that you'd been injured."

"I'm sorry to have worried you. I'll be fine."

"...I see."

"Was there something else, your lady?"

"..."

Mahiru shook her head.

"No, nothing at all," she said, softly. "I'll go now."

Mahiru gave Guren one last look and then turned to go.

"I almost forgot," said Guren, calling after her. "Congratulations on your engagement. Shinya told me all about it."

Mahiru froze mid-step. Her back stiffened as if she had been struck.

"…Thank you," she said.

She left the room without turning around.

Guren stared at the empty doorway, and at the empty room and the white walls.

"What the hell did I say that for?" he muttered to himself.

Chapter Five

Deadly Wars and Supermarkets

"Listen up, everyone," said the teacher, rapping on the blackboard with her fist. "Exam week begins tomorrow."

The qualifying exams. The exams were one-on-one spell duels that pitted students against each other to determine class ranking.

The exams didn't account for a student's total evaluation, but they did hold significant weight. The class buzzed with excitement.

"Of course, some of us are luckier than others," said Shinya, sitting next to Guren. "They won't be kicked out no matter how badly they do."

Guren glanced over at Shinya.

"I don't know what you're worried about. You nearly killed me with one punch the other day."

"Ha. You should have gotten out of the way," said Shinya, turning toward Guren. "Unless you really were unable to dodge my blow?"

" . . . "

"You'd have to be pretty stupid to take that blow. Either that or…"

"…I'm actually the pathetic mutt that everyone says I am? Well, I am. So why don't you get it through your head that you've overestimated me."

"In my experience," said Shinya, "people who can deprecate themselves like that are the most dangerous."

"You're being paranoid. Do you really think there's any freak out there who's strong enough to take you on? The Hiragi Clan chose you. They even chose you to be Mahiru's fiancé."

"..."

"No one chose me for anything. Whatever idea you've got, it's all in your head. Stop wasting your time on me."

Shinya laughed.

"Either you are acting or you've got serious self-esteem issues."

"Maybe my parents never hugged me as a child."

"If you say so. But then I have to wonder what Mahiru sees in you."

Guren gave Shinya one last glance and turned his eyes back toward the teacher.

Ms. Aiuchi was still talking about the qualifying exams. She urged the students to fight their hardest and to not lose any of their matches. When a lot of students from one class lost, it reflected poorly on their teacher.

"By the way, I heard you ran into Mahiru the other day," said Shinya.

"..."

"How was your reunion? You two still close?"

"Not really," answered Guren, without looking at him.

"Hey now, you don't have to worry about hurting my feelings. I may be her fiancé, but it's not like I'm her boyfriend..."

"..."

"You know, after your meeting, Mahiru seemed like she was in a bad mood. She doesn't get depressed easily. Did something happen?"

Apparently Mahiru had met with Shinya after she had met with Guren. Guren laughed and shook his head.

"I guess she was disappointed at how weak I've become."

Shinya stared at Guren with an exasperated look on his face.

"You really do have self-esteem issues, don't you?"

"I guess I do. If you've got a problem with that, then maybe you should stop talking to me."

"Ha!"

Shinya shook his head and laughed. Guren ignored him.

The teacher suddenly rapped her fist on the blackboard again.

"The one thing you must remember is that you must not—absolutely must not—lose to anyone from another class!"

Finally, the bell rang, signaling the end of class.

"Dismissed!"

The students all stood up. It was the last period of the day. Some students headed home. Some talked with their friends. Others began cleaning the classroom. There were no after-school clubs at First Shibuya. Everyone was too busy studying spellcraft or training to have time for that.

Guren grabbed his bag and stood to go.

"Wanna walk home together?" asked Shinya.

"Get lost," snapped Guren.

He glanced toward the classroom door. His two guards were already there, waiting for him and trying to stay out of sight. Sayuri spotted him first.

"Ah, Master Guren!" she shouted.

"Sayuri!" hissed Shigure, tugging on her sleeve. "Master Guren told us not to draw attention to ourselves. You don't want to make him angry again, do you?"

Shigure glanced over at Guren and nodded quietly. The truth was that they both stuck out like sore thumbs.

"I'm gonna have to have a talk with those two," muttered Guren.

Mito Jujo was still in the classroom. She glared at Guren.

"Why do you need two girls to protect you? Are all Ichinoses such cowards?"

The other students laughed.

"Seriously," chimed in Norito Goshi, saddling up next to Guren. "But at least they're easy on the eyes. You should introduce me."

The other students glanced around uncomfortably. They weren't sure whether to laugh this time at what Norito said or just pretend they hadn't heard.

Shinya Hiragi, Mito Jujo, and Norito Goshi were among the top four students in the class—both in terms of individual ability and clan prestige.

The fourth student was Aoi Sangu, a girl from the Sangu Clan. Aoi, however, was very quiet, and always left immediately when the bell rang.

With the top students—Aoi aside—acting so friendly with Guren, the rest of the class wasn't sure how to treat him anymore.

Not that Guren was getting picked on any less. The students and teachers from the other classes were still abusing him.

"Come on, Guren, tell us the truth," said Norito. He was sporting his usual, mischievous expression. "You're banging one of them, aren't you?"

Guren leveled his gaze at Norito.

"Since when are you interested in girls from the Ichinose Clan? I thought we were all just filthy mongrels?"

"I make an exception for hotties."

"I bet you do."

"Come on, spill it. They're your bodyguards, right? So they do what you say? You ever sneak in at night and let them guard your body, if you know what I mean?"

Mito's face flushed beet red.

"You're such a pervert!" she shouted. "If you're gonna behave like a dog at least do it out in the street!"

"Th-That's right!" Sayuri shouted angrily, from outside the classroom. "You shouldn't talk about Master Guren that way! He hasn't laid a hand on me. I should know, I've been waiting!"

"..."

The whole class suddenly fell silent. Norito looked at Guren in surprise. Even Mito stared at him like he was some creature from outer space.

Shinya, meanwhile, couldn't help laughing.

"Should I pass that bit of info on to Mahiru?" he asked.

Fed up, Guren sighed and began walking away.

"Do whatever you want... I'm going home."

"Hey, what's the big deal?" Norito shouted after him. "Don't keep all the girls to yourself, Guren! Ichinoses should learn how to share!"

Guren ignored him and left the room.

Shigure nodded to Guren as he approached.

"I'll see to it that Sayuri gets a talking to…" she said.

"Make sure you do," approved Guren.

"Wh-What?!"

Sayuri spun around in flustered circles. Guren just walked past her. He was ready to head home.

Unfortunately, that was easier said than done. Guren realized that someone was staring at him from the other side of the hallway. And it wasn't a friendly stare.

"…"

Guren continued walking, pretending he hadn't noticed. He had to keep up his charade of incompetence.

Of course, Sayuri and Shigure also noticed that something was amiss. They had both undergone years of training in order to protect Guren, and were very capable guards.

They both leapt forward, ready to act.

"Don't," whispered Guren. "I'll take care of this."

"But…!" Shigure turned toward Guren in surprise.

Before she could finish speaking, however, Guren was suddenly hit in the side of his face. Someone had kicked him.

"Ngh!"

Guren fell to the ground awkwardly, skidding sideways with a groan. He clutched his face and lifted his head up to see who had kicked him.

A boy was standing there, accompanied by his own entourage of lackeys.

He had brown hair and narrow, serpentine eyes. There was even a piercing through his lip. He stared down at Guren with a haughty expression on his face.

"Sorry," he said. "I guess my foot slipped."

His lackeys all burst into laughter.

"You son of a…!"

Shigure stepped forward, furious. She swung her fist at the boy.

Guren tried to stop her, but before he could one of the boy's followers—a girl—stepped forward and caught Shigure's fist.

Shigure's face went blank with surprise. Her punch had been pretty fast. It was amazing that the girl had managed to catch it.

"Do you have any idea what you were about to do?" the girl said. "This is Seishiro Hiragi. Show some respect!"

Apparently, the boy with the piercing was yet another Hiragi.

The Hiragis were like gods at the school.

"Raising your fist against Master Seishiro is punishable by death…"

"Forget it, Yumi," said Seishiro, waving the girl off. "It's no use talking to Ichinose scum as if they were human. The best way to train an animal is to beat it."

Seishiro raised his hand. Shigure's reflexes kicked in and she tried to parry. However…

"Haha! Too slow, shorty!"

Seishiro's punch was faster. In fact, all of Seishiro's movements were faster than Shigure's. There was no way Shigure was going to block him in time.

"Dammit," said Guren, getting ready to leap to his feet. He had to block Seishiro's punch before it could hit Shigure. Before he could act, however, the fist stopped in mid-swing.

Someone had reached out and grabbed Seishiro's arm.

It was Shinya. He had come out of the classroom at just the right moment.

"Master Seishiro, this hardly seems a fair fight for someone of your stature," Shinya said. "If it got around that you were beating up on little girls from the Ichinose Clan, it might reflect poorly on the Hiragis."

Seishiro glared at him.

"If I wanted your opinion I'd ask for it, you stray. You're forgetting your place."

"My apologies. But…"

"But nothing," said Seishiro, snatching his fist away. He swung again, this time at Shinya.

Shinya didn't attempt to dodge. The punch landed with a thud, and blood trickled from Shinya's lip.

"Ha, looks like you know better than to fight back," said Seishiro. "You know you're no match for me."

"…"

"The only reason pops chose you to be Mahiru's fiancé is because you're obedient. You better not forget that."

"…Of course not, Master Seishiro."

"You're in the same class as this Ichinose mongrel, right? So what's the deal? Is he strong? They put him down as my second fight in the qualifying exams…"

Now it all made sense.

That was why Seishiro had approached him in the first place. He was trying to figure out if Guren posed a threat, before the exams started.

"I thought he was, at first," said Shinya. "After all, he is the next head of the Ichinose Clan. You'd expect him to at least be capable…"

"Hmph."

Shinya turned toward Guren and glared at him with an icy stare.

"…but I was clearly wrong. What kind of trash would just sit there while a girl under his command is about to get hit? He lets his friends get hurt? In the end, he's just another two-bit jerk from a second-string clan."

Seishiro laughed. "Ha, is that so? I should've figured. When his dad was at this school, they say he used to hide in the corner with his tail between his legs… Like father like son, I guess."

Seishiro's lackeys burst into laughter again.

Guren's other classmates had also come out into the hall. They all laughed, too. Now that Shinya had stopped treating Guren with respect, they felt comfortable making fun of him again.

"Come on, this is getting boring," said Seishiro, turning to go. "We're wasting our time messing with this loser."

The other students laughed. Guren could hear them making fun of how pathetic and weak he was.

Norito was also in the hallway. He stared at Guren with something like pity in his eyes.

"Now you've gone and done it," he said. "If you can't even stick up for a girl, how can you expect anyone to respect you?"

Mito had also come out into the hall.

"Why don't you say something back?" she asked. She looked angry. "Don't you even care what they're saying?"

Guren looked up at her sheepishly.

"They told me at home never to go against the Hiragis..."

"And if they told you to jump off a bridge would you do that too?!" she shouted.

She turned around and stormed off. Apparently she was too angry even to be looking at him.

Guren finally stood back up. He stared at Mito's back as she left.

Now that the show was over, the other students all seemed to lose interest. They all went their separate ways.

Only Shinya remained.

"What a waste," he said, staring at Guren.

"..."

"I really expected more from you."

"I guess you shouldn't have gotten your hopes up, then."

"I guess not. I was a fool to expect anything from a weakling like you."

"..."

"You know what, I'm done with you. Don't ever talk to me again—"

"You're the one who's doing all the talking," interrupted Guren.

"Am I?" said Shinya, coldly. "In that case, stay away from Mahiru while you're at it."

"..."

"You don't have the right to talk to her. You don't have any power or self-respect. Someone who can't even put in the effort shouldn't have come to this school in the first place. You're not fit to walk the same halls as Mahiru."

In other words, he had to earn the right to show his face to Mahiru. It might have sounded harsh…but Guren agreed.

They lived in a world where only power mattered. A world where it took strength to realize your dreams.

Happiness was a privilege. A privilege that demanded strength.

But that was something that Guren still lacked. Power. Enough to destroy the Hiragi Clan. He would need a lot more of it if he was ever going to realize his dreams.

"What am I supposed to do?" said Guren. "I never wanted to come to this school. I know I don't belong here. It's you Hiragis who made me come. I just obeyed. If I don't belong, then why did you bring me here in the first place? What do you expect me to do?"

Guren knew he sounded childish. But he needed to keep up his act.

"…"

The disgust was evident on Shinya's face. He turned around without saying another word.

Only Guren, Shigure, and Sayuri were left in the hallway.

The other students had lost interest. Guren doubted Shinya, Mito, or Norito would be bothering him anymore. He was back to being just another filthy Ichinose mongrel.

"I'm sorry, Master Guren…" said Shigure. "I wasn't strong enough."

"M-M-Master Guren," said Sayuri, on the verge of tears, "I don't understand why you have to put up with them. Not when you're actually so much stronger than all of them put together…"

"Sayuri…" Guren said quietly.

Sayuri stopped talking. She clenched her jaw in an attempt to appear stoic. She couldn't hold back the tears, though, which began spilling down her face.

"…"

Guren watched her cry. He knew it must be hard for her to see her master subjected to such treatment.

"...I'm sorry."

He knew it was poor comfort, but he didn't know what else to say. Sayuri shook her head, flustered.

"N-No, it's nothing... I just got some dirt...in my eyes."

Shigure rolled hers.

"It's a little late to pretend, now," she said.

"B-But..."

"I know. It hurts to see Master Guren be made fun of. I feel the same way."

"Shigure..."

"But try to hold it together. It's even harder on Master Guren. But you don't see him crying, do you? If he can be strong, so can we."

"But..." sniffed Sayuri.

"You don't want me to report this behavior to your family, do you?"

"Augh!"

"So stop crying. We're here to protect and comfort Master Guren, not the other way around."

Although the tears continued to spill down her face, Sayuri seemed to cheer up at Shigure's words.

"Th-That's right! I can go to Master Guren's room tonight and comfort him!"

"Don't even think about it!" said Guren, conking Sayuri on the skull with his knuckles.

"Ow!" said Sayuri, holding her head.

Guren laughed. "Besides, you two weirdos cheer me up enough just by being yourselves. Come on, let's go home."

"Yes, sir!" they shouted.

Guren put a hand on Sayuri's back, steering her forward as they walked.

His mind, however, was already on other things.

Namely, the boy he had met moments before. Seishiro Hiragi.

Seishiro was part of the Hiragi Clan. That meant he was probably Mahiru's brother, related to her by blood.

He had heard that Mahiru had a twin brother. Since Seishiro was in the same year as them, maybe this was him. It would certainly explain the chip on his shoulder.

Guren recalled how Seishiro had dealt with Shinya and Shigure.

His movements had been sharp and fast. But it was impossible to tell from just those few seconds how powerful he really was. Still…

"…he's clearly a member of the head family," muttered Guren.

Guren wondered if Seishiro was more powerful than himself. Either way, Seishiro was scheduled to be Guren's opponent in the second round of the exams.

And those exams were starting tomorrow.

The sun was just beginning to set, bathing the town in dusky red.

Guren stood in front of a small supermarket. It was in a residential neighborhood, along the way home from school.

Not many people were about.

Sayuri and Shigure were inside, shopping for dinner. Guren waited outside, leaning against a guardrail with his arms crossed.

He could hear a young boy nearby, shouting. He sounded excited.

"Mr. Saito! Mr. Saito! Can I really buy whatever I like?"

Guren glanced in the boy's direction. He was just a kid. He had blond hair, white skin, and a cherubic face. He didn't look Japanese. Possibly he was mixed race, from Japan and somewhere else.

"What about the other kids at the orphanage? What do you think they'd want?" asked the boy. "Do you think the teachers at the orphanage would get mad if we brought back ice cream?"

The boy's smile stretched almost from ear to ear.

"I don't know," said the man beside him—the one he had called Mr. Saito. "Is there a freezer at the orphanage?"

"Of course there is!" said the boy.

"Then I don't see any problem. After all, I did get permission from your teachers before we left."

"All right!"

"Here, Mikaela, take this money. The supermarket's right over there. I can trust you to buy the treats on your own, can't I?"

"Of course," said the boy, who was apparently named Mikaela. "I'm not a baby. I'm already eight, you know!"

Mr. Saito handed him a 10,000-yen note. Mikaela looked at the money in shock.

"That's too much," he said.

Mr. Saito laughed and told him, "You need to get enough for everyone, remember?"

"But still, ten thousand yen is a lot of money..."

"It's fine. You just worry about spending it. Go on, now."

"Okay! But if we're buying that much, we should've brought Akane along to help carry everything."

Mikaela dashed off into the supermarket, a huge grin on his face.

"..."

Arms still crossed, Guren watched the boy disappear from sight.

Once he was gone, Guren turned his eyes toward the man named Mr. Saito.

He was dressed in a black suit, just like the man who had attacked him ten days ago.

"..."

It wasn't just the suit that was the same. It was the man himself. The very same assassin from the Brotherhood of a Thousand Nights that Guren had fought in the elevator.

"Mr. Saito?" said Guren, staring at him calmly. "You told me your name was Kijima."

The man laughed in response.

"The kids at the orphanage all know me as their friendly Uncle Saito."

"Hmph. But Kijima is your real name?"

"I don't have a real name."

"In other words, you're an assassin."

"That is correct."

"So, what? You spend your free time playing Daddy Warbucks to a bunch of orphans?"

"Ha, so it would appear. Anyway, now that you see what a nice guy I really am, maybe you'll be more willing to listen to what I have to say—"

"Go stuff yourself," said Guren, cutting him off.

"Fine, have it your way," said the assassin, laughing. "But do me a favor and call me Mr. Saito for now. We don't want to confuse young Mikaela."

Guren turned his eyes back toward the supermarket, where Mikaela had disappeared.

"What exactly are you planning to do with that boy?"

"I don't know what you mean."

"Everyone knows that the Thousand Nights carries out human experiments. Don't play dumb with me."

"Now, now, you've got the wrong idea there. The Thousand Nights runs Hyakuya orphanage as a purely charitable endeavor…"

"Then explain where you came from. Who did that to your body? Where did they make you? And don't tell me you were raised in a loving home, by two doting parents."

"…"

The smile disappeared from Saito's face. A serious expression appeared in its place.

"It's true, I am from Hyakuya Orphanage. But I volunteered for experiments. This body was my choice."

"Then I guess they brainwash their kids, too."

Saito ignored him. "The Thousand Nights is dedicated to ensuring our country's future. You may not be aware of it, Guren Ichinose, but if Japan continues on the path it's on, it will face ruin. The trumpets of the apocalypse are soon to sound."

"There it is. 'The end of the world.' The Thousand Nights is just another fly-by-night cult, isn't it? Let me guess: Only true believers, who join your religion, will be saved. Am I right? Our clan pulls the same kind of tricks. So do the Hiragis. Everyone has the same gimmick. Did you think that was all it would take to trick me into joining you?"

"You've mistaken me," said Saito. His expression remained unperturbed.

"Then what are you trying to say?"

"Only the truth... If things continue on their current path, a viral outbreak will occur. Forbidden magics that no man was meant to meddle in will be unsealed, and our world will become one in which humans can no longer survive."

"And you're saying you guys are here to stop that?"

"That is correct."

Guren smirked.

"Only repentance will save me? Sinners will be destroyed by the virus, while those who join the Thousand Nights will be saved?"

"I'm not trying to convert anyone," said Saito, laughing and shaking his head. "It would be pretty silly, in any case, to try those kinds of tricks on you."

"If you're not talking about religion, then what are you talking about?"

"War. It won't be gods who spread this virus. It will be man. Humans. And ones that you know very well. The Hiragi Clan."

"That's crazy..."

"The Imperial Demons are desperate to overtake the Thousand Nights as the leading magical syndicate in the country. In their panic, they have begun pursuing forbidden arts. We are doing all we can to stop them."

"..."

"So you see?" said Saito, his face suddenly breaking into a smile. "Our interests are aligned, after all."

Saito extended his hand toward Guren.

"Why don't you join us? We can bring down the Hiragi Clan together, before they bring this world to an end."

Guren stared at Saito's outstretched hand.

According to Saito, the Hiragi Clan was pursuing forbidden magics that would bring about the end of the world, and the Thousand Nights was working to stop them.

And once the Hiragis were removed…

"…where will that leave the Ichinose Clan?" Guren asked.

Saito smiled.

"If the illustrious Ichinose Clan were to assist us in our endeavors, the relationship between your two clans would be reversed. That would leave the Ichinose Clan in charge of both the Order of the Imperial Demons and the Order of the Imperial Moon."

"Hmph. So you're looking for cooperation from the entire Ichinose Clan? Not just me, but the Imperial Moon as well?"

"Obviously."

"Then why are you speaking to me? The head of the Ichinose Clan…"

"…is your father, correct? But your father is a moderate."

Guren laughed.

"Are you saying I'm a radical?"

Saito smiled, apologetically.

"As I mentioned before, we've been investigating you. You and your father. We decided to approach the person we thought would be most receptive to a…constructive discussion."

"You mean me."

"Correct."

"So, what, you thought I'd just roll over and accept everything you say?"

Saito shook his head.

"Of course not. But we figured there was no harm in at least speaking with you, before everything begins."

Before everything begins. In other words…

"You're saying this war will start, with or without the Ichinose Clan."

Saito shrugged his shoulders.

"The Hiragi Clan has already started it."

"And if you're telling me all this," said Guren, "that means the war will be out in the open before very long."

Saito nodded, smiling again.

"Only ten days. In ten days, the war between the Thousand Nights and the Hiragi Clan will begin."

"So I have ten days to give you an answer…"

"I'm afraid not. We need your answer, now or never. We've already begun moving forward. Either you are with us, or you are against us."

Saito stared at Guren. Guren stared back.

"You're asking for too much," Guren said. "How am I supposed to take your word for things? I don't know whether the Hiragis are really trying to unlock forbidden magics or not. And even if they are, how do I know they need to be stopped? For all I know, the Thousand Nights could be working with the Hiragis, and this is all a trap. I can't answer you until I know more."

"I see," said Saito, nodding. "Then I guess we have nothing more to discuss."

"We're not finished yet."

"We're not? So then you *are* willing to join us? Decide one way or the other, and do it quick. Whatever you choose, it's no skin off our backs…"

Guren understood what Saito was implying.

If they were going to war, they would want as many allies as possible. But as far as the Thousand Nights was concerned, a minor player like the Ichinose Clan would have little effect on the war's outcome, one way or the other. Guren couldn't argue with their logic.

After all, the Ichinose Clan had been under the Hiragi Clan's thumb for years. The Brotherhood of a Thousand Nights, meanwhile, dwarfed even the Hiragi Clan in size. The Ichinoses had been kowtowing to the Hiragis for so long that it was laughable to think they could make a difference now.

The Thousand Nights was simply making contact with them before the war began. If the Ichinose Clan could answer immediately, there was no harm in having them on their side.

Guren tried to figure out what he should do. What choice would keep the Ichinose Clan—and everyone else in the Imperial Moon—the safest?

Their whole future could hinge on this one moment, and how he answered Saito's question.

What was the right choice?

What should he do?

Guren played out the different scenarios in his head before answering.

"Give me one hour, at least."

"No," said Saito.

Guren narrowed his eyes.

"Then I refuse. We don't need any allies who aren't interested in honest negotiation. Go find another toady. I refuse."

"I see... That's unfortunate."

"No, the misfortune will come later. You're the ones who will pay the price for this. You should have given me more time. One day you'll regret not having me on your side."

"Ha. That's some sense of humor you've got there."

As Saito finished speaking, the supermarket's automatic doors swung open. The little blond boy, Mikaela, came stumbling out.

"Mr. Saito!" he called. "H-Help! I think I bought too much. It's too heavy for me to carry!"

Guren turned his head in the boy's direction. Mikaela noticed him staring.

"Hey, Mr. Saito, who's that guy next to you? He's got a nasty look in his eyes."

Saito laughed.

"I don't know," he said, without turning to look at Guren. "I thought maybe you knew him."

"Not me."

"You better watch out, then. He's probably some kind of pervert."

"He does look pretty creepy!" cried Mikaela.

Guren guessed that was Saito's way of letting him know their talk was at an end. Saito said he didn't know who Guren was. In other words, they no longer had any business to discuss.

Saito and Mikaela turned around and began walking away. They were probably heading back toward the orphanage. Guren stared at them, silently, until they disappeared from sight.

"I wonder if I made the right decision," muttered Guren.

He would need to look into what Saito had said. At the very least, he should contact the Ichinose Clan and have them investigate whether there was any truth to Saito's claims.

In ten days, a war between the Thousand Nights and the Hiragi Clan would begin. That is, if Saito was telling the truth. If he was, then how should the Ichinose Clan respond when the time came? How far should they get involved? They needed to decide, and soon.

Unless that's precisely what the Thousand Nights wants us to do. Maybe they're simply trying to create chaos between our two clans, so they can swoop in when we're least prepared.

For now, it was important that they tread carefully.

A voice suddenly interrupted Guren's thoughts.

"Master Guren! I'm sorry we took so long!"

It was Sayuri and Shigure. They exited the supermarket, both of them carrying a full bag of groceries in each hand.

Still leaning against the guardrail, Guren uncrossed his arms and stood up straight. He glanced warily at the shopping bags.

"That looks like a lot of food. Are you two planning on feeding an elephant?"

"After everything that happened today we thought we should treat ourselves to a party!" Sayuri said happily. "We bought stuff to make barbecue, curry, and yakisoba!"

"And who's going to eat all that?" chided Guren.

"Those are all Sayuri's favorites," Shigure told him. "Obviously, we're also planning to make whatever you'd like, Master Guren. Isn't that right, Sayuri?"

"Of course! Just name your pick, Master Guren!"

"Anything's fine."

"That's what you always say! How are we supposed to know what you really want if you always say that? Remember, the qualifying exams start tomorrow. It's important you get a good meal to build up your strength."

After his talk with the man from the Thousand Nights, the qualifying exams no longer seemed so important. After all, in ten days' time a war was going to break out between two of the most powerful magical syndicates in the country.

Sayuri hopped from foot to foot in excitement, unaware of what Guren was thinking.

"Come on, come on, there must be something you want," she said, leaning in close in anticipation. Guren figured it would be easier to just pick something.

"Fine, how about curry and rice."

"Indian style, or European?"

"...Japanese style."

"Just leave it to me! Today we'll have the most delicious Japanese curry and rice ever made! Ah! But for Japanese curry we'll need those little green onions. Shigure, hold my bags, I'll be right back!"

Sayuri spun on her heel and went rushing back into the supermarket.

After she left, Shigure narrowed her eyes and peered up into Guren's face.

"Master Guren?"

"Yeah?"

"I don't know if you remember, but we had curry and rice yesterday, too."

"We did? I guess I forgot."

"Is…something bothering you? If it's about what happened at school today, I'm here anytime you need to talk…"

Guren shook his head.

"No, it's something else. I might need to talk to you about it in the next few days, but for now don't worry."

"The next few days?"

"First I need to contact the clan. Is my cellphone secure?"

Shigure realized that something urgent was afoot. Her expression quickly grew serious.

"We've taken all precautions to ensure your communications stay secret. But…"

"But this is Hiragi territory."

"Yes, sir."

"Then we can't be sure."

"I don't believe so, sir."

"Fine. Once we get back home I'll write a letter. Arrange for a messenger."

"Understood. Should I go now?"

"Yes…better to do it at once."

Shigure nodded. She was about to rush off when she realized she was still holding the grocery bags.

"Ah…"

"Give them to me," said Guren, taking the bags from her.

"Thank you, sir."

"Now hurry."

"Yessir!"

Shigure dashed away. Sayuri came back outside just as she was leaving. She looked around, confused.

"Was that Shigure just now?"

"I had something for her to do."

"Master Guren, you shouldn't be carrying the bags. Here…let me have them."

"It's fine. Come on, let's go."

"But…"

"I said it's fine." Guren began walking toward home. A moment later, Sayuri came running after him.

"Umm…Master Guren?" she said.

"Yeah?"

"Just the two of us…walking alone together like this… Do you think we look like boyfriend and girlfriend to other people?"

"If you're gonna talk nonsense, then keep it to yourself."

"Augh… Y-Yes, sir."

◆

That night, Guren wrote a letter home.

In it, he explained that the Brotherhood of a Thousand Nights had approached him.

He mentioned how the Hiragi Clan might be courting disaster, the possibility the world might end, and the virus that Saito had described.

He also mentioned the war between the Thousand Nights and the Hiragi Clan, and that it could be starting in ten days' time.

Finally, he mentioned how he had refused the Thousand Nights' invitation.

The letter would likely reach the Ichinose household by nightfall. A problem this wide-reaching called for a strategy meeting attended by all of the leaders—not just of the Ichinose Clan but of the entire Order of the Imperial Moon.

They would begin gathering intelligence to ascertain the truth of what Saito had said.

Guren expected these measures to take three days. That would leave them one week to prepare.

If Saito was telling the truth and they had only ten days left, then there was no time left to spare.

A war was brewing.

A war that, if handled poorly, could result in the total annihilation of Japan.

When that war came, what hand would the Ichinose Clan be able to play?

"More importantly, how can we turn the confusion to our advantage?" murmured Guren.

Head in his hands, Guren sat thinking, long into the night.

Chapter Six

The Qualifying Exams

The qualifying exams began at 8:00 a.m.

They were being held in the schoolyard, but it was a schoolyard in name only. In truth it was a vast training ground, large enough for military maneuvers.

All of the students were gathered there.

The exams were an elimination-style tournament. Every student in every grade had to compete. The whole process would take an entire week.

Students in the same class didn't have to face each other unless they had already won several matches and moved up in the ranks. This meant that, for the first matches at least, there was a sense of team spirit among students from the same class.

In the end, each match came down to individual ability. But for now there was a sense that they were all in the same boat, together. Their teacher, Saia Aiuchi, was spending the morning psyching her students up.

"Whatever happens," she said, "you absolutely must not lose to anyone from another class! This is your week to show those other classes why we're number one!"

"..."

Guren sat a little apart from the other students as she spoke.

Ever since the incident in the hallway, Shinya, Norito, and Mito had all stopped speaking to him. He had become a total outcast.

Fortunately, Guren preferred it that way.

"…"

He stared at the other students with a look of boredom on his face.

The first match in their division had already begun. It was between a girl in his class—whose name he didn't even know—and a boy from Class 1-2.

The match was dragging on. The two were equals in skill.

All matches were full contact, with no techniques barred.

The rules for victory were simple:

The winner would be determined by the judges, entirely at their discretion.

The judges would choose whoever appeared to be the most capable.

Accidentally killing your opponent would result in a lower evaluation.

Otherwise, combatants were free to use any weapons or spells of their choosing. While killing your opponent was frowned upon, it would not result in expulsion. No charges would be filed, and the police would not be informed.

That was the kind of school they were at. The rule of law didn't extend to First Shibuya.

In fact, in a way the school was its own separate country. It may have been inside of Japan, but the Hiragi Clan ruled over it like gods.

In order to minimize the chance of death, five teachers were assigned as judges to referee each match.

"The winner is Midori Sugiyama, Class 1-9!"

The girl from Guren's class had won her match against the boy from Class 1-2. Apparently, her name was Midori.

Guren glanced toward the ring. The girl had thrown her opponent to the ground and was holding a knife against his throat.

"Yessssssssssssss!"

Ms. Aiuchi tossed her hands up in a victory pose. The other students in the class all cheered.

"Great start, let's keep it up," she said.

The next combatants stepped forward. All of the students from Class 1-9 and Class 1-2 would be facing off against each other today.

Guren glanced across the yard, where the students from Class 1-2 were huddled together.

One of Guren's guards, Shigure Yukimi, was in that class, but Guren couldn't see her among the other students. He shrugged his shoulders.

"She is a munchkin, after all..."

A voice spoke up from Guren's side.

"Who's a munchkin, after all?"

Guren turned his head. Shigure was standing right next to him. She stared up at him with her usual, stone-faced expression.

"What are you doing over here?"

"I just came over to say hello."

"Is that all?"

"My class and yours are up against each other today."

"I can see that."

"Of course. But I thought you might not know what class I'm in... I'm happy you took an interest."

Guren sighed.

The second match had already begun. It was another classmate whose name Guren didn't know. He seemed to be giving the fight his all.

His movements, however, were slow. As was his spellcasting. He didn't look very skilled in the use of his weapon, either.

"Is that really one of the school's elites?" asked Shigure.

Guren smiled in response.

"You don't seem very worried about your match."

"Well, an opponent like that..."

"...would be no threat?"

"No."

"Glad to hear you say that. Who is your opponent?"

Just then, another student interrupted them.

"What are you two whispering about?"

The girl who spoke had crimson red hair. She stared at Guren and Shigure suspiciously.

It was Mito Jujo.

"Were we whispering?" asked Guren, turning toward her.

Mito thrust a finger in Shigure's direction.

"You were! She may be your bodyguard, but she's my opponent today!"

Guren turned his attention from Mito back to Shigure.

"Is that true?"

"Yes, sir," said Shigure, nodding.

"I see. Well, that should make for an interesting match."

"Is it okay if I beat her?" asked Shigure.

"You? Beat me?!" exclaimed Mito. "Fat chance! Even your master is a wuss. What chance do you think you'll have against me? I'm a Jujo, you know!"

Shigure glared at Mito.

"Watch your tongue when you speak about Master Guren…"

"Or you'll do what?"

"I'll cut it out," threatened Shigure.

Her voice practically dripped daggers. Shigure's tone of voice would have been enough to petrify most people.

Mito, however, seemed unfazed. She just laughed the threat off.

"I look forward to seeing you try," she said, turning her back and walking away. Guren watched her go.

"Shigure?"

"Yes, sir?"

"Do you really think you can beat her?"

"Of course I can!" she shouted, uncharacteristically enthusiastic. She stood up straight and thrust her chin out.

It seemed like she was rearing for a fight.

Shigure didn't rely on a lot of spellcasting when fighting. Instead she excelled at assassin's tricks and knifework. That meant she would be able to use her strengths without revealing Ichinose Clan spells to their enemies.

She could fight without holding anything back.

Even so...

"You know, Mito Jujo is no pushover, either."

"Whose side are you on, Master Guren?"

"Whose side? I guess I don't really care who wins."

"You mean you're not going to root for me?"

Guren laughed.

"Do you need me to root for you in order to win?"

"No," said Shigure, with a dissatisfied look on her face. "But it would make me sad if you didn't."

"Ha. Anyways, we've got more important things to talk about. Remember—"

"I know," said Shigure, cutting him off, "don't use any Ichinose magic. There's no reason for us to tip our hand to our enemies. I'll only use spells that the Hiragis already have at their disposal."

"Glad you understand. In that case, give her hell. It will be a chance to vent off some of the anger we've been building up over the past few days."

Just then, one of the judges called out Shigure's name.

"Shigure Yukimi, Class 1-2. Come forward."

Shigure began walking toward the ring. She stopped midway and turned back toward Guren.

"Do you think you could root for me anyway, even if it isn't important?"

"Fine, just get in there already."

"Yes, sir!"

Next, the judge called out Shigure's opponent's name.

"Mito Jujo, Class 1-9. Come forward."

Mito stepped into the ring. She flicked her crimson red hair over her shoulder, no doubt to show off her lineage as a Jujo.

"Aristocratic snob," hissed Shigure.

Mito flashed a confident smile.

"I'm sorry, I don't speak to peasants."

"Get ready to die," said Shigure.

"Not by your hand," said Mito.

Before Mito even finished speaking, Shigure had already slipped a hand behind her own back. Guren guessed she had a weapon hidden up her sleeve.

Mito, meanwhile, was muttering quietly. She was probably casting a Hiragi Clan spell. The Jujo Clan used magic to power themselves up physically and push their bodies to their limits. The spell's structure seemed similar to the invocation magic Shinya had used against Guren. A fiery, three-pointed halo began to materialize over Mito's head. It was bright crimson—even brighter than her hair.

"What demon is she using... Vajrayaksa?" muttered Guren, watching carefully.

One of the judges stepped forward. He explained the rules of the fight. A signal would be given to stop the match, if necessary.

He also reminded them that killing the opponent would result in a lower evaluation.

"Look at that," said Norito Goshi, whistling. "It's hottie versus hottie. I wouldn't mind being in the middle of that catfight."

Norito was surrounded by a throng of students. Shinya was standing next to him.

"I'm more interested in catching a glimpse of the Ichinose Clan's spells," he said.

Guren wasn't surprised to hear that. But Shinya didn't really seem all that interested. Perhaps he really had written off any hope for Guren.

"Begin!" shouted the judge.

Shigure and Mito both leapt into action.

Mito's movements—amplified by her spell—were incredibly fast.

Shigure, however, was able to react in time. She jumped backward and flung her hand outward. A stream of *kunai*—small ninja dirks—

came flying from her hand. The hilts of each dirk had threads attached to them, which fluttered like magic in the air.

Each thread had a *fuda*—a magical paper charm—attached to it. If anyone came into contact with a thread the *fuda* attached to it would explode, sending the *kunai* leaping back into the air toward whoever had set off the trap.

Mito stared down at the dirks contemptuously.

"Cheap assassin's tricks... I should've expected as much from an Ichinose retainer."

Mito continued to barrel ahead, running straight through the trap that Shigure had set.

One of Mito's long, slender legs came into contact with a thread. Instantly, the *fuda* exploded, sending the attached dirk hurtling straight toward her.

Mito dodged it easily.

One after another, the *fuda* exploded and dirks came flying toward Mito's head. But one after another, she dodged them. If she wasn't fast enough to dodge a strike, she simply knocked it out of the way as she charged forward.

"Man oh man, look at her go!" said Norito.

Shinya, however, looked bored. Apparently neither Mito's speed nor Shigure's cunning was enough to impress a Hiragi.

Mito quickly closed the gap between herself and Shigure.

"Time to end this," sneered Mito, raising her hand in a fist.

Shigure only smirked.

"Nice try, but get ready to be knocked down a peg," she said.

Shigure snapped the fingers on her right hand. In response, one of the *kunai* which Mito had knocked aside exploded, leaping back into the air.

Before Mito knew what happened, the string attached to the end of the *kunai* had wrapped itself around her wrist, holding her tight.

"Ngh!"

Mito couldn't move.

The thread had been hexed. It paralyzed anyone it touched, almost like an injection of anesthetics.

It looked like Shigure had won.

But she wasn't satisfied yet.

She drew one last *kunai* from behind her back and raised it high, ready to throw it straight at Mito's throat.

Guren jerked forward in surprise. He opened his mouth to order Shigure to stand down.

The judges all began shouting at Shigure to stop, as well.

Before anyone could stop her, however....

"Let...me...go...!!" screamed Mito.

The crimson halo above her head grew brighter and began to spin. Suddenly, Mito's fist jerked forward, despite the thread binding her.

"H-How?!"

Shigure's eyes widened in shock.

Mito's fist hurtled forward, landing squarely on Shigure's jaw.

"Ngh!"

Shigure tossed her *kunai* just as she was hit. It veered wide, barely scratching Mito's cheek.

The force of the punch sent Shigure's body soaring through the air. She landed in the dirt and rolled several feet before coming to a stop. It didn't look like she was getting back up. It had been a devastating blow. Shigure's brain had probably shaken inside her skull, leaving her stunned.

Mito, however, was still able to move. She ran toward Shigure's prone body.

"Stop!" shouted the judge. "The winner is Mito Jujo!"

The match had been decided.

"Hmph," said Guren, watching with arms folded.

Ms. Aiuchi struck another victory pose.

"All right, Mito! I knew you had it in you!"

Mito, however, remained where she stood. She stared down at Shigure sadly.

"You can leave the ring now," said the judge.

Mito shook her head. She raised her hand, as if she had something she wanted to say.

"I...I think it should be a draw."

"What?!" The judges all turned their heads sharply toward Mito.

She pointed to the nick on her cheek.

"She injured me, too. But she's an assassin. If this were a real fight..."

"...the weapon would have been coated with lethal poison?" asked the judge.

"Yes. Because of my training I'd still be able to move, even after being poisoned. I could've taken her out while she was still on the ground..."

"But in the end, you would have died too?"

"Yes."

"I see. You have a point. But all decisions are final. Victory is still yours."

"But..."

"The decision is in our hands, Ms. Jujo. Keep your opinions to yourself. Remember, these rules were set by the Hiragi Clan. You're not trying to question them, are you?"

"...Of course not, sir."

Mito left the ring without saying anything more.

Guren watched her go before walking over to Shigure. She was still lying motionless on the ground. He stared down at her.

She was conscious.

However, she was clearly upset. She was biting her lips, either to hold back anger or tears. Guren sighed.

"Looks like you lost," he said.

"Ngh... I'm sorry, Master Guren."

Shigure's face crumpled up in defeat.

"After everything that happened, I wanted to at least win this match. I...I embarrassed you again, Master Guren..."

Shigure choked up mid-sentence, and tears began spilling down her cheeks. Guren just smiled.

"Mito was a strong opponent."

"Yes, sir. It was stupid of me to underestimate her."

"Hey, at least it was a draw."

"I'm from the Yukimi family…one of the Ichinose Clan's body-guards. A draw is the same as a loss, as far as I'm concerned."

"Have it your way, then. It was a loss."

"…"

"Can you stand on your own?"

"…ngh."

Shigure tried to stand and failed. Mito's punch had really been in-credible.

"Are…are you all right?" It was Mito. She approached them timidly from behind. She sounded worried.

"Just…leave me alone, please," said Shigure.

Guren turned toward Mito.

"I guess she wants to be left alone," he said.

"But…"

"Look, she's upset that she lost. She doesn't want you to see her cry. Have a little sympathy, okay?"

"…"

Mito looked down at the ground, embarrassed. Apparently, she was a nice enough person deep down.

She turned on Guren suddenly, however. Her eyes flashed with an-ger.

"Why don't you stay out of it?! I don't need to be scolded by some weakling!"

"If you say so."

"I do. I was talking to Shigure Yukimi. She's strong. She just proved it. But you're…"

"…just in the way?"

"That's right."

"I guess you've got me there. Fine, I'm going. I'll see you later, Shigure."

Shigure raised herself into a sitting position, finally able to move again.

"I'll go with you…" she said.

Mito rushed over to her side.

"A-About earlier…"

"If you're about to apologize for punching me, don't bother. It was a fair fight—"

"Not that," said Mito, cutting her off. "I want to apologize for what I said before the fight. I shouldn't have underestimated you just because you work for Guren. You're stronger than you look."

Shigure opened her mouth as if to say something, but Guren gave her a warning look. Guren figured she was going to say something stupid, like how he was actually even stronger than her.

Catching Guren's glance, Shigure closed her mouth without speaking. She frowned, looking dissatisfied.

Mito didn't seem to notice.

"Have you ever thought of becoming a bodyguard for the Jujo Clan? You're too talented to waste on such a spineless master."

"Don't speak about Master Guren that way…"

"I admire your loyalty as well. Won't you at least consider it?"

"I told you—"

"Come visit our compound. We can discuss it there…"

"Master Guren!" called Shigure, embarrassed. Guren ignored her and began walking back toward his classmates. Shigure could deal with Mito on her own.

The next match was already underway. This one was between Norito Goshi and a boy from Class 1-2.

"Couldn't I have a girl instead?" said Norito. "It's no fun fighting a boy."

"What, you'd rather hit a girl?" said Shinya, laughing from the sidelines.

"Who said anything about hitting her?" Norito shot back laughing. "If she were cute, I could wear down her defenses with my special kissing technique!"

"C-Come on, this is no fair!" cried Norito's opponent, from the other side of the ring. "What's the deal pairing me up with someone from the Goshi Clan on my first match? I don't stand a chance..."

It sounded like he had given up before his match had even started.

"Don't worry, kid," said Norito, "I'll make it quick. The sooner this ends, the sooner I can get back to scouting for hotties."

Norito crooked his finger at his opponent, inviting him to attack.

The boy drew a longsword from his belt. Apparently he was also from a clan that trained in swordcraft.

His movements were fluid. He seemed to at least know his way around a sword.

Norito just stared at him with bored, half-lidded eyes.

"Are we gonna do this or what?"

"Get ready," said the boy.

"Hurry it up, already."

"Here I come...!"

The boy lifted his sword to strike. The instant he did so, however, the sword disappeared.

Norito appeared behind the boy, in a flash. He was holding the boy's sword. He leveled it slowly at the boy's neck.

"Are we done here?" he asked.

The boy stood in place, frozen in shock.

"He's fast..." muttered Guren.

Shinya, who was standing next to Guren, glanced at him out of the corner of his eyes and sighed.

"No, he isn't," he sneered.

"What?"

Shinya turned back toward the fight without explaining.

But Guren already knew what Shinya meant.

Norito had actually used illusion magic.

Norito's movement hadn't been fast at all. His illusions had just been very convincing. The actual Norito had slowly walked toward his opponent, slowly stolen his sword, and slowly pointed it at his neck.

Guren had made his comment on purpose, so that it would appear that he couldn't tell what was happening. It was all for Shinya's sake, to ensure that the Hiragis continued to underestimate Guren.

Guren's plan appeared to be working. Shinya now clearly despised him. He barely even bothered to look in his direction anymore.

Guren shrugged, satisfied.

Shinya's name was called next.

"Shinya Hiragi, Class 1-9."

"I'm here," said Shinya, raising his head.

Shinya stepped forward into the ring. Murmurs of excitement spread through the crowd.

—*It's Shinya Hiragi!*
—*Shinya Hiragi is fighting next!*

The students whispered his name in admiration.

"You'd almost think he was a celebrity," said Guren, laughing to himself.

Shinya's opponent stepped forward next. The poor kid was practically shaking in his boots.

For some reason, Shinya glanced toward Guren one more time before the fight began. They made eye contact.

It seemed like some sort of challenge.

"Hmph. I thought he had already given up on me," muttered Guren. "Maybe he wants to show off just how much stronger than me he actually is..."

At last, the match began.

"Lord Shinya...I'm ready!"

"Let's make it a good fight."

"Yes, sir!"

Shinya's opponent smiled, happy that Shinya had deigned to speak to him. He drew several *fuda* from his uniform. Apparently, Shinya's opponent was primarily a spellcaster.

The boy tossed the *fuda* into the air and began casting a powerful spell.

While the boy readied his spell, Shinya simply stood his ground. He didn't seem to be doing anything—but waiting patiently.

Shinya's opponent began to grow worried.

"Umm…"

"Yes?"

"Aren't you going to attack?"

"Oops. I guess I forgot."

"My spell is already finished…"

"Is it? You'd better cast it then."

"But it's a pretty big spell… If it hits you full-on, I'm pretty sure it would kill you…"

"Really? This should be interesting then."

"But…I don't want to kill you, Lord Shinya. Are you…conceding defeat? I don't mean to be impertinent…"

"Cast your spell," said Shinya. "It won't affect me."

A look of surprise appeared on the boy's face. After all, it was a pretty unbelievable claim.

It was only natural for the boy to be concerned. Everyone at First Shibuya studied Hiragi spellcraft. But even by the school's high standards, the spell the boy had prepared was impressive.

It looked like it had been designed for widespread destruction. Usually, a spellcaster would need to be protected by teammates in order to have enough time to prepare a spell of that magnitude.

The boy fighting Shinya, however, was able to ready his spell in just a few seconds. He was clearly very skilled. Once he let the spell loose, victory was almost assured.

After all, no normal person could survive a blast from a spell that huge. And once a spell like that was prepared, it was too late to dispel it.

Hence the boy asking Shinya to concede defeat.

"I can't kill someone from the Hiragi Clan," said the boy, glancing anxiously at the judges. "Can I just be disqualified instead?"

The judges turned toward Shinya.

"Is that acceptable?"

"I already told him," said Shinya, "to cast the spell."

"But…"

"But what? Do you all doubt my power?"

"…"

The judges looked startled. A moment later, one of them turned back toward Shinya's opponent.

"Cast your spell," he said.

The boy looked uncertain at first, but then he furrowed his brow in determination.

"Fine, but don't hold me responsible for what happens!"

The boy activated the spell.

The *fuda* floating in the air flickered, and a great ball of fire appeared in their place. The fireball went hurtling toward Shinya.

Shinya raised his hand, lazily, as the fireball approached.

"Begone," he said.

Amazingly, the ball of fire disappeared.

The crowd was speechless.

What had just happened? Nobody knew. Even the judges seemed at a loss. They were so surprised they forgot to announce the winner.

But it was already clear to everyone there who the winner was.

Shinya turned slowly on his heel and exited the ring. He was walking in Guren's direction.

"Th-The winner is Shinya Hiragi!" announced one of the judges, at long last.

Cheers of applause rang out among the students. Shinya glanced at Guren and smirked.

"I'm guessing you don't know what happened there, either."

Guren opened his mouth to answer, but Shinya just walked past him without waiting for a response.

It seemed that Shinya was no longer interested in what Guren had to say.

Shinya's technique had been very impressive. But Guren understood how he had done it. It had simply been an illusion. His casting hadn't even been any faster than Norito's. His timing had just been more clever.

Shinya had weaved the illusion while he was still conversing with the boy. He had then used the illusion to interrupt his opponent's spell at several points.

The spell had actually been sabotaged, in advance, so that it would fail.

It was dirty fighting. Shinya had been in control the entire time. Guren wondered whether he would be able to defeat Shinya if they ever came to real blows. After what he had just seen, he honestly wasn't sure.

"How did you do that?" said Guren, keeping up his act, just in case.

Shinya, however, didn't bother turning around.

Apparently he wasn't interested in watching Guren's match, either.

Just then, the judge called out Guren's name.

"Next up, Guren Ichinose. Come forward!"

Shinya had already headed back toward the classroom. Guren smirked to himself.

"Guren Ichinose! Come forward now!" repeated the judge. Guren turned back toward the schoolyard.

"Sorry," he said, stepping into the center of the ring.

"Master Guren, go get him!" shouted Shigure from the sidelines.

The other students all laughed in response. Even Ms. Aiuchi snickered.

"I suppose we can afford to lose one match," she said.

The students from his opponent's class were even worse. Instead of shouting at Guren they shouted at his opponent, saying how he'd never live it down if he lost to some mangy Ichinose dog.

" . . . "

Guren, however, wasn't planning on losing this time. He wanted to face Seishiro Hiragi in the second round. Of course, he did plan on losing his match to Seishiro. But the fight would give him a chance to judge just how powerful the Hiragis really were.

First thing first though, he had to win today's match.

But only by the skin of his teeth.

Guren's opponent stepped forward. He looked nervous, and his stance was clumsy. He held a spear in his hand.

Guren placed his hand on the sword at his hip.

"Let's make it a good fight," said Guren, bowing.

"Don't talk to me, mongrel," said the boy, snorting through his nose.

"My apologies."

"Whatever. Just get ready to lose."

"Go easy on me, at least."

The match began.

The match, however, was barely worth commenting on.

Guren fought as poorly as possible, staying on the defensive the entire time. He stumbled around the ring and ran from his opponent whenever he could. He only won in the end thanks to what looked like a lucky, wild swing that happened to knock his opponent out.

"The winner is Guren Ichinose!" shouted the judge. A massive groan broke out among the students.

Even Guren's classmates booed and jeered, complaining that he had embarrassed them. Norito rolled his eyes.

"You're even weaker than I thought," he said.

"Aren't you embarrassed to have someone as strong as Shigure follow you when you're so incompetent?" said Mito. "You could at least put in some effort, instead of relying on your followers to cover for you."

Mito seemed personally offended by Guren's weakness. Apparently, she had been so impressed by Shigure during their fight that now she felt the need to look after her.

"I guess I do rely on Shigure a lot…" said Guren.

"Then why don't you release her from your service?" Mito suggested. "You've got no right to be in charge of someone so skilled!"

"…"

"Stop it," said Shigure, cutting in. "I won't let you talk about Master Guren that way!"

The other students all burst into laughter. A girl coming to his defense made him look even weaker.

Mito glared at Guren.

"See? Aren't you ashamed of yourself?"

"Of course I am. But I am weak. What am I supposed to do about it?"

What Guren said was part of his act, but it was also partly true.

It bothered him every day. That he lacked the strength. That he lacked the power to take down the Hiragi Clan. It made him feel ashamed.

"If you'd just put in some effort!" bemoaned Mito.

Why didn't he just put in more effort?

"…Whatever," said Guren, turning to go.

As he did so, a shout of excitement rose up from the next ring. The cheering was as loud as the one that had greeted Shinya's entrance.

The ring was where Class 1-3 and Class 1-5 were holding their matches.

Class 1-3 was Mahiru's class.

Guren peered in their direction.

Just as he thought, Mahiru was currently fighting.

She was fast. Even faster than Shinya. Every one of her moves was perfect.

Mahiru's opponent seemed to be at about the same level as Mito. Mahiru defeated her easily.

Mahiru's strength had skyrocketed over the past ten years.

Guren wondered if it was due to effort, or just inborn Hiragi talent.

Maybe it was both.

"Effort, huh?" muttered Guren, still staring at Mahiru.

Guren's thoughts were interrupted by the sound of someone screaming. The scream came from a different ring. Guren recognized the voice. It was one he knew very well.

"Sayuri…?"

Guren turned in its direction.

The scream had come from the ring where Class 1-1 and Class 1-4 were holding their matches.

Guren could also hear the sound of cheers.

The crowd was cheering as enthusiastically as they had for Mahiru and Shinya.

"Kill her! Kill her!" chanted the crowd.

"Do it, Lord Seishiro!"

"Kill the filthy Ichinose bitch!"

Guren finally spotted them.

Sayuri was in the ring, and she was fighting Seishiro Hiragi.

Sayuri looked like she was on her last legs. She was battered and bruised. Her lip was split, probably from a punch, and blood streamed from the cut. Her shoulders heaved as she panted for breath. The front of her sailor uniform was torn and her left hand was clutched to her chest, desperately trying to keep her shirt from falling open.

Her opponent, Seishiro Hiragi, grinned maliciously at her.

"I must be going too easy on you," he said. "You seem more worried about hiding your tits than fighting me."

The other students burst into laughter.

"Strip her naked!"

"What's a pig need clothes for anyways?"

Seishiro spread his arms out wide, showboating for the crowd.

"If that's what the crowd wants, that's what the crowd gets… Let's strip the she-piggie!"

Seishiro took a step toward Sayuri.

Sayuri stumbled backward, but Seishiro was too quick for her. His hand reached out toward Sayuri's chest.

"Ngh."

Sayuri tried to smack his hand away.

Her parry, however, missed. Midway, Seishiro's hand closed into a fist and changed direction. He landed an uppercut square on her chin.

"Nggh!"

Sayuri's head snapped back and her uniform fell open, exposing her bra.

Seishiro wasn't finished yet.

"She-piggies should keep their filthy bodies to themselves," he said, punching her in the stomach this time.

"Ngh!"

Sayuri doubled over in her pain. As her face fell forward Seishiro brought his knee up, bouncing her head backward like it was a soccer ball.

The blow had almost certainly knocked Sayuri out.

It was hardly a fair fight. Sayuri was clearly no match for Seishiro.

With Sayuri knocked out, the fight should have ended there.

"Not so fast," said Seishiro. As Sayuri collapsed he began hitting her with a flurry of punches and kicks. The force of his blows tossed her around like a ragdoll, keeping her on her feet.

Seishiro laughed maniacally as he continued to beat the unconscious Sayuri.

"Dammit," hissed Guren. He broke into a run, heading straight for the ring.

"Why won't you stop the match?" he shouted at the judges.

The teachers—who were supposedly refereeing the match—only smiled coldly at Guren.

Like everyone else at the school, they were all on Seishiro's side.

Seishiro glanced at Guren and smirked.

He grabbed Sayuri's neck and began to squeeze.

"There you are. I was wondering what was taking you so long. You're just in time to see one of your followers die."

"You son of a bitch…"

"Haha, such anger. Do you think a weakling like you can stop me? Fine then, let's go. There's no need to wait for our match tomorrow. We can see who's stronger—Hiragi or Ichinose—right here and now."

Guren narrowed his eyes.

"Dammit," he muttered, "I guess it can't be helped."

Guren took a step forward.

"Wait…!" Someone grabbed Guren's arm, holding him back.

He turned around to be met by Mahiru. Guren had no idea when she had gotten there. She'd been fighting her own match just moments before.

"You're not strong enough to beat Seishiro. If you fight him now you'll be killed."

Guren stared into her eyes. She smiled back at him, wanly, before turning her attention toward Seishiro.

"My ears must be deceiving me," she said. "I thought I just heard you say you were planning on killing that girl."

Seishiro glared back at her coldly.

"…This is none of your concern, Mahiru. Stay out of my business."

"This is my business. I won't let you dirty the Hiragi name…"

"I told you, stay out of it!"

Mahiru sprang forward in a flash. Her movements were graceful and perfect, leaving no opening for a counterstrike.

Mahiru's left hand stretched out toward Seishiro.

Seishiro swung wildly, trying to bat her arm away. Mahiru changed direction effortlessly, reaching instead for Sayuri, whom she easily wrested from Seishiro's grasp.

"Ngh!"

Seishiro gritted his teeth. He balled his hand into a fist, ready to swing at Mahiru. Mahiru stared at him from beneath hooded eyes.

"Are you sure you want to take this any further?" she said menacingly.

Mahiru's eyes flashed with venom. It was just a split second, but Guren saw it. He wondered if any of the other students had seen as well.

The look would have been easy to miss. It was only there for a brief moment.

Seishiro seemed to get the message, however. His fist stopped in mid-air. He glared hatefully at Mahiru.

"You brat... You think just because you're dad's favorite you can..."

"...do whatever I want? I don't have any interest in making father happy and I never have."

"You stupid, little..."

"This conversation is over, Seishiro. Judges. I believe the match is over."

"Ah...f-forgive me..." one of the judges stammered.

"Your apologies are unnecessary. Just end this disgusting match."

The judge announced Seishiro's victory.

Mahiru walked back toward Guren. She was still carrying the unconscious Sayuri in her arms. She handed Sayuri's limp body to Guren.

"Your follower," she said.

Guren took Sayuri from Mahiru's arms.

"I'm sorry—"

"I don't want you to apologize to me," interrupted Mahiru. "Especially not this weak you, who can't protect the girls in his life."

Mahiru walked away without saying anything more.

This weak you...

Mahiru's words echoed in Guren's head.

But no matter how many times he repeated them, he couldn't pin down Mahiru's meaning.

Was she saying that Guren couldn't protect Sayuri...or was she talking about herself? How he had never come back for her?

"..."

Guren stared at her as she walked away.

"Wh-Where am I...?"

Sayuri's eyes fluttered open. She was still lying in Guren's arms. Her face was black and blue.

She was covered in bruises. They seemed out of place on a girl her age.

Despite her bruises, Sayuri's face broke into a smile as she stared up at Guren.

"You came to save me…" she said.

"…"

"I'm…I'm sorry, Master Guren. I lost my match…"

"…"

"B-But…I tried my best, and I didn't use any Ichinose magic."

"…"

"I shouldn't have lost in such an embarrassing way, though—"

"Try not to speak," said Guren, interrupting her. "You'll open your cuts back up. And you didn't embarrass anyone. You did well. It's this place that's wrong."

"B-But…"

"I told you, don't speak."

Sayuri fell silent.

Shigure came rushing up from behind.

"Master Guren! Here, let me take Sayuri from you…"

"It's all right. I'll carry her. Let's go home. Our matches are already over for today."

"Yes, sir."

"You both did well today."

Guren couldn't help but feel that his words were inadequate. He cursed his own weakness.

Seishiro, however, wanted to add insult to injury. He shouted after them as they walked away, "That's right, losers, run home and cry!"

The other students all burst into laughter. Every single one of them.

A sorrowful look appeared on Sayuri's and Shigure's faces.

Guren didn't mind being made fun of. But he couldn't stand to see Sayuri and Shigure hurt.

"…"

Laugh now… thought Guren, *but one day, I'll kill every last one of you Hiragi scum.*

How great would it feel? To throw all his ambitions away and just give in to anger and revenge? Thoughts of what he could do to them flashed through Guren's mind. He turned around and glared at the other students...

"Why do you guys always have to make fun of me?" he said, purposefully sounding as feeble as possible.

The students only laughed harder. They looked like they were about to piss themselves with laughter.

Sayuri clung to Guren's chest, whimpering. Guren looked down at her and frowned.

Mahiru's words echoed once more in his head.

I don't want you to apologize to me, she had said. *Especially not this weak you, who can't protect the girls in his life.*

"Dammit," cursed Guren.

As he walked away from the school and the courtyard, he felt more troubled than ever before.

It was the next day.

Another round of qualifying exams was being held in the school-yard.

The students' shouts and cheers filled the air.

The elite students in Guren's class—Class 1-9—were dominating their matches. The class's winning streak continued as they easily over-powered their opponents.

By tomorrow, or possibly the day after that, they would begin facing off against each other.

For now, however, team spirit was still high.

After going through two days of exams together, the students in the class had begun to grow close.

"….well, except for me, of course," muttered Guren, staring up at the sky.

He chuckled to himself.

The weather had been sunny for the past few days. The sky was clear today, too.

Not a single cloud was in sight.

Underneath that peaceful sky, meanwhile, the students were pitted against each other in vicious grudge matches.

The exams might not have been as bad as human experiments, but every two or three years at least one student was killed.

So in a way, they were a kind of human experiment in their own right.

"Is this really any different than what the Thousand Nights does?" muttered Guren.

It wasn't to say that the Ichinose Clan didn't carry out similar training. He wasn't going to start getting picky now.

Someone shouted at Guren from nearby.

"Hey, Guren!"

It was Shinya.

"Huh? I thought you weren't talking to me anymore."

"I did say that, didn't I?" laughed Shinya. "I have to admit, I was pretty disappointed in you."

"So why don't you leave me alone?"

"I'm just a softie, I guess. You're so weak, I thought I should lend you a helping hand."

"What do you mean?"

"Today's match. Just forfeit it. I'll make sure there's no problem if you do."

Guren glanced at Shinya out of the corners of his eyes.

"What do you mean, forfeit?"

"I heard about yesterday," said Shinya. "Your bodyguard...what's her name?"

"Sayuri Hanayori."

"Yeah, her. I heard she was hospitalized..."

Sayuri's wounds had been pretty severe. After leaving the school they had taken her straight to the hospital. Guren had asked Shigure to stay at the hospital with her. As a result, neither Sayuri nor Shigure was at school today.

"How is she doing?" asked Shinya.

"...She's fine," replied Guren, turning his eyes back toward the matches. "Don't worry about her. My followers are well-trained. It would take a lot more to do them in."

"Haha, they train that hard even though their master is so weak?"

"...Yes."

"Well then, what about you? Aren't you ashamed that even your own followers are stronger than you?"

Guren glanced at Shinya without answering. Shinya went on, not expecting an answer.

"After what happened to your followers, a normal person would want payback against Seishiro, no matter how bad the odds were. Don't you feel that way at all?"

Guren grimaced in reply.

"What good would that do?" he said.

"What good?!"

"Obviously I don't stand a chance against him. I don't believe in wasting my time on pointless fantasies."

"Hmph."

"And my followers...Sayuri...wouldn't want it, either. They wouldn't want me to do something rash and get injured, too—"

"Enough," said Shinya, raising a hand to stop Guren. "I've heard your excuses. Long story short, you were born a loser and you'll die a loser. Right?"

"..."

"I guess I was right about you, then. If you had at least shown some spine, I would have told you Seishiro's weaknesses instead. But I guess there's no point. Forfeit the match. If you try fighting with that attitude you'll just be killed."

"..."

"That's the kind of person Seishiro is. He'll humiliate you, and then he'll kill you. The teachers won't stop him, either. They wouldn't even lower his evaluation for killing you."

"So I should forfeit?"

Shinya nodded.

"You mean I should run, without fighting."

"Yeah. After all, it's what you do best, isn't it?"

Guren thought about it. Should he do what Shinya said? He was hoping to trade at least a few blows with Seishiro, so he could judge firsthand how fast the Hiragis were with their spells.

But the circumstances had changed.

After what had happened to Sayuri yesterday, Guren wasn't sure he'd be able to control himself.

If he fought Seishiro...

He would have to continue acting weak, while Seishiro showboated for the crowd. Seishiro would show off some of his techniques, and then Guren would close the act by losing.

But he didn't think he was mature enough to do that this time. He could feel the anger building up in his chest already, just thinking about the day before.

His sense of pride?

His need to assert himself?

What he really needed was power. All the anger and pride in the world would only get in his way. He would end up throwing away everything he had worked for, all for one brief moment of gratification.

Hold it in, he told himself. *Be patient. Your real goal lies elsewhere.*

He wouldn't accomplish it by playing their childish games.

Guren glanced at Shinya.

"So you'll help me forfeit the match?" he said, bowing his head.

Shinya fixed Guren with an icy stare. A look of disgust appeared on his face.

"You're pathetic," he said.

"But you're the one who told me to forfeit..."

"What a waste of space," he said, ignoring Guren's words and turning away with a rueful expression. "I can't believe that Mahiru..."

Whatever he was going to say, he stopped mid-sentence.

"Fine, I'll help you forfeit your match," he spat. He slapped Guren on the shoulder once and walked away without saying anything more.

The current match was just coming to an end. The judge called out the names of the next students.

"Seishiro Hiragi, Class 1-4. Come forward!"

Seishiro stepped into the ring.

"Guren Ichinose, Class 1-9. Come forward!"

Guren didn't move. Instead, Shinya stepped forward to face Seishiro.

A murmur passed through the crowd.

Norito and Mito, who were standing nearby, glanced at Guren in confusion.

"What the heck is going on?" said Mito.

"Why is Shinya in the ring instead of you?" said Norito.

"I'm forfeiting the match..." said Guren, a self-deprecating smile on his face.

"What?!"

"I don't stand a chance against Seishiro."

Norito's eyes widened in shock.

"You're not serious, are you?"

"This is going too far," said Mito, glaring at him. "Don't you even care what he did to your follower yesterday?!"

"Seriously! Forget about the odds, you can't just forfeit! She fought hard, for your sake. She didn't care about the consequences! You can't just tuck tail and run! I don't care how strong Seishiro is. You need to get in there and fight!"

"Listen to Norito! Even if you lose, we'll stop him before anything bad happens... If you don't fight, everything your followers did for you will be wasted—"

"Dammit, why can't you guys just leave me alone?" said Guren, cutting them off. "I don't need you two telling me what to do. I'm forfeiting the match. I'm weaker than Sayuri. So what point is there in fighting?"

Mito was at a loss for words, hardly able to believe what she had just heard.

Norito glared at Guren. He had a look on his face like he had just stepped in something.

"Ha! He's forfeiting? You've gotta be kidding me!" cried Seishiro. Apparently Shinya had explained the situation. "I can't believe he's running. Not after what I did to his woman. The Ichinoses really are pathetic."

Word of Guren's forfeit quickly spread through the crowd. The other students began laughing viciously. They taunted Guren, throwing every insult they could muster at him.

"..."

Guren didn't budge. He just stared up at the sky, refusing to meet anyone's gaze.

He could still hear them, however.

—*Look at him. I think he's scared stiff!*

—*I didn't know anyone could be so pathetic.*

—*Isn't he the one whose bodyguard got the stuffing kicked out of her yesterday? He's got a lot of nerve coming to this school. How low can you get?*

Their laughter grew louder and louder.

They were all laughing at Guren and making fun of him for being weak.

Guren laughed along with them, like a fool.

He tried to come off as exactly what they said he was. Someone with no pride, no ambition, and no strength. A mongrel.

Eventually they would tire of laughing and turn their attention elsewhere.

Guren was used to this routine.

He had three more years of it to look forward to.

But suddenly, everything changed.

"...Ngh?!"

Guren sensed danger. He reacted instinctively, turning his head toward the source of the attack. He was lucky he did.

Something was wrong.

Something in the sky.

Guren spotted a beam of red light. It was hurtling through the sky on a collision course straight toward them. Guren tensed, preparing to dodge.

Just a step to the side…

As soon as he began to move, he realized a girl was standing right close to him.

It was Mito Jujo. And next to her was Norito Goshi. They were both standing directly in the ray's path.

They still hadn't noticed. They were completely oblivious to the coming attack.

At the speed the beam was moving, Guren doubted anyone could see it coming.

If he didn't save them, they would die.

Guren's face twisted up in frustration.

"Dammit!" he said.

He thrust his hand out, reaching for Mito's shoulder.

"Ahh!"

Mito cried out in shock. She was thrust backward, bumping into Norito.

"Dude, what the hell?!" said Norito, staring at Guren in surprise.

"What do you think you're doing?!" shouted Mito, tumbling off her feet.

Her cries were cut short as the light made impact.

It passed right before Mito's eyes and crashed into a small group of students standing behind them. The students were tossed like ragdolls, engulfed in a fiery burst as the red light hit the dirt and exploded.

Luckily, the explosion wasn't very large. Whatever the attack had been designed to do, apparently it wasn't mass destruction.

The blast was enough to kill more than a few people, however.

Not just people—students. Someone was killing the students.

The attack wasn't over. More beams were incoming.

A score of fiery blasts rained down upon the schoolyard, sweeping through the students' ranks.

Explosions broke out across the yard. The ground shook, and a deafening roar filled the air.

For a moment all was silence. And then…

—*Auggggghhhh!!*

—*What happened? What in the hell just happened?!*

—*Oh god, my arm!*

—*They're dead, they're all dead!*

Screams filled the air. Guren could hear other students crying in pain. Their voices shook with fear.

This was no time for crying, though.

Someone was attacking the school.

Guren stared back toward the sky.

One after another, men in black suits came floating down from overhead. It was happening.

The war had begun.

The war between the Brotherhood of a Thousand Nights and the Hiragi Clan.

According to Saito, the war would begin in ten days' time. It had only been two days since they'd last met. Saito had lied.

Not that Guren had taken him at his word in the first place…

"…but I didn't think anything would happen so soon."

He scanned the surrounding carnage.

The other students and teachers were still caught off guard. Visibility was also limited. The explosions from the surprise bombing had created smokescreens. Apparently the main purpose of those red beams of light had been to blind the students.

Guren lost sight of Mito and Norito. Only Shinya and Seishiro still remained in his field of vision.

Guren could hear screams, however. Beyond the smoke, the screams of students surrounded him on all sides.

—*Don't kill me! P-Please, don't kill me…auughhhh!*

—*I don't know who you are, but you won't get away with this. This school is run by the Order of the Imperial Demons! You…you'll…aieeeeeee!*

They were being slaughtered.

The students had never seen real combat. It left them complacent and defenseless. The attack, on the other hand, was deliberate. The enemy had come well prepared.

"At this rate, everyone will be killed," muttered Guren.

He placed his hand on the sword at his hip.

As he did so, a lone man in black came floating down from the sky. He landed in the center of the schoolyard's temporary fighting ring where matches were being held only moments ago.

Guren recognized the man's face.

He had last seen him two days ago. It was the man called Saito, the assassin from the Thousand Nights.

As Saito landed he cast a glance around him and then smiled wryly.

"Excellent. They can all die," he said, spreading his arms out wide.

"Who the hell is that?" said Shinya.

"You made a big mistake, chump," said Seishiro. "You think you'll get away with attacking the Hiragi Clan like this?"

"That's exactly what I think. I hate noisy brats like you," said Saito.

Chains sprouted from Saito's body. They were the same kind of chains as the one he had used to attack Guren. This time, however, there were several of them. They went shooting toward Seishiro.

Seishiro dodged. First one chain. Then the second. Then the third.

"Ha! You've got some nerve attacking me with such a pathetic weapon," mocked Seishiro.

Seishiro didn't realize it was a trap. Saito was herding him. He had Seishiro exactly where he wanted him.

And Saito's chains could move faster than that. Much, much faster.

"Checkmate," smirked Saito. "When you meet your maker, tell him it was pride that was your downfall."

A fourth chain darted from Saito's body, hurtling at full speed toward Seishiro.

There was no way for Seishiro to dodge. Saito had tricked him into cornering himself. He could have saved himself the trouble, though. His chain was moving so fast that Seishiro wouldn't have been able to dodge it even without the trap.

Seishiro didn't stand a chance.

"S-Stop!" he screamed. His face twisted up in horror.

"Move, you fool!" shouted Guren.

He was standing behind Seishiro. He leapt forward and kicked Seishiro as hard as he could, sending him flying out of the way.

"Ngh!"

The kick was so strong it tossed Seishiro into the air and through one of the smokescreens created by the initial blast.

He disappeared from sight.

Seishiro may have been gone, but Saito's attack continued. The other chains—the ones he had used to trap Seishiro—whipped into the air to join the assault.

All of the chains were moving at full speed now. More of them appeared. One had been too fast for Seishiro to dodge. Now there were eight, all together. They writhed like tentacles in the air, each hurtling toward Guren from a different direction.

"…"

Guren stopped watching the chains.

He couldn't focus on each of them, individually.

If he tried to block them in turn, he'd never be able to react to all eight. Instead of focusing on the chains he stared ahead blankly. It wasn't until one of them entered his field of vision that he drew his sword.

Guren's spells were already active. There was magic to make his blade unsheathe faster. Magic to sharpen its edge. And magic to curse anything the blade cut.

For most casters, even one of those spells would have been difficult to weave. Guren had activated them all in the blink of an eye. He drew his sword and slashed away the chain with a single strike.

Guren heard a gasp from behind him. It was Shinya.

"H-How did you do that?"

Guren glanced over his shoulder. Shinya was standing there with a look of astonishment on his face.

"…Dammit. You're the last witness I ever wanted."

"If you're so powerful, why have you been hiding it for so long?"

"Be quiet," snapped Guren, "unless you want to be on the receiving end of this sword next. I know better than to trust someone who can't keep his trap shut."

Shinya's eyes widened in shock.

"Now you know the truth," said Guren. "But answer me one question. Were you serious when you said you wanted to destroy the Hiragi Clan?"

"…"

"You've seen my strength. If you were lying, I'll cut you down right now, where you stand."

Guren reversed his blade, leveling it at Shinya and holding it against the nape of his neck.

Shinya never had a chance to dodge. Guren had swung the sword with perfect timing.

"Ngh."

Shinya stared at Guren in shock. Guren smiled in response.

"Of course, if you were serious about what you said, then I guess I could use you as a servant. What do you say? Follow me, and we'll take out this jerk in the suit together."

Shinya glanced down at the blade thrust against his neck and smiled. He actually looked pleased.

"Heh. Don't get ahead of yourself, Guren. Who says I'm not just as strong as you are?"

"I do."

"Don't be so sure—"

He didn't get to finish. Saito was coming in for a second attack.

He shot one of his chains at Guren, who dove out of the way. The chain was fast. It had been too fast for Seishiro to dodge only moments before.

Bur right now it was either dodge or die. A few of the chains were also directed at Shinya. Guren didn't look back to make sure he was all right. If Shinya couldn't take care of himself in a fight, then it was a waste of time for Guren to bother saving him.

Fortunately…

"…well? How should we take down the guy in the suit?"

It was Shinya. Guren spun around to see him standing there, alive and whole.

Shinya had slapped several protective *fuda* onto Saito's chains, sealing them into the ground. Apparently Guren wasn't the only one who had been hiding his full strength.

"Hmph. I still think I'm stronger than you," said Guren.

"Wanna put that to the test?" said Shinya.

"Just my luck," said Saito, interrupting their exchange. "I picked the worst spot to land. There's only seven people on the list of dangerous targets at this school, and I'm stuck handling two of them."

"I see," said Guren, turning his attention back toward Saito. "So you already investigated me and Shinya before coming here. Didn't you, Saito?"

"Of course. We wouldn't start a war with the Hiragi Clan without doing our homework first."

"Wait a second, Guren, you know this guy?" said Shinya.

"He's from the Brotherhood of a Thousand Nights. They're waging a war to crush the Hiragis. They contacted me a while back, to ask me to join their fight."

Shinya didn't seem particularly surprised by the revelation.

"Ahh, now it all makes sense. I probably would've figured it out for myself if I'd given it some thought. After all, how many people out there are capable of attacking the Hiragi Clan head on…"

"…other than the Thousand Nights?" Guren completed the sentence. "Quit asking stupid questions. You've got the brain of a monkey."

"Keep flapping your gums and maybe I'll take care of you before the suit here gets a chance."

"You and what army?"

"Haha. Anyway, back to the matter at hand," said Shinya, scanning their surroundings. "It looks like we're surrounded by smokescreens. None of the other students or teachers can see us…"

Guren glanced around out of the corners of his eyes. What Shinya said seemed to be true.

It almost looked as if the smokescreens had been set up to quarantine them from the other students.

From beyond the smokescreens came the sounds of screaming and explosions. A fierce battle was being waged.

"Why are we the only two on this side of the smokescreens, Guren? It almost seems intentional. We're the two students who hate the Hiragi Clan the most, and we just happened to get stuck together? When you stop to think about it…"

"It's so much easier negotiating when your partner is intelligent," said Saito, flashing them a grin. "Obviously I'm here to talk, not to fight."

"Hmph. So talk."

"…Join us. Let's crush the Hiragi Clan together. Once the Hiragis have been beaten into submission, you two will be left in charge. Any who remain will be your slaves."

That seemed to have gotten Shinya's attention.

"Well, that's certainly an interesting proposition," he said, "but who would be in charge of this new empire? Me or Guren?"

"That's not my concern," said Saito. "You'll have to fight it out between yourselves."

Shinya turned toward Guren.

"Well, you heard the man. What do you think?"

"…"

"Don't tell me you've already made a deal with them? Are you working for the Thousand Nights? What were the terms?"

Guren cast a sidelong glance at Shinya. "I told you, you talk too much. If you want to accept so much then go ahead and accept. Become king of your little empire."

"Well—"

"For my part, I'm not interested in being a puppet for the Thousand Nights," said Guren, interrupting Shinya. "I've already had enough of bowing my head. My answer is right here!"

Guren suddenly leapt forward, brandishing his sword.

"I'll destroy anyone who tries to control me!"

He swung his katana with full force. He didn't want to just cut his opponent. He wanted to wipe him off the face of the planet.

Saito stared at the blade calmly as it descended.

"We've been through this before," he said. "Don't you remember? Physical attacks don't affect me. My body has been altered to resist such tactics."

Saito's chains writhed into the air, and his body began to diffuse into mist.

Guren hadn't forgotten.

What they saw before them wasn't Saito's true form.

Guren suspected that Saito's human form was only a disguise, and that his actual body was made of the black mist now enshrouding his chains.

Guren carried through with his strike, undeterred.

Saito's chains twisted in the air, ready to block.

"Ahh, these chains won't be enough to stop that blow," hissed Saito.

Saito was right. Guren's blade sliced clean through the chains.

The blow landed on Saito's shoulder, digging into his flesh.

Saito just smiled, apparently unfazed.

"I told you, physical attacks are useless…" he said.

Guren wasn't finished yet, though. He slipped a *fuda* from the sleeve of his uniform and pasted it onto his sword. Instantly, the scarlet blade flared to life, glowing a deeper crimson, like blood and fire.

"Kujakumaru…release!"

The blade exploded with energy.

The dark curse inside the sword came to life, undulating in tendrils through Saito's body.

When they had fought before, Saito had protected himself from

Guren's physical attacks by transforming his body into mist. This time, Guren was using a different approach.

Guren's sword was named Kujakumaru. It had been wielded by the leader of the Ichinose Clan for generations. According to legend, the angry souls of all those felled by the sword remained trapped as a curse inside the blade.

A curse that could be released with the correct spell.

"Gh...ngh... Wh-What's happening?!" shouted Saito. He stared at Guren in shock. "I can't move..."

"..."

"My body was designed to resist all Hiragi Clan magic..."

"I'm not a Hiragi," growled Guren, glaring back at Saito.

The curse was gnawing away at Saito, consuming him from within. Little by little it invaded his mist form, devouring him in a mass of red light and turning his chains to rust.

A gruesome smile spread across Guren's face.

"Look at what's happening to you, Saito. Do you know why you're glowing red? The curse is feeding on you. The curse changes you, and then it devours you. Once it has finished consuming you, you'll be trapped for all eternity inside the sword."

A look of fear spread across Saito's face.

"S-Stop...!"

"If you want me to stop, then you'll answer my questions. Why did you choose to attack the school? Why attack a bunch of helpless kids? The Hiragi Clan's power isn't concentrated here. It doesn't make any sense."

As Guren spoke, screams echoed through the yard. It was the screams of students dying.

Only moments earlier, those same students had been laughing in mockery at Guren.

"B-Because..."

"If you lie to me, I'll kill you on the spot. If I even suspect you of lying, I'll kill you. So think carefully before you answer. Why are you here?"

"I guess I've got no choice," said Saito, staring at Guren.

Saito closed his eyes and sighed. A moment later he opened them again.

A pattern had appeared in the center of his eye, like a coiled snake.

It was a spell.

There was a spell inscribed directly onto Saito's eye.

Guren tensed, ready to leap backward out of the way. Before he could, however, Shinya stepped forward.

"You don't need to retreat," he said, plastering a protective *fuda* straight over Saito's eye. "There, it's sealed."

"Ah…!" Saito gasped stupidly.

"I want to hear your answer, too," said Shinya. "I don't really care what happens to the other Hiragi Clan students…but there doesn't seem to be any reason for you to attack here. You didn't bring that many troops with you, either. Once the Imperial Demon Army shows up they'll have no problem clearing you out. What are you trying to accomplish?"

Saito sighed again, this time in real distress.

"Dammit. I thought this would be easier. For a couple of kids, you two really are strong… I told my bosses to send more than one guy to deal with you two—"

Guren cut him off mid-sentence, driving his sword deeper into Saito's chest.

"Nrggh!"

Guren let him suffer for a moment before speaking.

"No more stalling. Answer my questions, and keep the small talk to yourself."

"…"

"Why? Why did you come here?"

"…There's something here we want," Saito said.

"Here?"

"Yes."

"What is it?"

"Research materials."

"…"

"It's a long story. One of the students here betrayed the Hiragis. This student has been selling secret magics to the Thousand Nights, behind the clan's back… The research project was an experiment we've been carrying out together with the student."

The corner of Guren's mouth twisted into a smile.

Apparently the Hiragi Clan had even more enemies than Guren had thought. Their position didn't seem to be as stable as the clan let on.

However powerful an organization grew, there were always other organizations out there waiting in the wings to take it down.

And of course, individuals who disagreed with the organization and who were willing to sabotage it from within always existed too.

"You're not the one who's been selling them information, are you?" asked Guren, turning toward Shinya.

Shinya shrugged his shoulders. His *fuda* was still plastered across Saito's face.

"This may come as a surprise, but it's the first time I've ever come into contact with the Thousand Nights. I wonder why they didn't approach me, too."

A smile crept across Saito's face.

"The Hiragi Clan was betrayed by someone important," he said.

"So, what, you're trying to say I'm not important?" snickered Shinya. "Fine, but you're saying it was someone higher up. Who? One of the seniors? Was it Kureto Hiragi, the student council president?"

Saito shook his head.

"Even more important. Someone who despises the Hiragi Clan."

Guren had no idea who Saito could be referring to. Which was only natural. He wasn't familiar with the inner workings of the Hiragi Clan. The Ichinose Clan lacked the power and resources necessary to spy on the Hiragis.

The Order of the Imperial Moon, from the Ichinose Clan on down, continued to exist because the Hiragi-led Imperial Demons allowed it, though the price was constant scrutiny and displaying some degree of obedience.

Only an organization such as the Thousand Nights, which dwarfed even the Imperial Demons, was large enough to spy on the Hiragis.

Unless, of course, you were someone on the inside.

"…"

Guren glanced toward Shinya.

The expression on Shinya's face had changed. Apparently he had guessed who Saito meant.

"Do you know who it is?" asked Guren.

Shinya didn't answer.

It didn't matter, though. There was already someone else for Guren to question.

"Fine. You answer, Saito. Who's been working with the Thousand Nights?"

"Hmm? Why ask me? It looks like young Shinya here has already figured it out…"

Guren pushed the sword in deeper.

"Nggh!"

Saito's face twisted up in pain.

"I'm asking you," said Guren. "Talk or I'll kill you."

"Ha. I'm so terrified. But if you're going to kill me, maybe you should just get it over with already."

"What?"

"My mission is almost complete. We came here to recover the research materials and to pick up our collaborator. Both objectives should be nearly complete. You two were deemed the students most likely to interfere. My job was simply to keep you busy. I've already succeeded. You two were so busy dealing with me that you never had a chance to meddle in our real plans…"

"Dammit! I should've known," cried Shinya. The blood drained from his face and he ran off suddenly, through one of the smokescreens.

Guren watched him go before turning his attention back toward Saito.

Guren had mostly grasped the situation by this point.

Everything he needed to know to figure it out was already out in the open. Specifically:

Someone powerful within the Hiragi Clan had sold information to the Thousand Nights and was collaborating with them on an experiment.

That powerful person held a deep grudge against the clan.

The Thousand Nights had to keep Guren and Shinya busy while they collected that person, because Guren and Shinya were the two who seemed most likely to interfere.

When you put it all together, the answer was as plain as the nose on Guren's face.

"Mahiru. The traitor was Mahiru, wasn't it?"

"Hmph. You're taking that information better than I thought you would."

"Why should I be upset?"

"Well, she is your girlfriend, isn't she?"

Guren snorted.

"I'd have to be an idiot to think a girl I hadn't seen in ten years was my girlfriend."

"Oh. Is that so?"

"It is."

"You still think about her, though."

"Wrong again."

"No…I don't think I am. You're powerful. Too powerful for someone your age. You built up your strength in hopes that one day you might take Mahiru back from the Hiragi Clan…"

"I said you're wrong!" sneered Guren. He drove his sword deeper into Saito's chest.

"Haha! Have it your way. But you realize that Mahiru is still in love with you, don't you?"

"..."

"The only reason she grew so strong, and betrayed her own family, was so that she could return to your side. It was very brave of her, don't you think? All these years she's remained true, working hard to be reunited with you."

"..."

"Don't you think it's time you rewarded her devotion? All she wants is for you to hold her again..."

Guren recalled his meeting with Mahiru in the nurse's room, a few days back.

The happiness on her face...

And the disappointment, when she saw how weak Guren had become and how he seemed not to have been thinking of her the way she had been thinking of him.

When Guren told her she was pretty, however, her face had lit up with joy.

"Let me guess," said Guren. "The Brotherhood of a Thousands Nights is going to pave the way for us."

Saito smiled and nodded.

"Indeed. Any two people as accomplished as yourselves would make a welcome addition to the Thousand Nights. Of course, we would insist that the rest of the Hiragi and Ichinose Clan members also surrender to us."

"..."

"If you help us defeat the Hiragis, you and Mahiru will be free to reign as king and queen over whatever remains of the clans afterward. We won't bother you with petty things like family or position. You can be in love, or whatever else it is you like."

Guren stared into Saito's face.

He was smiling. Although his chest had been torn open by Guren's katana and his body was half consumed by dark magic, he still felt confident enough to smile. Guren narrowed his eyes.

"This is part of your mission too, isn't it?"

"Of course it is," said Saito, laughing. "I was told to wait for this moment, and then extend our invitation once more."

"So the one who convinced Mahiru to betray her clan…"

"…was me. She told me how she still loves you. She wants to create a world where the two of you can be together. She said she would do anything to achieve that goal. Even sell out her own family."

"…"

"Make your decision, Guren. Come with me, and I can take you to Mahiru—"

Saito was interrupted by the sound of more explosions from beyond the smokescreens.

A great shout suddenly rose up among the students.

—*The Imperial Demon Army is here!*

—*W-We're saved!*

—*Kill them! Kill them all! They'll regret having attacked the Imperial Demons!*

Guren could also hear other voices, coming from a different direction.

—*L-Lady Mahiru! They've taken Lady Mahiru!*

—*Q-Quickly! We must protect Lady Mahiru with our lives…aieeee!*

It was all a farce. The entire scenario was unfolding just as the Thousand Nights had planned.

Apparently Mahiru was planning to escape the school without the Hiragis ever discovering that she betrayed them. She wasn't going to scamper away as a traitor. Instead she was going to be abducted as a prisoner. Which meant she could be planning to come back at some point in the future.

"It looks like we're out of time," said Saito. "We can't fight the Imperial Demon Army without exposing the Thousand Night's involvement. A tactical withdrawal seems in order."

"What are you talking about? You already told me everything…"

"But like you said, you're not a Hiragi. You won't rat us out…"

"…"

"Besides, if you care for Mahiru at all, you wouldn't want to say anything that would put her in danger."

"…"

"I'll tell you our location. You can meet Mahiru there, tonight. If you come, the Thousand Nights will greet you as a hero. A hero who will help us crush the Hiragi Clan."

"…"

"What do you say? Remove the sword from my chest. Everything is already prepared. After ten years, you and Mahiru will be reunited at last."

Guren glared at Saito.

Saito was still smiling. Guren deliberated. What should he say? What should he do? How far could he even trust what Saito was saying?

There was no time.

If he was going to accept Saito's offer he had to release him, now, before the Imperial Demons found them. Once the Imperial Demons got their hands on Saito, the Ichinose Clan would lose access to him.

Guren thought it over carefully.

What should he do?

Which choice was the best one?

Was he even sure what he wanted?

He weighed all his options before answering.

"Something about this just doesn't sit right. I've got a feeling you people from the Thousand Nights are manipulating us…"

A cold smile spread across Guren's face. He drove the sword in even deeper.

"Ngh!"

"I'm not letting you get away," said Guren. "I'll wring the truth out of you while I've still got you captured."

"You'll never learn the meeting place that way," said Saito.

"You'll talk when you're being tortured."

"Heh. I won't talk, not even then. I've been trained to resist torture. My brain has even been altered to kill me if I ever leak information."

"Huh, is that so? Then I guess you're about to die."

A hint of panic crept into Saito's face.

"If you kill me, you'll never see Mahiru again…" he said, staring up into Guren's face.

"I'm fine with that. You got the wrong idea. I didn't grow stronger just so I could see Mahiru again—"

Another voice suddenly interrupted them.

"I'm really sad to hear you say that, Guren," it lamented.

It was a girl's voice.

Guren drew his sword from Saito's chest and leapt backward as fast as he could.

He had sensed something dangerous and powerful coming his way fast. He had a feeling that if he didn't pull back it would spell his doom.

Whatever it was, it was still there. It continued to pursue Guren, even after he leapt backward.

Guren squared off in its direction and swung his sword in defense.

The sound of metal clashing against metal filled the air. Guren blinked, clearing his eyes.

And found himself staring face to face with a beautiful girl.

A girl with long, sleek, ashen hair.

A commanding stare.

And soft, pink lips.

It was Mahiru.

Mahiru Hiragi.

She wielded a katana in her hands. Its blade was as black as night.

Her jet-black blade and Guren's crimson Kujakumaru crossed. Mahiru pressed forward. The two lengths of metal made a screeching sound as they ground against each other.

"…Mahiru."

Mahiru smiled. Her eyes seemed to twinkle.

"Back in the nurse's room you called me Lady Mahiru. I'm glad you've dropped the formalities…"

"There's no need for me to keep up the act with someone who betrayed the Hiragis," said Guren. "Besides, you've seen my true strength, now."

Mahiru nodded. She seemed happy.

"That's true… There aren't many people who could block a strike from my sword."

Mahiru leaned forward into her strike. She was strong. It was hard to believe a girl her size could be that strong. In fact, it was hard to believe any human could be that strong. Guren wasn't sure if she was using magic to amplify her powers, or if the strength came from somewhere else.

Guren flashed Mahiru a grin.

"This is interesting. Maybe we should fight, figure out which of us is stronger?"

Despite Guren's bluster, he was forced back another step.

Suddenly he parried Mahiru's blade to the side and countered with a rapid succession of blows.

Mahiru met him blow for blow. In the blink of an eye, their blades clashed multiple times.

Mahiru was quick.

She was stronger than Guren, and faster.

Guren's technique, however, was better. He managed to hold his own against her strikes.

However…

"Nngh… You gotta be kidding me…"

He was losing ground, steadily. Although he was able to meet her strike for strike, she was still outmaneuvering him.

"Hmm?" said Mahiru. "I thought you said you wanted to fight. Weren't you going to show me how strong you are?"

"Don't get cocky," hissed Guren. He retreated another step, and then reached into his sleeves, pretending to draw out a *fuda*.

Mahiru saw the move.

"If you can't beat me with swordcraft—"

"Be quiet!"

Guren didn't draw out a *fuda*. It had all been a feint. Instead he thrust with his sword, at full strength.

"Ahhh!"

Caught off guard, Mahiru moved to parry. She wasn't fast enough. Guren's blade lunged in a straight line, aimed directly at Mahiru's heart.

"..."

He stayed his hand just moments before the blade would have pierced her chest.

Mahiru stared down at Guren's sword and then laughed.

"Impressive! You really have become strong, haven't you, Guren? Was it all for my sake?"

Guren lowered his blade.

"No," he said.

"No?"

"No. How many times do I have to say it?"

Mahiru bit her lip and frowned. Guren recognized the look. She used to make the same face when they were children. Mahiru would ask Guren, over and over, whether he liked her or not. And Guren, annoyed, would refuse to answer. She had made the same face then.

"I see..." she said. "All I ever wanted was to be with you again, Guren. That's why I grew stronger."

Mahiru's voice trembled, seductively, as she spoke. Guren's face, however, remained neutral.

"And so you joined with the Thousand Nights to start a war?" he asked her.

Screams continued to fill the air. They were surrounded by the sounds of battle.

It was the sound of the Imperial Demon Army fighting the assassins from the Brotherhood of a Thousand Nights.

But at the center of that carnage...

Mahiru seemed in ecstasy, surrounded on all sides by the screams of students. She smiled at Guren, bewitchingly.

"Ahaha. Once I began acquiring power, I enjoyed the feeling. You understand, don't you, Guren? You've grown so strong, but you're still flesh and blood. You must feel the seductive pull of power…"

"…"

"There's a limit to flesh and blood, though, isn't there? To become truly powerful, you have to be willing to transcend to the next level."

"…Transcend? What are you talking about?"

Mahiru raised her sword up into the air. She narrowed her eyes as she spoke.

"Transcend to something higher," she said.

She swung her sword downward.

It shone with a dark light as it descended. In its wake, the very space behind it seemed to rend in two. The ground beneath her, where the sword aimed, suddenly split in two, and a huge fissure ripped open in a massive arc, snaking outward until it was lost from sight beyond the smokescreen.

It was power beyond human comprehension.

If Mahiru had used her full strength earlier, Guren would have been obliterated by her very first strike.

Mahiru turned her eyes back toward Guren and smiled.

"You look surprised. Amazing, isn't it? A cursed weapon. It's a combination of Hiragi and Thousand Nights magic. We learned how to make contracts with high-ranking demons that were formerly out of reach, and to bind them into weaponry…"

It was a simple explanation, but Guren understood.

He had heard of such "demon curses" before.

They were thought to be the most difficult of all magics.

Creating a demon curse involved calling directly on Bodhisattva, black demons, or other supernatural entities and sealing them into sacred items so that they could serve the wielder.

The items used to seal demons were almost exclusively weapons.

They could be swords, axes, or even bows.

The weapons needed to be consecrated and purified—a process that took years—before a demon could be trapped inside.

This was all in theory, however. According to current spellcraft, creating such a weapon was supposed to be impossible.

Or rather, even if it was possible, it would require sacrificing thousands—maybe even tens of thousands—of lives in human experiments.

Previous attempts had all resulted in failure. Instead of getting sealed into a weapon, the demon possessed the wielder's body and soul, causing them to go on a destructive rampage.

Once people became demons, their human memories and reason disappeared. They became mere monsters and delighted in consuming the flesh of mortals.

The Order of the Imperial Moon, which was led by the Ichinose Clan, had absolutely forbidden all research into demon curses. Of course, the Ichinose Clan also lacked the technical prowess and funds to pursue such research in the first place.

"..."

According to Mahiru, however, the weapon she was wielding was a demon-possessed sword.

Mahiru still appeared to be human, as far as Guren could tell.

"So you're saying you've perfected cursed gear?" he asked.

Mahiru grinned.

"I knew that would interest you, Guren. It's hard to resist something so new and powerful, isn't it?"

"Answer my question."

"So forceful," said Mahiru, laughing. She lifted the obsidian blade into the air.

"It's not quite perfected...but I think we're close. Just think of it, Guren. With a weapon like this, what is there left to fear?"

"..."

"The Hiragis are powerless ants in comparison."

"..."

"Even vampires would be no threat. They think of humans as no

more than mere cattle, but with a weapon like this we could kill them. It just needs to be perfected. Look at it. It's so beautiful—"

"I think you've gone mad," said Guren, interrupting her. "Tell me, how many people did you sacrifice to create that blade? How many lives were lost to your experiments?"

Mahiru fixed Guren with her stare.

"Since when did you become so high-minded? You act as if you've never sacrificed anything. But I have a feeling you've given up more than your share to gain the strength you have now."

"..."

"It's a lesson we learned together, Guren. That day, on the grass, when the sky was so blue. Without strength, you can't protect anyone. Not the ones you love, and not the things that are most precious. All that matters is power. I know that, now. And so do you, Guren…"

Mahiru stretched her hand out toward Guren.

"Come with me. I can give you power, Guren. We can perfect this strength together. We…we can—"

Mahiru suddenly broke off, mid-sentence. Her face contorted in pain, and she gripped her chest over her sailor-suit uniform.

"S-Stay away, Guren!" she shouted suddenly. Her voice had changed. She sounded more like the girl he had known years ago, trembling and near tears.

"It's too late," she said. "Too late… The demon, it's already possessed me. The cursed gear…our experiment… W-We failed… This isn't me. I…I… Shut up! Shut up! No one is possessed! I just need power…more power…"

Mahiru's right arm began shaking.

It jerked and twitched uncontrollably.

Black tendrils appeared on the blade's surface and began writhing along Mahiru's arm.

As if the sword's curse was feeding on her.

The blackness began eating away at Mahiru's arm. It began to change shape. Her nails sprouted into talons, and her hand twisted up like a beast's claw.

"Oops now, that's no good," observed Saito.

He was still standing behind Mahiru. One of his chains shot out, wrapping itself around Mahiru's arm several times.

"We're out of time. We have to go now, my dear. You've used that sword about as much as you can for one day."

Mahiru's expression seemed to return to normal. She grew calm.

"…As you say. Let's go."

Guren glared at Saito.

"What did you do to her?" he said.

"If you really want to know, then you'll join us. The Thousand Nights—"

"I asked you what you did to her!" shouted Guren, cutting him off. He leapt forward, swinging his crimson blade at Saito.

Mahiru intercepted him.

She stepped in front of Saito, brandishing her dark sword.

Guren's scarlet blade and Mahiru's inky black blade clashed against each other one final time.

This time, however, there was no sound of metal hitting metal.

Guren's sword, the Kujakumaru, was severed in two. Mahiru's sword cut through it like it was butter.

Mahiru thrust her cursed black sword at Guren's neck, stopping just inches short.

She could have easily cut Guren's head off.

"You spared me earlier, so I guess that makes this a draw. Not that getting stabbed in the heart would actually kill me…"

What was Mahiru saying? If she really could be stabbed in the heart without dying, was she even human anymore?

Guren glanced down at the tip of Mahiru's sword.

"Well, maybe getting my head cut off wouldn't kill me, either," deadpanned Guren.

"Haha. I doubt that. You're still human, after all. I'm glad you still have your sense of humor, though."

"Who's joking?"

"Ha! Oh, and Guren?"

"Yeah?"

"I love you."

Mahiru leaned forward suddenly and embraced Guren. Her arms were draped around his neck. She was so close that Guren could hear the sound of her breathing and her heart beating.

The sound hadn't changed. He remembered it from when they were little.

When they lay on the grass.

Beneath the clear blue sky.

Everything else, though, had changed.

Everything was different. It left a bitter taste in Guren's mouth.

Mahiru stepped back and stared at Guren.

"Last chance, Guren," she said. "Please come with me."

"I don't think so."

"I can give you power…"

"I'm not interested."

"Heh. All these years I've waited, and in the end you hate me."

Guren could hear the sorrow in her voice.

"I don't hate you," he said. "But the power I'm pursuing is different from yours."

"Is it?"

"Yes."

"I see… I wonder when we grew apart."

Guren couldn't answer. It had been ten years. They had lived their own lives. It was too late to go back and find the turning point now.

Maybe that was a good thing. Maybe it was sad. But it was the way things were.

For her own part, Mahiru seemed sad.

"…I want to tell you something important, Guren," she said.

Saito suddenly seemed to panic.

"Mahiru, wait…"

She ignored him.

"The truth is, this year at Christmas, the world will come to an end."

"What?"

"The trumpets of the apocalypse will sound, and a virus will spread. When that time comes, a new world will arise. One that, more so than ever, requires power. When that time comes, I know you'll need me once more... We'll meet again, Guren, when the world comes to an end."

"Mahiru, I don't understand..." Guren trailed off.

But Mahiru had said all that she was going to say. She leapt backward, nimbly, like a feather floating away.

She gave Guren one last smile.

"I love you, Guren," she said. "That much is true. A day will come when you need me again... Until then, I'll be waiting."

Mahiru passed through one of the smokescreens and disappeared from sight.

"We've gotten pretty far off schedule," said Saito, a tired look on his face, "but I guess it doesn't really matter anymore. In any case, you remember the boy I was with when we met last time? If you want to get in touch with the Thousand Nights, speak to the director of the orphanage where he lives. The Hyakuya Orphanage. I think you know the place."

"..."

"He'll be able to put you in contact with me. Goodbye, Guren Ichinose."

Saito turned and walked away.

Guren was suddenly left alone, surrounded by white clouds of smoke.

He stared at the point where Mahiru had disappeared. Mahiru, however, was already long gone. Finally, Guren turned his gaze toward the broken sword in his hand.

Kujakumaru had been laced with powerful magics. Its metal had been forged using the esoteric Buddhist magic of the Deva Kings. Nothing should have been able to break it.

"She cut through it like paper...damn..."

Guren sighed in disgust.

He was trying to make sense of what just happened.

What was Mahiru trying to achieve?

What was going to happen at Christmas?

And how much power lay hidden in those cursed weapons?

None of it made any sense.

"Dammit..." said Guren, his face twisted up in childish annoyance.

The smokescreens began to dissipate, almost as quickly as they had appeared. Apparently, only magic had been keeping them in place. When the Thousand Nights made their retreat, the smokescreens faded with them.

"..."

The sight that awaited Guren once the smoke cleared was like a scene from hell.

The sprawling schoolyard was drenched in blood.

Injured students lay in the dirt.

Girls lay weeping and screaming.

Boys stood dazed among the carnage.

Some were desperately trying CPR on friends who were clearly long dead.

There were also bodies.

The bodies of students and teachers littered the schoolyard.

Guren didn't spot any of the men in black suits among the bodies. Despite their boasting—despite the way they had ridiculed Guren—it seemed that the other students hadn't been able to defeat even a single assassin from the Thousand Nights.

Unless the Thousand Nights had taken the bodies of their fallen comrades with them when they left, in order to keep their identity secret.

Either way, the Hiragi Clan was clearly on the losing end of this first battle.

The attack had thrown them into total chaos. They couldn't even identify their attackers. One look at the carnage around them was proof of how badly they had lost.

"They never even stood a chance..." muttered Guren.

He returned his broken sword to its sheath.

A girl's voice suddenly shouted in Guren's direction.

"Ah... Y-You! You're alive!"

Guren turned around to see Mito Jujo. She was covered in blood. Guren couldn't tell if it was her own blood or an enemy's.

"That blood..." said Guren.

He was going to ask her whose it was. Before he could, however, Mito ran toward him. She burst into tears and threw herself into his arms.

"Th-Thank heaven you're alive!"

Mito was shaking. Her slender body convulsed uncontrollably.

"Th-They're all dead... I tried so hard to save them, but...but..."

Guren wasn't sure how to react. He gripped Mito's shoulders lightly, waiting for the shaking to stop.

Once she had calmed down a little he spoke.

"Everything's fine now. Listen to me."

"...?"

"Are you hurt? The adrenaline's still coursing through your body so you might not feel it yet..."

Mito shook her head.

"I-I'm fine. It's nothing serious..."

"Good."

"B-But, everyone else...our classmates... If you hadn't pushed me out of the way, I'd be dead too...in that first blast..."

Mito's face twisted up in horror, and she clung tight to Guren's chest once more.

Another voice interrupted them.

"Huh? When did you two get so close?"

It was Norito Goshi.

Guren turned toward him. Norito stood there with his usual flippant expression on his face.

"Norito!" shouted Mito, overjoyed. "You're alive, too!"

"If staying alive is all it takes to get a hug from a pretty girl, then come to papa!" shouted Norito, holding his arms out wide.

For some reason, though, Mito didn't go running to Norito like she had to Guren. Norito frowned.

"Well, that's not fair. How come you get all the girls, Guren?"

"Hmph. I don't know why you're acting so friendly all of a sudden," said Guren, "but I don't think I like it."

Norito laughed.

"Hey, what can I say? If it hadn't been for you, I'd have been dead back there for sure. You're my hero!"

"So what? You're gonna bake me a friggin' cake now?"

"Hey, you should be happy! After all, it's not like you have many friends to pick and choose from."

"Get bent."

"Ha! Anyway, joking aside, we really took one on the chin here, didn't we?"

Norito cast his eyes around the schoolyard.

It was littered with the bodies of his friends.

Many of the surviving students lay in pools of blood.

The soldiers from the Imperial Demon Army were trying to help the wounded, but the schoolyard was still in a state of chaos.

"It's hard to believe this is all happening in the middle of Shibuya," said Norito. He turned his attention back toward Guren. "By the way, I'm kind of surprised someone as weak as you was able to survive."

Mito finally let go of Guren. She looked up into his face and nodded vigorously.

"How *did* you manage to avoid the chains those guys in black suits were wielding?"

Guren hadn't been able to see through the smokescreens. Judging by Mito's comment, however, he guessed that the men from the Thousand Nights had been pretty fearsome.

"Well…" said Guren, "the truth is, I just stayed down."

"Huh?" said Mito.

"What?" said Norito.

"I just stayed down and waited for everything to end."

An exasperated look appeared on Mito's face. Norito and Mito made eye contact.

"I should have known…" she said.

"But how did you notice the attack before it hit us?" asked Norito.

Guren shrugged.

"I was already staring up at the sky when it happened. I was just bored, I guess."

Norito and Mito suddenly burst into laughter.

It wasn't like before, though, when they had been laughing at Guren. This time, the tension had been broken, and they were laughing to release their anxiety.

They laughed so hard they nearly cried. And then they grew silent.

"I guess this is no time for laughter," said Norito, staring at the injured students around them.

Mito nodded.

"They picked the wrong school to attack," fumed Norito. "We're not gonna just let them get away with murdering our friends like that."

Mito nodded again.

"We'll get revenge," Norito swore.

Mito paused for a moment and then nodded once more, solemnly.

"We will," she said.

Guren stared at the two.

Revenge. But revenge against who? Against the Thousand Nights? Or against the person actually responsible for what happened—Mahiru?

Guren suddenly found himself remembering what Mahiru had

been like as a child. She had an innocent face, and a confident smile. Like most children, she believed—mistakenly—that she could be anyone or do anything that she set her heart on.

—Hey Guren...

Her voice was always so happy when she called his name.

—Do you think the two of us could get married?

She seemed even happier than usual, that day.

—We could be together, forever...just like we are now...

Guren lifted his head up.

Standing in the center of the blood-strewn schoolyard, he looked up at the sky. It was still as clear and blue as before.

In Guren's mind, however, everything was gloomy and gray.

It all seemed so hopeless. It felt like there was a heavy weight on his chest.

"Guren!"

Guren turned his head.

It was Shinya.

Apparently he had survived as well.

He was covered in blood, like the others. He looked distraught.

"Mahiru...she's gone..." he said.

"..."

"They said she was kidnapped!"

Of course, Shinya knew that Mahiru was really the traitor. Pretending that she had been kidnapped was proof that he really hated the Hiragis. Apparently he had been serious when he said that he wanted to destroy them.

"What should we do?"

Guren wasn't sure what to say. So much had happened, he couldn't find the strength to explain it all just yet.

"Why are you asking me about Lady Mahiru..." he said instead. "She's your fiancée, isn't she?"

Shinya's eyes widened in surprise. He realized Mito and Norito were standing there, and an exasperated expression appeared on his face. After everything that had just happened, it was hard for him to believe that Guren was trying to keep up his act.

"You know, Guren, sometimes…"

"…I can be really annoying?" Guren said, grinning.

"At least you admit it."

"Haha. I'm just tired now. We can talk later, okay?"

"Later might be too late."

"I think we're past the point of it being too late."

Guren gestured toward the bodies lying around them.

The enemy had already gotten the drop on them. It would take time, and patience, before they could catch up. Right now they needed to use their brains, collect what information they could, and prepare carefully.

Mahiru and the Brotherhood of a Thousand Nights already had a big head-start.

Shinya nodded.

"Fine then, I'm with you."

He turned on his heel and walked away.

"What was that all about?" asked Norito.

Guren shook his head.

"Who knows," he said.

"But is it true what he said, that Lady Mahiru's been abducted? What are we going to do?"

Guren, however, wasn't listening anymore.

The sky above him was blue.

A deep and piercing blue.

A single cloud floated gently across the sky.

"…I guess the war has started," he muttered distantly.

"Master Guren! Master Guren! School starts again today. This time I'm not leaving your side, not even for a second!"

"..."

"I can't believe that the very day after I got put in the hospital you got caught in the middle of a war. As soon as we heard, me and Shigure just looked at each other and then rushed to the school as quickly as we could. We're your guards. If there's danger, we should be there to protect you! S-So..."

Sayuri stepped in close, pressing herself to Guren's side.

"So..." said Shigure, pressed against Guren on his other side, "starting from today we're going to stay by your side every second of every day."

Guren stared at the two, in their sailor uniforms, in turn.

"Whatever, but do you have to stand so close?"

"It's a state of emergency," said Shigure.

"We're in the middle of a war," said Sayuri.

Guren placed a hand on each of their shoulders and pushed them open like swinging doors.

"You're in the way. I can barely walk. Besides, I'm stronger than both of you."

"Master Guren, wait! You have to stay close!" said Sayuri.

"Obviously we're not nearly as strong as you are, Master Guren," conceded Shigure, "but we could still take a bullet for you. Sayuri's right. Please stay close."

Sayuri's and Shigure's eyes darted around, warily, scanning for the next enemy or attack. They were on full alert. Really, they just looked like a pair of suspicious weirdos.

The three were walking toward school along their usual route.

The road leading to First Shibuya High School.

The school had shut down for two weeks, after being attacked by an unidentified organization during the qualifying exams. Today was the first day that classes were being held again.

According to the latest reports, the attackers had been an obscure terrorist organization that no one had ever heard of.

The Imperial Demons claimed to have hunted down every last member of the group and killed them all in one fell swoop. They said it was an example of the fate that awaited any who defied the Imperial Demons.

The reports put school officials at ease. The other followers of the Order of the Imperial Demons also seemed satisfied.

But of course, it was all a lie.

The actual attackers had been the largest magical syndicate in Japan, the Brotherhood of a Thousand Nights. And the Thousand Nights could not be dealt with so easily.

Either the terrorist group was a red herring set up by the Thousand Nights, or the stumped Imperial Demons had concocted a fictitious enemy to cover for their failure.

Neither possibility changed how things really stood.

Either way, a war was brewing between the two largest magical syndicates in the country.

The Order of the Imperial Moon, which was led by the Ichinose Clan, was determined to take advantage of the conflict for its own benefit. The aim was to slip in when conditions were favorable, to destroy both organizations, and then to take their rightful place at the top of the new food chain.

The knowledge that the two organizations were hurtling toward a war had only been communicated to the highest-up in the Order. Strict secrecy was being imposed. Meanwhile, full-scale intelligence-gathering operations were underway behind the scenes.

Operatives from every branch of the Imperial Moon were now risking their lives to infiltrate and sabotage the enemy.

Meanwhile…

"…we won't let you fall into danger again, Master Guren. I swear it," said Shigure.

It sounded like a resolution. Apparently she was speaking to herself.

Just as she finished speaking, however, the enemy struck unexpectedly.

Fortunately, it wasn't a life-threatening attack.

"Huh…?"

Guren lifted his eyes up. A plastic bottle full of cola was hurtling toward his head. The cap was off. If it hit him he would be drenched.

It was like the first day of school, all over again.

From across the street he could hear the students from the Order of the Imperial Demons laughing at him.

They were in the middle of a war, but no one had told these fools. They were all happy to believe that the attack had been by a random terrorist group that had already been dealt with. In the meantime, they had nothing better to do than to pick on Guren.

Guren stared at them through half-lidded eyes.

He leaned toward Shigure, planning to tell her to let the bottle hit him.

After all, there was still no reason for Guren to reveal his true strength. In fact, after these recent developments, it was more important than ever that he conceal his full power.

Plus, in the end, it looked like he wouldn't have to put up with their bullying for three years, after all.

Because the war had already started.

The two behemoth organizations Guren wanted to destroy had turned against each other, just when it suited him the most.

For now, however, Guren would let the other students continue to despise him.

It was important that he keep up the act.

The fools could strut around and sneer at the Ichinose Clan all they liked. After all, they were strutting toward their own deaths.

Which is why Guren decided to let the cola bottle hit him.

Unfortunately, Shigure was so on edge that she sprang into action before Guren could hold her back. With split-second timing, she threw one of her *kunai*—her assassin dirks. She was ready to strike down anyone, or anything, that came too close to her master.

The *kunai* was flying on a collision course for the cola bottle.

Seeing the bottle get pulverized in midair would certainly shut them up. You didn't want to be on Shigure's bad side. Shigure's bad side was deadly.

Unfortunately, it would be a counterproductive display.

Guren was going to have to have a talk with Shigure later…

Fortunately, he was saved the trouble.

"Yo!" came a voice from the side.

He seemed to come out of nowhere, reaching out and plucking the *kunai* from the air before it could hit its target.

It was Shinya Hiragi.

With the *kunai* out of the way, the cola bottle was free to strike Guren on the head. Its contents spilled out, drenching him from head to foot in cola.

The other students all burst into laughter. They began calling Guren names.

—*You're supposed to drink cola, you idiot, not wear it!*

—*Go home, weakling! This school's not for you!*

—*Yeah, go home! We don't want Ichinose mongrels here!*

Shinya turned toward Guren, smiling faintly.

"Heh. Some people never learn. Can't you even dodge a bottle of soda?"

The other students laughed even louder. Shinya was a Hiragi. With him on their side, they felt even bolder.

Apparently, Shinya had decided that he was going to help Guren keep up his act.

"You'll pay for that!"

Sayuri and Shigure stepped forward in anger. Guren put his hand out to calm them down.

"Thanks for the help, Shinya," he said.

"Hey, that's what friends are for."

"Friends? Are you planning on joining the Imperial Moon, then?"

"Not a chance."

"In that case, we're not friends."

"Hmph. You know what they say, the enemy of my enemy is my friend. See you in class, Guren…"

Shinya turned and walked away. Shigure turned toward Guren to ask him what that was all about. Before she could, however, they were interrupted again.

"Look at you, you're all wet!"

It was Mito Jujo. She approached them from behind.

She stepped past Guren and stood in front of him as if to protect him from the students who had thrown the bottle.

"Aren't you people ashamed of yourselves?!" she shouted indignantly.

The students suddenly didn't seem so brave anymore.

—*Look at that hair… She must be a Jujo…*

—*That's not right… Why is a Jujo sticking up for some Ichinose punk?*

—*Who cares? Lord Shinya's on our side!*

—*So is Lord Seishiro! Everyone hates that Ichinose mongrel…*

To bully or not to bully? The students began arguing amongst themselves. None of it really mattered to Guren.

"Geez, Guren, what the heck happened to you?"

This time it was Norito Goshi. He walked up to Guren and sniffed his shoulder.

"Dude, you smell like cola."

"What can I say, it's my favorite drink."

"Haha! But seriously, don't tell me you're getting bullied again. Tell me who did it. You saved me the other day, it's my turn to do you a favor."

Norito glared at the group of students who had thrown the bottle. He narrowed his eyes in a threatening manner.

"Ahh!"

Startled, the students cried out in fear.

—C-Come on guys, let's get to class.

—Y-Yeah, we don't wanna be late!

The students scampered off, still making excuses as they went.

"…"

Guren watched with disinterest as they left. He turned toward his new saviors, Norito and Mito, and said, "I need to speak to you."

"What is it?" said Norito. "Did you want to thank us?"

"There's no reason to thank us," said Mito. "After all, you saved us first."

"You're right, I've got no reason to thank you," said Guren, nodding his head. "What I was gonna say is, just stay away from me. I don't need any friends."

Mito and Norito's eyes widened in surprise.

"I never knew you were so shy," laughed Norito.

"You're worried we'll get bullied too?" said Mito. "Is that why you want us to stay away?"

"What? No…"

"You don't need to worry about us," said Mito. "But it's nice of you. I feel like I understand you a little better now."

One thing was certain: Mito definitely didn't understand anything about Guren.

"Ah, Shigure. How are you?" said Mito, turning toward Guren's follower.

"I'm not interested…" said Shigure.

"Can't you come to the compound, just for a visit? I told my father about you, and he'd really like to meet you…"

"I'm not interested..."

"Of course, of course. But you could come today, right after school..."

Norito, meanwhile, was more interested in Sayuri.

"Hey, it's Sayuri, isn't it? Say, you don't have a boyfriend, do you?"

"H-H-Hold on a second, get away from me!" stammered Sayuri. "Don't make me hit you!"

"Come on, don't be that way. Let's you and me go on a date today, after school..."

"Not a chance!"

"So you do have a boyfriend? Is that it?"

"W-Well...no...I don't have a boyfriend. But there's someone very important to me... M-Master Guren..."

Sayuri blushed beet red, stealing glances out of the corners of her eyes at Guren.

"..."

They're acting like they don't have a care in the world, thought Guren. *Haven't they realized we're in the middle of a war?*

Why was it that everyone Guren knew talked so much? He thought about telling them all to shut up, but he knew it would do no good.

He stared at them for a moment and then sighed. He brushed his cola-drenched hair from his face.

And looked up at the sky.

It was clear and blue and peaceful. Suddenly, everything seemed so absurd.

"...Heh."

Guren chuckled softly to himself.

He just couldn't help it.

And so, Guren's story began.

A story of war.

Of death.

Of despair.

Of love and hate.

A story of human kindness, and human folly.

A story of desires...

And the consequences they bring...

Desires that grow and swell, until only the end of the world can contain them.

This is a story of those last days, before the fall of mankind.

A story of the last pains and struggles of man, before the trumpets of the apocalypse sounded, and the hammer of fate came crashing down upon the world.

A High School Fantasy! At least, that's how they billed it.

I guess it's a pretty accurate description.

But this is also a story where it's already been decided that the world is going to end. It was interesting writing a story where I knew the world was definitely going to come to an end. I enjoyed writing it.

But before I get ahead of myself, since this is the start of a new series, maybe I should introduce myself.

Hello! My name is Takaya Kagami.

I've written other works such as *The Legend of the Legendary Heroes* and *A Dark Rabbit Has Seven Lives*.

Whenever I start a new book it usually turns into a long series, so I don't get many opportunities to begin a new one.

In fact, I think this is my first time writing a completely new work in four and a half years. It's also my first time writing a book for a publisher other than Fujimi Shobo Fantasy, so I'm a little nervous as well.

But that's also why I'll try my best to make this series really great. I hope you all enjoy reading it!

Now seems like a good time to explain how this series came to be.

Some of you probably first became aware of the series after seeing the cover or an advertisement. But there's also a *Seraph of the End* manga series running at the same time in Jump SQ magazine.

In fact, this book is being released at the same time as issue one of the manga (I'm also writing the script for the whole manga series, so I hope you'll check that out too!).

The manga occurs in the same world, eight years later—after the world has already come to an end.

In other words, when Guren is twenty-four. All grown up! (LOL)

Guren plays a big part in the manga, too—as Lieutenant Colonel of the Japanese Imperial Demon Army (fancy title!)—so you should definitely check it out.

Of course, eight years later the world has already been destroyed. The story starts after the fall. Wild demons run rampant, and humans, controlled by vampires, have had their population reduced to a tenth of their former numbers.

In other words, the catastrophe is certain.

But why did the apocalypse occur?

How did mankind face this tragedy? What struggles did they face?

What happened to Guren and his friends along the way, and how did they handle it?

I want to write a story that paints these last days of humanity as seen through Guren's eyes.

It would make me very happy if fans read the novel and the manga at the same time. But since both the protagonists (the hero of the manga series is named Yuichiro Hyakuya) and the concept are different, you can definitely enjoy one without reading the other.

But…I still hope you'll check out both!

And for those of you who have already read the manga…

What did you think of Guren when he was fifteen—the same age as Yuichiro in the manga? (LOL)

After getting my start at Fujimi Shobo, I don't want to make them mad by jumping ship. So once you're done with *Seraph of the End*, why not check out *The Legend of the Legendary Heroes* as well?

There's one last thing I want to say. Since it's something I say whenever I start a new series, those of you who have read my other works might be a little sick of hearing it already. But here it goes:

I believe that my books are something we create together. It's thanks to you, the fans, that these books come together. That's why I want to thank those of you who are reading. Without you, there would be no book in the first place.

What do you think will be in store for Guren, Sayuri, Shigure, Shinya, and Mahiru? I hope you're looking forward to finding out what happens!

There's definitely more I'd like to say, but I've already used up most of the space that's been allotted for the afterword.

Luckily, we'll have a chance to meet again soon.

Like I said before, Guren plays a pretty big role in the *Seraph of the End* manga series coming out in the April edition of Jump SQ. If you like the manga series, don't forget to fill out the reader survey!

Until then!

Takaya Kagami
Website:
"Healthy Living with Takaya Kagami"
http://www.kagamitakaya.com

Book Two

When was it when I first realized I was in love?

In love with someone beyond my station.

I was born to the Hanayori Clan. Master Guren was born to the main clan. My family had sworn their lives to protect his.

I was born a servant.

I had no business falling in love with someone like Master Guren. But still...

I remember that day, ten years ago.

The day when everything happened.

"...M-Master Guren? Are you okay?"

Maybe I had spoken too softly. Master Guren didn't seem to hear me.

He was lying down in one of the rooms in the Ichinose Clan compound. I could hear him groaning, painfully, on the other side of the sliding paper door.

My father told me a crowd of grownups from the Hiragi Clan had beaten Master Guren up. Several of his bones were broken and his face was covered in bruises. He was running a high fever.

As loyal followers of the Ichinose Clan, the Hanayori Clan had been summoned immediately. The adults were still busy discussing how they would prevent something like it from happening in the future.

Then there was me. I was being trained as one of Master Guren's personal bodyguards. I was ordered to stay by Master Guren's side while the adults spoke.

But I was only five years old.

I didn't really understand what the grownups were talking about. And I was still too young to feel any real loyalty to Master Guren.

But my parents had drilled it into my head that the whole reason I had been born was to serve the Ichinose Clan. I figured this was all part of what was expected of me.

I was sitting outside Master Guren's room, because that's what I had been told to do.

Master Guren was just a boy, too. When I heard him groaning in pain on the other side of the sliding doors I felt sorry for him. But I wasn't angry that somebody had hurt my master.

It was just my job.

My mission, given to me by parents. To guard.

I tried calling to him again.

"...Master Guren? Are you in pain?"

Before I could finish speaking, I heard a loud thud from inside the room. It sounded like something was being punched.

The noise surprised me, but I reacted immediately. I was afraid something had happened to Master Guren. I leapt to my feet and reached out to open the sliding door.

My daily training had been so thorough that even though I didn't feel real loyalty yet, my first instinct was to protect Master Guren. My body seemed to move of its own accord.

I put my hand on the sliding door and opened it, just a crack.

As I did so, I heard the thudding sound again. Like something being punched.

But this time I could see what had made the noise. I stared through the sliver in the door.

Master Guren had crawled free from his blankets and was punching the tatami mat floor with his fists.

He was just a five-year-old boy, with broken bones. His face was swollen and blue. As he punched the floor he spoke, spitting the words out angrily.

"D-Dammit! Why aren't I stronger?"

That's when he noticed me standing in the doorway.

I'll never forget Master Guren's face that day.

No, not his face. His eyes. I'll never forget the look in his eyes.

Although his face was twisted in anger, his pupils were black and moist. His eyes shone beautifully.

Master Guren was crying.

His face was battered, bruised, and in tears. He seemed so angry. So frustrated. And so lonely.

I felt like I had seen something I shouldn't have. I quickly shut the door.

But Master Guren called out to me as soon as the door shut.

"Sayuri? Is that you?"

"…Y-Yes, sir."

"Open the door. I'm up."

"…Y-Yes, sir."

I reached for the door, as ordered.

To be honest, I didn't want to open it. It was awkward seeing my master cry. I wasn't sure how to react. I don't think I had ever seen a boy my age cry so hard.

While I was hesitating, the door slid open from the other side and Master Guren stepped out.

"…Ah."

I looked up into Master Guren's face and gasped. He wasn't crying anymore.

His face was still swollen. He was really too injured to be standing. But he stared down at me calmly as he spoke.

"I didn't mean to worry you, Sayuri," he said. "You can go now."

"But…"

Guren stepped past me without answering.

I wasn't sure what to do, so I followed my master from behind.

Master Guren walked out into the garden, barefoot, and stared absently at the night sky.

There was a beautiful crescent moon overhead. I still remember it vividly.

The moon was just a sliver, like the drawing of the moon on the Order of the Imperial Moon's coat of arms. The Imperial Moon was the magical syndicate to which we belonged. The moon in the sky was so slender, it looked as if it would cut your hand if you could reach out and touch it.

"Sayuri?" said Master Guren, as he stared up at the crescent moon.

"Yes, sir?"

"How long have I been asleep?"

"Almost a whole day."

"Have you been waiting outside my door that entire time?"

"Yes, sir."

"I'm sorry I put you through so much trouble. You can go home, now."

I shook my head from left to right.

"It's my duty to stay by your side and assist you, Master Guren," I said.

Guren chuckled.

"Your duty? You're just a kid, what do you know about loyalty?" he said.

To be honest that made me a little angry. I wanted to tell Master Guren that he was just a kid, too.

After all, every day I was told to dedicate myself to Master Guren. My only value seemed to rest in how loyal I could be.

So how dare he say that I didn't know what loyalty was?

Almost as if he knew what I was thinking, Master Guren turned around suddenly and spoke to me.

"...I'm sorry. Forget what I just said. I only said it because I was embarrassed that you saw me cry."

"Ah…"

"I shouldn't have let you see that. I know it puts you in a tough spot to see your own master in such a sorry state. I promise I won't give into my feelings like that again. Forgive me, Sayuri."

As he spoke, Master Guren flashed me an embarrassed smile.

"…"

It was at that moment that my fate was sealed.

It wasn't because I had seen the burden that my master carried. Or because I suddenly understood the pressure he was under as the next head of the Imperial Moon. There was no rational reason for it.

It was just that I fell in love.

In love with a boy my age who was there in front of me.

A boy with a cute smile and a delicate frame who was so strong it broke your heart.

Ten years passed, as if they were nothing.

And still, today, I'm just as much in love.

I never saw Master Guren cry again after that. He became even stronger, growing up into the type of person that anyone would be proud to have as head of the clan. For me, though, the change was a little sad.

I couldn't help but wonder if Master Guren would ever open up to me again like he did on that day.

It wasn't until years later that I understood everything that had happened that day.

Everything that happened between Master Guren and the girl from the Hiragi Clan, Mahiru Hiragi.

When I first heard the story, it felt like I had been stabbed in the heart. I couldn't sleep. I also knew that the two could never be together. I was both relieved, and ashamed of myself for feeling that way.

When I thought about it, really, they were both in the same boat as me.

In love, with someone beyond them.

With someone they could never be with.

"…"

The more I thought about it, the less I could sleep.

But there was one thing that I had that Mahiru Hiragi didn't…

"…At least, I get to be by Master Guren's side," I muttered to myself, taking a step closer to him as we walked to school.

We were on the road toward First Shibuya High School, a magical academy run by the Hiragi Clan. It was a place rife with enemies of our clan.

When I took a step closer to Master Guren he reacted just like I expected.

"Sayuri!" he said.

"Yes, sir?"

"You're in the way."

"But I have to stay close, Master Guren! How else will I protect you?"

"Not this close. I can barely walk!"

I took another half-step closer.

"Ugh… Why don't my followers ever do what I tell them to do?"

"Tee-hee ♡"

"Don't 'tee-hee' me. Just give me some space, already."

"No, Master Guren. I have to stay close so I can protect you…"

"Enough, already!" shouted Master Guren.

I just laughed.

For now, for today, this was enough for me.

Until Master Guren had a love of his own…

It was enough to just be by his side, for a little while.

Chapter One

Waiting to Pounce

The sun was bright in the sky.

It was early summer.

"..."

"Man, it's hot," muttered Guren Ichinose, unbuttoning the top of his high school uniform collar with one hand.

He was standing in the training yard at First Shibuya High School.

He was staring at the ground to keep the hot sun off his face. He lifted his head up suddenly.

A beautiful young girl, high-spirited and with crimson red hair, was standing in front of him. She shouted at him in a high-pitched screech.

"What are you staring at? Do you think you can afford to take your eyes off your opponent at your level?!"

She had slanted, almond-shaped eyes and milky white skin. Her delicate frame was dressed in a sailor-suit school uniform.

Her name was Mito Jujo.

She came rushing toward Guren, closing the distance between them with incredible speed.

"Hyah!"

With a fierce shout she balled her hand into a fist and swung at Guren.

Her punch was fast. Probably too fast for any of the other students in the courtyard to react.

Of course, Guren could have dodged it easily.

"..."

Instead he pretended that he didn't even see it coming.

"Huh? What?"

He acted as if he was too slow and weak to counter.

Mito's fist stopped just a hair's breadth away from Guren's cheek. She glared sharply at him out of the corners of her beautiful eyes.

"Come on, you're not even trying, Guren! How am I supposed to believe you're gonna be the next head of the Ichinose Clan if you can't even dodge a punch?"

Guren glanced down at Mito as he answered.

"Believe what you want, I guess," he said.

"Get real! Don't you know that if you take over the clan at this level, people are gonna treat you even worse than they do already?" sneered Mito.

She was trying to coax a reaction out of Guren.

Guren just shrugged his shoulders.

"Probably," he said. "Everyone in the clan has already given up on me. They all say I'm just a stupid brat, and the only reason I'm going to head the clan is because of my family."

That was a complete lie, of course.

The truth was, ever since Guren was born, he had been saddled with expectations from the whole Order of the Imperial Moon. The Imperial Moon was the magical syndicate headed by the Ichinose Clan.

Guren had shown an in-born gift for spellcraft and martial arts. As a result, they had been grooming him as the perfect leader ever since birth. If Guren developed his talents then maybe one day he could crush the Order of the Imperial Demons, which was led by the Hiragi Clan.

That was also why the Hiragi-led Imperial Demons had remained unaware of Guren's existence. It had been a closely guarded secret. Even now, the fact that the next leader of the Ichinose Clan harbored so much power was kept a secret from the Imperial Demons.

But even if they hadn't kept the truth a secret, the Hiragi Clan might not have taken much of an interest in Guren.

Any organization run by a branch family as small and weak as the Ichinoses was probably beneath their notice to begin with.

Guren snickered, amused at his own insignificance. Mito noticed immediately.

"You know what they call someone who grins like an idiot while other people pick on him and call him weak?" she said.

"I don't know, what?"

"A jerk."

Guren laughed.

"So that's why you guys keep calling me that," he said.

Mito raised her fist again and angrily swung at Guren. The punch wasn't very fast this time, but Guren still pretended he couldn't dodge it.

It landed on his left shoulder.

Guren felt the pain spread across his shoulder. He hesitated. Should he make a big show of how much it hurt? Or would that make it too obvious that he was faking it? While he was still trying to decide, Mito spoke.

"Why are you laughing, then?! Doesn't everyone making fun of you like that bother you?"

Mito seemed genuinely angry for some reason.

"…"

Guren wasn't sure how to respond.

The truth was that it didn't bother him.

He wasn't powerful enough yet to destroy the Hiragi Clan. As far as he was concerned, being made fun of was just something he would have to deal with until he became stronger.

Of course, you could argue that Guren took that attitude too far. But what good would it do for Guren to tip his hand too early, just so that he could show off and have people tell him how strong he was?

"Doesn't it ever occur to you to try and become better?" asked Mito.

"…"

"Maybe if you put in a little effort people wouldn't make fun of you so much!"

" …"

"Doesn't it ever occur to you to act like a man?!"

Mito grew angrier with every sentence.

The other students practicing on the training ground all stopped what they were doing.

Most of them were laughing. They stared at Guren with contemptuous smiles on their faces.

Nothing had really changed since Guren first entered the school in April. He was still an Ichinose, a pathetic mongrel from a lowly clan.

That was his place in the school's food chain.

For some reason, though, Mito Jujo—first daughter of the Hiragiloyal Jujo Clan—had taken an interest in him.

"All right…try and concentrate now," she said. "I'm here to help. We can train together."

Guren stared at her, grimacing inwardly. *I made a mistake saving her life*, he thought to himself. Really he had just been in the right place at the right time. Now Mito seemed to feel she owed him a debt. She wouldn't leave him alone.

"Hey, Mito…" said Guren.

Mito raised her hands up in fists. There was a fighting glint in her eyes, but her smile was playful.

"You finally ready to get serious?" she said, but Guren waved it off.

"There's something that's been bothering me for a while now. You don't have a crush on me, do you?"

Mito's eyes widened in shock, and her cheeks flushed beet red.

"O-On you? D-Don't be ridiculous!"

She shook her head, and then clenched her jaw in anger.

"You don't have a crush on me, then?" teased Guren.

"Of course I don't! The Jujos are one of the most prestigious clans in the order. You don't think a Jujo like me could really fall for a lowly Ichinose?"

"So then…why do you keep bothering me?"

"That…that's because I can't stand to watch you make a mess of everything!"

"Hmph. Maybe you should try minding your own business for a change."

"Well, maybe you should try being serious—"

"You're really pretty clingy, you know," Guren cut her off.

"Ahh…"

Mito's face fell slightly in shock. Guren's comment seemed to have hit home. A touch of sadness, maybe even loneliness, appeared on Mito's face.

"I'm not interested in becoming stronger," said Guren. "And I hate hard work. Instead of wasting your time on a mongrel like me, why don't you stick with all the other wunderkinds from the other top clans? You don't want your rivals to outpace you, do you?"

Mito narrowed her eyes and glared at Guren.

"You know what, you're right. It was my mistake for expecting anything from a loser like you."

"Now you're getting it."

"Once an Ichinose mongrel, always an Ichinose mongrel. Right?"

"Exactly. Now that that's settled, how about you leave me—"

Mito suddenly stepped forward and raised her hand in a fist again. Guren saw the punch coming, of course.

But he still didn't try to dodge.

This time Mito's punch landed on Guren's left cheek.

"Ngh!"

Guren tumbled backwards and landed on the ground with a groan.

"I'm through talking to you, you jerk!" shouted Mito, standing over him. "So don't try to talk to me, either!"

She stormed off in a huff. Guren stared absently at her back as she walked away.

"What a pain in the neck…" he sighed.

Guren wasn't out of the woods yet, though. There was still one more "pain in the neck" Guren had to deal with, and he was staring down at Guren right now.

It was a boy from the same class. Another student from one of the famous clans, whom Guren had saved along with Mito.

Norito Goshi.

Most people at the school treated Guren like roadkill. Like Mito, however, Norito had taken an interest in Guren and refused to leave him alone.

"Man, you sure pissed her off," he said. "I think you went too far this time, Guren."

"How so?" said Guren, staring up at Norito.

"With what you said. You saved her life. She was just trying to help you in turn. These past two weeks all she's been doing is trying to help you not get bullied so much."

"Well, no one asked her for help."

Norito laughed.

"I can't say I don't sympathize. I don't really like hard work either. But still…"

"Hmph," Guren snorted in response. He raised himself up into a sitting position and said, "For someone who doesn't like hard work, you sure seem pretty strong."

"Trust me, it wasn't my doing," grinned Norito. "My parents forced me to work hard. Son of the great Goshi Clan, and all that. You probably had to deal with the same thing from your parents, right?"

Guren made a sulking face in reply. "So that's all it took?" he said. "A little hard work and *poof*, now you're strong? No wonder you're so smug. You know, for us normal people, sometimes training just doesn't pay off, no matter how hard we try."

"In other words," said Norito, raising an eyebrow, "you used to make an effort?"

"…"

"Let me guess. You didn't get the results you wanted, so you gave up on trying? Ran away from life?"

Norito was half right, half wrong.

Guren had spent his whole life trying, putting so much effort into growing stronger that it consumed everything else. But it was true that Guren still hadn't gotten the results that he wanted.

He still couldn't destroy the Hiragi Clan.

And he hadn't been able to prevent Mahiru from getting wrapped up in her lust for power, or from falling in with the Brotherhood of a Thousand Nights.

As long as Guren lacked power he would be unable to save anyone.

In other words, he was nowhere near the results he wanted. But he was already in too deep to think of running now.

Guren wasn't looking for sympathy from anybody, either, though.

"In the end, Guren," said Norito, "the more you run the harder things get. You know what I mean?"

"Heh. What, you're gonna lecture me now, too? Don't make me laugh."

"I'm not trying to lecture you."

"What I don't get is why you two are so determined to make my life harder."

Norito laughed.

"You say that now...but hey, you saved our lives. We owe you. Either way, we're gonna be in the same class for the next three years. By the time we graduate you're gonna be stronger, and I bet you'll be thanking us then..."

"If you really think you owe me, how about you just leave me the hell alone? I don't need any allies and I don't need any friends."

Norito laughed, unfazed by Guren's rejection. "I've been where you are, Guren," he said, nodding his head sympathetically. "I never wanted to be part of a big clan, or be forced to grow stronger. The truth is I was sick of the whole thing."

Being born into a famous clan probably brought its own set of troubles. But Guren wasn't interested in Norito's life story and made an exaggerated show of looking annoyed.

Norito just laughed in response and said, "Either way, there's no harm in being friends. We are classmates, after all."

Then he turned and walked away.

Guren watched him go. The other students waited until both Norito and Mito were clearly out of sight before they started picking on Guren.

—*Hey, Ichinose mongrel! What are you doing on the ground? That's no place to take a nap!*

—*Why don't you stand up and fight me? I'll make sure you never stand up again!*

Guren stared at the students surrounding him and smirked inwardly.

Look at these idiots, he thought. *I could probably take them on with my hands tied behind my back.*

The faces in Guren's class had changed since the first day of school.

Which was only natural. The school had been attacked by a mysterious organization during the qualifying exams in April, and more than half of the students had been killed.

Casualties had been especially high among the freshmen, who were still too inexperienced to defend themselves. Before the attack there had been 600 freshmen. Now there were only 180.

The freshman year had been cut down to only five classes in total. As a result, more than half of the faces in Guren's class were new to him. But since he had never really bothered to remember any of his classmates in the first place, it didn't really matter either way.

They were all Imperial Demon students. Their faces might have changed, but they still acted the same.

They looked down on the Ichinoses as a minor family, made a big fuss over their own importance, and practically worshipped the ground that the Hiragis walked on.

"Hey, jerkface, are you listening to us?" shouted one of the students. He stepped forward and kicked Guren in the chest.

"Ngh!"

Guren didn't try to move out of the way. Instead he groaned as loud as he could, so that all the students could hear.

They laughed.

"Hey, don't pick on the weakling too much," said one of the other students. "You wouldn't want to catch any Ichinose loser germs."

The boy's voice stood out from the other students. It sounded classier and more grownup.

Guren turned his head toward the source of the voice. But the other students spotted the speaker first.

—Lord Shinya!

The girls in the group all squealed in excitement. They stared at him with hungry eyes.

It was Shinya Hiragi. One of the most privileged of them all.

He was dressed in a high-collared school uniform, with snow-white hair and a broad grin that almost seemed plastered on. There was a quick-witted glint to his eyes.

Those eyes now stared at Guren as he spoke.

"Leave this sorry piece of trash to me. The rest of you should get back to your training."

That was all it took. The students stopped picking on Guren and quickly dispersed.

The unwritten rule at First Shibuya High School was that lineage came first. The one thing that mattered most was your last name—what family you were born into.

The Hiragi Clan occupied the top rung of the Imperial Demons hierarchy. The students and teachers at the school would obey any order from a Hiragi without question, even if doing so might cost them their lives.

Case in point: during the attack on the school, hundreds of kids—only fifteen or sixteen years old—had died.

The attack had been an absolute massacre, and it had occurred in the very heart of Shibuya.

However, not a single mention of the incident was ever made on the news.

The Imperial Demons placed an immediate gag order on all information related to the attack. Afterward, in order to restore order, they circulated a fake story throughout the order claiming that they had completely wiped out the organization responsible for the attack.

All of the students swallowed this story blindly. Just as they had been trained to do.

The other students were scurrying away at Shinya's order like baby spiders fleeing from a nest.

"Look at them run," said Guren, watching the students go. "Do they know you're just a foster kid?"

It was true. Shinya Hiragi didn't actually carry the Hiragi bloodline.

Essentially he was a stud horse, trained since childhood to be used by the Hiragis to breed more powerful children for the clan.

The Hiragis planned to marry him to a pedigreed Hiragi—namely, Mahiru Hiragi.

But Mahiru had disappeared.

"..."

Shinya stepped in close to Guren. He stared down at him as he spoke.

"You're one to talk," he said. "You think they all know you're just pretending to be such a slacker?"

Guren laughed.

"Maybe I really am a slacker," he said.

"Haha! I don't know how you put up with them, when you could tear them apart if you wanted."

"I'm patient. I was born that way. Unlike a certain brat I know who takes every chance he gets to show off."

"Oh, and who would that be?"

"You, obviously."

Shinya laughed.

"If you're trying to offend me you're gonna have to try harder than that."

"No offense intended," said Guren, standing up. "I'm just pointing out the facts."

Guren turned toward Shinya. The two were about the same height, and nearly the same weight and build. Shinya was at the top of the curve when it came to magical skill. Otherwise he would have never been selected as Mahiru's fiancé.

But how do we compare? wondered Guren.

" … "

They had never fought each other seriously. If they were to ever fight to the death, would Guren be able to defeat him?

"Look at what you're doing right now," said Guren, still sizing Shinya up. "Why do you keep talking to me? If you really hated the Hiragis and wanted to destroy them so bad you'd be doing it by now, instead of wasting your time shooting the breeze with me."

Shinya grinned, as always.

"Come on, don't be such a hard-ass," he said. "Why don't we go get a cup of coffee, and talk over our plans for what to do next—"

"You gotta be kidding me," said Guren, cutting him off.

"I thought you'd say that," laughed Shinya.

"I don't have time for your nonsense," said Guren. "Just get lost already."

"All right, but we could at least share information."

"What, did you hear something?"

"Well, that got your attention. It's nothing very important…"

"Then get lost."

"Hold on. I thought you were patient? I figured you might be interested in hearing what the Hiragis know."

Guren figured he meant how the Imperial Demons were responding to the attack in April.

Guren already knew that the attackers were from the Brotherhood of a Thousand Nights. They had approached him directly, before the incident, asking him to join their side. But during the attack, at least, it seemed as if the Hiragi Clan were still unaware of their assailants' identity.

But that had been over a month ago. They should have pieced some information together by now.

"How much do the Hiragis know?" asked Guren.

"They've identified the attackers."

"You mean the Thousand Nights?"

"Exactly. And they're not taking it well. Together, the Thousand Nights and the Imperial Demons are the two most powerful magical syndicates in Japan. Now they're at war. If things go off course, the whole country could be destroyed."

"Save the commentary," said Guren. "Just tell me what's going on."

The Ichinose Clan was actually in favor of the war. It would be an opportunity to even the odds. If the two largest syndicates came to blows, neither of them was likely to come out the better for it. That would open up a chance for a smaller organization, like the Imperial Moon.

Shinya was almost certainly aware of what Guren was thinking. He probably even approved of the plan. But Guren still wasn't sure where Shinya's own ambitions lay in all of this. Or how far he was willing to go to get revenge against the Hiragi Clan.

"Well?" said Guren.

"I already gave you one piece of information," said Shinya, grinning. "Don't you think you should tell me something in return?"

"No."

"Heh. Why, wasn't my information worth anything?"

"Unlike a certain moron, I'm not stupid enough to go running my mouth off to someone when I'm not sure what side he's on."

"A certain moron? Who, exactly, are you referring to?"

"You, obviously."

"Haha!"

Shinya seemed more amused than angry.

"Well," he said, "maybe I should share one more tidbit. I've got to earn your trust, after all."

" ... "

Guren just stared at Shinya.

"They've started an internal investigation," Shinya said.

Guren nodded. "Of course they have. An attack like that couldn't have been pulled off without inside help. But if they're going to the trouble of carrying out an investigation, that means…"

"Exactly. They have no idea that it was Mahiru who betrayed them. Tenri Hiragi is the head of the clan. He's Mahiru's father and he has complete faith in her."

"…"

"Everyone says she shows even more potential than Kureto, her brother who's a senior here. They've always had high hopes for her."

Kureto Hiragi was also president of the student council.

Guren laughed.

"You must be so proud of your future bride," he said sarcastically.

Shinya just shrugged his shoulders.

"She's your ex-girlfriend."

"We were just kids. That's all forgotten now."

"Really? Because Mahiru never stopped talking about you."

"Hmph. So what? It made you jealous?"

"Ha! Maybe just a little."

Guren peered into Shinya's face once more. But Shinya was still grinning, like always. Guren found it impossible to figure out what he was really thinking.

Shinya carried on with his explanation.

"The internal investigation is being run by a special team led by Kureto," he said. "They're probably going to be watching you, too."

"Why?" said Guren, staring at Shinya. "I've been doing my best to look weak."

"True, but if anyone's got a motive, it's you."

"…"

"If they're searching for outsiders at the school who have a reason to bear a grudge against the Hiragi Clan, it's pretty obvious who they'll think of first…"

"The Ichinose Clan."

"Exactly."

"Not just me then. My followers, too…"

Guren frowned. Shigure and Sayuri could be in trouble.

Now that the number of classes had been cut down after the attack, Shigure and Sayuri had been moved to the classroom next to Guren's.

"I wouldn't worry too much," said Shinya. "After all, they'll probably be looking at you first. They've already seen what Shigure and Sayuri can do. After the qualifying exams, it was pretty clear that neither of them is capable of causing an incident like that."

"But I'm supposed to be even weaker than them. Shouldn't that let me off the hook, too?"

"I snuck a peek at your file. There seems to be some doubt that someone of your ability could have survived the attack. That's why they've got you in their sights. In fact you're being watched right now. Do you see him?"

"You're gonna have to be more specific than that," said Guren. "I'm always being watched."

"The window of the school building. Class 3-1. Don't look now, though. He'll notice."

Guren was no fool. He didn't need Shinya to tell him to be careful.

Guren had spent his whole life, ever since he was little, learning how not to draw attention from the Hiragi Clan.

To avert suspicion, Guren stretched his neck around as if it was feeling stiff. He caught sight of the window for just a split second.

There was a lone boy standing in the window.

Guren knew he was always being watched. But he hadn't noticed the observer in the window. If Shinya hadn't pointed him out, Guren might have never spotted him.

The boy in the window had dark black hair and cold, intelligent eyes.

"…It's the student council president, isn't it?"

"Yeah, it's Kureto. He's a senior, in competition with Mahiru to be

the next head of the clan."

"Hmph. Is he strong?"

"If we were to fight tomorrow, I'm not sure I could beat him…"

"Ha. Luckily I'm stronger than you."

"Haha! Let's hope you are…" said Shinya.

Guren still couldn't feel Kureto's eyes on him. But Shinya was right, Guren was clearly being watched. Being watched for any sign of disobedience. Any sign of strength.

Kureto's eyes searched for the ambition that lay hidden in Guren's soul.

"By the way, Guren…"

"Yeah?"

"I'm gonna have to punch you now."

"Huh?"

"We're being watched. If you don't want Kureto to get suspicious that we're working together, you better take the punch like a good boy—"

Before Shinya could finish speaking, Guren raised his hand in a fist to strike at him.

But Guren moved slowly on purpose. Shinya caught his fist in midair and sneered in disgust.

"Too slow, you Ichinose parasite!" he shouted, shoving Guren backward with a laugh. Once Guren was off balance, he followed up with a swift kick to his face.

"You said punch, not kick…" Guren muttered as Shinya's foot flew toward him.

Shinya laughed, following through with the strike.

"Ngh!"

Guren groaned in pain, tumbling backward to the ground.

He could hear the other students laughing.

Guren was used to this act. It was how he convinced everyone that he was just a weak, pathetic loser.

"…But was it enough to fool the student council president?" Guren muttered as he tumbled over in a heap on the school's training ground for the second time that day.

They were on the road home from school.

"Master Guren! Master Guren! Nothing bad happened at school today, did it?"

"..."

"Ever since we came to this school I've been a mess. I keep worrying that something is going to happen to you while I'm not around, or that you'll have to deal with too much on your own..."

"..."

"I mean, I know it sounds silly for me to say I'm worried about you when you're so much stronger and cleverer than I am. But as your bodyguard, it's really difficult for me not to be by your side..."

It was Guren's bodyguard, Sayuri Hanayori. She was babbling, like she always did.

Sayuri was fifteen years old, about 5' 3" tall, with wheat-colored hair. She was dressed in a sailor-suit school uniform. She chattered constantly. But she was also pretty, with a very attractive face.

Guren glanced at Sayuri out of the corners of his eyes. He sighed, obviously wishing she would be quiet for a little while.

A look of shock flashed across Sayuri's face. For a moment, it seemed like she had actually gotten the message. But...

"S-Something did happen, didn't it? There was trouble while I wasn't around, wasn't there?!"

"Geez, nothing happened!" said Guren. His voice was louder than he meant it to be.

Sayuri kept talking.

"B-But...when you sighed just now, you made a face like something was really bothering you!"

"The only reason I sighed is because you won't stop babbling."

"Whaaaa?!" shouted Sayuri, throwing her hands up in surprise.

If there was one thing Sayuri knew, it was how to be loud.

Sayuri fell back into line behind Guren, sniffling like she always did when Guren yelled at her. A hangdog expression appeared on her face. Shigure Yukimi, Guren's other bodyguard, was already walking behind Guren. Sayuri saddled up next to her.

"Sh-Shigure... Master Guren said I was babbling again."

Shigure looked up into Sayuri's face. Shigure was only 4' 11", but she had already stopped growing. Like Sayuri, she was dressed in a girl's sailor-suit school uniform. Unlike Sayuri, however, Shigure had an air of composure about her.

"That's because you were babbling," she said. "You always babble."

"Wha.........?!" Sayuri threw her hands up in shock again.

"I agree with Master Guren. It's annoying."

"Wh-Wha.........?!"

"You know, sometimes I think you actually enjoy pushing Master Guren's buttons."

"H-Heehee," Sayuri giggled in response. Her hands were still raised in the air.

Shigure sighed. She turned toward Guren with a tired expression on her face.

"Honestly though, Master Guren," she said, "it's not just Sayuri. I'm worried, too. After the classes were cut in half due to the attack in April, we were moved into the classroom next to yours. But there's still no way for us to know what happens to you during class."

Sayuri nodded enthusiastically.

"Couldn't you at least tell us how your day went?" asked Shigure. "For instance, who gave you that small bruise on your face?"

Guren touched his cheek lightly. It was the bruise from where

Shinya had kicked him.

"Don't worry about it," said Guren. "Shinya was just helping me keep up my act in front of the other students."

Shigure grinned, apparently relieved.

"So it was that piece of Hiragi crap," she said. "Come on, Sayuri. How about you and me go take care of him!"

"Aye, aye!"

"No, what 'aye, aye'!" shouted Guren, holding out his hand to stop the two.

"See, this is exactly why I don't tell you two things," he sighed.

"But if Shinya is really as tough as he seems, he could've made it look good without actually injuring you. I think he kicked too hard on purpose…"

"It couldn't be helped," explained Guren. "We were being watched."

"Watched?"

"Apparently I've caught the attention of the student council president."

Sayuri and Shigure exchanged glances with each other.

"You mean…Kureto Hiragi?" asked Sayuri.

"You know him?"

"Just his name," said Shigure, answering for Sayuri. "The Hiragis are pretty good at keeping secrets so it's hard to gather information on them, but I've heard Kureto mentioned a few times since we started at this school. He entered as the head of his class, just like Mahiru Hiragi, and has kept the position ever since. He's supposed to be very strong, very smart, and very calculating. There's even a rumor that he might be selected as the next head of the clan."

"I see," said Guren, narrowing his eyes.

He thought back to the glimpse of Kureto he'd seen in the window. It was just a momentary glance, from far away. But Guren's impression lined up with what Shigure said. To be more precise, Kureto had made almost no impression.

Kureto wasn't just strong. He was strong enough to hide it.

"I doubt there could be anyone in the Hiragi Clan as powerful as you, Master Guren!" said Sayuri.

"That goes without saying," agreed Shigure.

The two completely believed what they said.

They were referring to members of the head clan of one of the most powerful magical syndicates in the country. Regardless, there was no doubt in either of their minds that Guren could wipe the floor with them.

It wasn't just Sayuri and Shigure, either. All of the leaders of the Order of the Imperial Moon expected great things from Guren. It was almost overwhelming.

"Hmph..."

Guren didn't bother contradicting them. He was already used to having such heavy expectations on his shoulders.

Instead he just sighed, a look of dissatisfaction on his face.

"Let's hope I can live up to your expectations," he said, flashing them a smile. "After all, what good am I to anyone otherwise?"

Sayuri gasped. A vague hint of regret crept into her face. But Guren had already turned away.

He continued walking forward.

He was mulling over the situation in his mind. Namely, that:

A war between the Brotherhood of a Thousand Nights and the Order of the Imperial Demons had already started behind the scenes.

Mahiru had betrayed the Hiragi Clan and joined the Thousand Nights, where she was researching demonic weaponry—a type of forbidden magic that far surpassed any power known to man.

The Imperial Demons had already identified the Thousand Nights as their enemy, but the conflict had yet to proceed to full-out bloodshed.

"..."

Guren recalled Mahiru's words, from the day of the attack.

I want to tell you something important... she'd said, causing a look of panic to appear on the face of Saito, an assassin from the Thousand Nights. Usually nothing seemed to ruffle Saito's fur.

Their entire meeting had been a trap, orchestrated by the Thousand Nights. But the look on Saito's face told Guren that Mahiru had spilled a secret that she wasn't meant to share.

Guren recalled what she had told him.

The truth, she had said, suddenly, *is this year, at Christmas, the world will come to an end.*

The trumpets of the apocalypse will sound, and a virus will spread. When that time comes, a new world will arise. One that, more so than ever, requires power. When that time comes, I know you'll need me once more... We'll meet again, Guren, when the world comes to an end.

Guren still couldn't figure it out.

Of course, he understood the meaning of the words she spoke.

A virus was going to spread, and the world was going to end.

That was simple enough. But still...

A virus? The end of the world? Was the Thousand Nights planning to carry out an act of biological terrorism?

Guren couldn't see what they stood to gain from such an act. The Thousand Nights was the largest magical syndicate in Japan. It already pulled the strings of government. There was no one who stood to lose more than the Thousand Nights should this world—and the current status quo—fall apart.

Even if the Thousand Nights held a vaccine against the virus, when the virus spread it would destroy all systems of power and authority in the world. Could such madmen exist? What would be the point?

"Total world domination?" muttered Guren. "It sounds like a bad movie script."

But that's what Mahiru had said.

There was certainty in her face when she said it.

A virus was going to destroy the world.

And soon. Christmas, of this year.

It was already June. That left less than half a year until the end.

"..."

And what did she mean by the "trumpets of the apocalypse"? In the Book of Revelations seven angels appeared, sounding seven horns to signal the end of the world. Was it a reference to them? Or a metaphor for something else entirely? Guren had no idea.

War

Virus

Christmas

"If the world is really going to end in half a year, you think there would be some sign..."

Guren stared at the sky while scrolling through the list of troubling keywords in his mind. A wry smile appeared on his face.

Technically, the rainy season had already hit Japan. But there still wasn't a cloud in sight.

It was almost unsettling, how clear and blue the sky was.

"If things have already come this far, maybe I should try to get in contact with the Thousand Nights while there's still time..." muttered Guren, still staring overhead.

After all, the Hiragi Clan already suspected that Guren might be a traitor.

Their suspicion actually worked to Guren's favor.

Because Guren wasn't the real traitor.

It was Mahiru who had betrayed the Hiragis. The Brotherhood of a Thousand Nights had actually approached Guren before the attack.

That meant that, out of all the players on the board, the Hiragi Clan was furthest behind in the information war.

However, the Hiragis were no fools. If Guren didn't act fast, they would catch up before long. And once they had their bearings, full conflict with the Thousand Nights was sure to follow.

Guren needed to find a way to shore up the Ichinose Clan's position before then.

Guren recalled what Saito, the assassin from the Thousand Nights, had said.

If Guren ever felt like joining with the Thousand Nights, he could contact them via Hyakuya Orphanage.

"If I'm going to contact them I should do it now, before the Hiragis start watching me any closer..." muttered Guren.

"Hm? Did you say something?"

Guren was pulled out of his reverie to see Sayuri staring up at him.

"It's nothing. You and Shigure wanted to stop at the supermarket on the way home, didn't you?"

"Yes, sir. We used up most of the groceries yesterday, and we try to go once every three days."

"You two should go on your own today. I'm going to head home first."

Shigure peered into Guren's face, trying to read his expression.

"Of course, Master Guren...but is something the matter?"

Guren nearly laughed.

So many things were the matter that he wasn't sure what to deal with first. Instead, he just nodded.

"I'll tell you about it when we get home."

"But—"

Guren cut her off. "Remember, we're being watched. Right now, you two would be more hindrance than help."

"..."

The bodyguards' expressions grew tense. Guren continued.

"We need to start gathering information. I'll have work for both of you when I get back. We'll each have our jobs to do and we're going to have to do them with zero mistakes."

The two didn't ask any more questions. Although they tended to be loud and obnoxious, both Sayuri and Shigure were more than capable. It was why they were serving as bodyguards for the next head of the Ichinose Clan.

"There is one thing I'd like to know, Master Guren…"

"What?"

"What would you like for dinner?"

"Curry and rice," said Guren. It was the same answer he always gave.

Sayuri frowned, scrunching her forehead.

"I know you don't want to waste time thinking about something so unimportant," said Shigure, "but you always say curry and rice…"

"Hey, I like curry and rice," retorted Guren, laughing.

Sayuri laughed awkwardly and said, "Fine. We'll figure out what to make on our own."

"Thanks. I'm sure it will be good. Whatever you guys make is always delicious."

Sayuri's and Shigure's eyes widened slightly and they both blushed. They seemed happy to hear Guren praise their cooking.

"Wait a second!" said Sayuri, pouting suddenly. "I knew you were just saying curry and rice because you didn't want to think of anything!"

Guren laughed, waving his hand as he walked away from the two.

He was headed in the direction of the high-rise apartment building where he was staying. The Ichinose Clan had rented several of the top floors for him.

Guren knew the spies tailing them would also split up.

One of the spies was barely competent. It was obvious all along that he was watching them.

The other spy was fairly skilled and did a much better job of hiding himself.

Guren figured that Sayuri and Shigure had probably also noticed they were being followed.

"Heh. Not too long ago they wouldn't have even bothered to spit in my direction," Guren said to himself, laughing. "Now I'm the center of attention."

Guren knew it would be easy to shake the man following him. Of course, if Kureto Hiragi, himself, had been following Guren, it would have been a different story.

Once they found out how strong Guren really was, they would begin watching him even more closely.

If he was going to make his move…

"…I have to do it now."

Guren began walking.

He turned onto the main street that ran next to his apartment building, then entered a small arcade located along the way. He flagged down one of the attendants and asked to borrow the bathroom. It was located past a back door in a staff-only area. There was also a back exit next to the bathroom door.

The Ichinose Clan had scouted the area in advance, identifying different routes that Guren could take in case he ever needed to shake a tail.

Guren slipped out the arcade's back door.

By this point he was pretty sure that he had already lost the spy.

But he decided to take one more detour, just in case there was someone else following that Guren hadn't noticed.

After he was sure he was safe he turned around in the other direction, walking back toward the supermarket where Sayuri and Shigure were shopping for groceries.

Hyakuya Orphanage was located in the same direction. The supermarket sat between the orphanage and Guren's apartment building.

Hyakuya Orphanage was a home for gifted children whose parents had been killed so that the kids could be brought to the orphanage and experimented on—at least, that was the rumor.

"…"

Guren walked down the narrow alleyway behind the supermarket, exiting on the other side.

He was confident now that he had lost the spy.

Guren nodded to himself as he turned onto a wider street. The orphanage was located in the middle of a quiet residential area. For all intents and purposes it appeared to be a normal orphanage. Guren

walked in its direction now.

On his way, however, he was interrupted.

The street he was walking on was flanked on either side by private homes. And smack dab in the middle of that street stood a small girl.

She looked to be about seven or eight years old.

Despite her young age she had clear, piercing eyes that seemed to stare out at the world. Her skin was so pale it was almost transparent.

The strangest thing about the girl, however, was her unusual, ashen hair. It was just like Mahiru's.

She was staring at Guren as he approached.

"..."

Guren stopped walking and stared back at the girl. Once he realized he was staring, he smiled and spoke to the girl.

"I'm sorry. Was there something you wanted?"

"You're Guren Ichinose, aren't you?" said the girl.

"And you are? You're not by any chance related to Lady Mahiru, are you?"

"Is it that obvious?" said the girl, reaching up to touch her locks. "I guess the hair is a bit of a giveaway."

The girl laughed self-consciously. There was something strangely grownup about her mannerisms. She bowed to Guren, introducing herself.

"My name is Shinoa Hiragi. I'm Mahiru's younger sister."

Mahiru's sister.

"Of course," said Guren, nodding. "But is there a reason Lady Mahiru's younger sister is gracing me with her presence?"

"I have a message for you from my sister," she said.

So she had been sent by Mahiru. That is, if she was telling the truth…

Guren smiled stiffly in reply and said, "A message from Lady Mahiru? I can't imagine why she would have a message for someone like—"

Shinoa cut Guren off before he could finish.

"You can stop making that silly smile," she said. "I already know all about who you really are. My sister told me."

"Hmm? I'm not sure what you mean…"

"I guess I can't expect you to take my word for it. Maybe if I tell you some of what I know? About the Brotherhood of a Thousand Nights? And the cursed weapons? The fact that my sister sold out the Hiragis in pursuit of power, all for the sake of some boy she loves? Well? Is any of this starting to sound familiar?"

It was all information that only Mahiru should have known. Even if the girl wasn't really Mahiru's sister, and was actually a spy for the Hiragis, if she knew that much there wasn't anything left to hide.

The fake smile disappeared from Guren's face.

"Fine. And? What do you want from me, kid?"

Shinoa giggled, amused.

"What a change!" she said. "I have to say, I like this Guren much more."

"I don't really need praise from some kid."

"If you say so. But I always wondered what kind of man had managed to capture my sister's heart. I'm glad it's not just some run-of-the-mill bore."

The kind of man who had captured her heart.

Is that how Mahiru felt? What had motivated her to pursue research that no humans were meant to dabble in, and to create her powerful cursed weapon?

More importantly, how did Shinoa know all this?

"Whose side are you on?" asked Guren.

Was she with the Hiragis? Or with the Brotherhood of a Thousand Nights?

"Whichever side is most interesting," said Shinoa.

"Huh?"

"I'm just a kid. To be honest, power and influence just seem boring to me. I was lucky enough to be born with a powerful sister, so I don't have to deal with the same expectations over leading the clan."

"…"

"That's between Kureto and my sister. I've had some training from the clan, mostly just as a backup in case both Kureto and Mahiru die. I'm still fairly capable, though. At least, for my age."

Shinoa suddenly sprang forward.

She held a *fuda*—a paper charm used to cast spells—in her hand. It seemed to appear from out of nowhere.

She was fast.

An aura of danger rippled from her small body.

It was hard to believe that such a small child could evince so much power.

This must be what people mean when they refer to a child as a prodigy, thought Guren. Whether it was due to her Hiragi blood, or to having Mahiru as a sister, the girl was clearly talented.

Guren, however, didn't react. He just narrowed his eyes and stared at her as she approached.

Shinoa stopped mid-stride, with a frustrated laugh.

"What are you doing? I was about to strike with full force. Aren't you even going to try to counter?"

"If you're that strong, there's nothing I could do about it anyways."

"I know."

"So? What exactly are you trying to prove?"

Shinoa slipped the *fuda* back into her pocket before speaking.

"I'm just trying to prove whose side I'm on. I'm not interested in the Hiragis. Or the Brotherhood of a Thousand Nights. But I love my sister… She's always been kind to me. And interesting. She tells me everything."

"So now I should believe everything you say and spill my guts to you?"

Shinoa shook her head.

"I'm just here to deliver a message."

"What is it?"

"Don't go to Hyakuya Orphanage. Mahiru is planning to betray the Thousand Nights, too."

"…"

"That's all. It caught me by surprise, to be honest. Apparently, my sister loves you so much that she's willing to leak important information for you," said Shinoa, laughing. "I don't think I've ever seen her act this way before. She's usually very rational and logical."

"…"

"I guess love makes people act impulsively. I don't quite understand it. But then again, I'm just a kid."

Guren returned Shinoa's gaze.

"I don't understand it, either."

"Ahh, is that so?"

"Yes."

"That's too bad. You're going to make my sister cry."

Shinoa laughed.

"Just one thing, Shinoa…" said Guren.

Shinoa cocked an eyebrow at him. "Well, I guess I'm younger than you, so it's okay for you to call me by my first name… Anyway, what is it, Guren?" she asked just using his first name in turn.

Guren smiled and said, "What exactly is Mahiru planning? What is she going to do?"

"I thought you weren't in love?" asked Shinoa, grinning. "What do you care?"

"Just answer my question."

Shinoa tilted her head.

"My sister is very clever. Whatever she's planning, it's way too complicated for me to understand."

"Then just tell me the basics. Whatever you do understand."

"I'm sorry, all I know is that my sister is trying to acquire enough power to ensure that no one ever comes between the two of you again."

"…"

"But she says you're doing the same. She said that you need her, that your paths are different but in the end your destinations are the same. She looked so dreamy when she said it. I've never seen her like that before."

In the end, their destinations were the same.

Mahiru's words flashed through Guren's mind once more.

Virus.

Christmas.

The end of the world…

"…Is that all you know?" he asked.

Shinoa nodded emphatically.

"It is," she said.

"In that case, can you also deliver a message from me to Mahiru?"

Shinoa laughed.

"What is it? Do you want me to whisper sweet nothings in her ear?"

"Tell her I don't like being manipulated. By anyone. Tell her that she's a fool, and if she really thinks she loves me she should stop playing games and tell me what she's planning."

"Do you really want me to put it in those words?"

"Yes."

"Hmph… I really don't understand grownup love. It all seems a bit twisted to me."

Shinoa crossed her arms and tilted her head again.

Just then voices rang out from behind her. They seemed to belong to a group of children of about the same age as her.

"I'll race you all to the park! You too, Akane!"

"You're on! You'll never beat me, Mika!"

Guren turned his eyes toward the children.

Among the group was one boy whom Guren remembered having seen before.

He had blond hair, and skin even paler than Shinoa's. He was probably mixed race, with family from somewhere outside of Japan.

It was the boy from the Hyakuya Orphanage. Guren had seen him before with Saito—the assassin from the Thousand Nights.

His name was Mikaela, Guren recalled.

The boy quickly noticed Guren staring at him.

"Uh oh."

"What's wrong," asked the girl standing next to Mikaela.

"That guy over there with the nasty look in his eyes, I've seen him before. Mr. Saito said he's the neighborhood pervert!"

"The what?!!" spit out Shinoa, overhearing their conversation.

Mikaela ran up to Shinoa from behind.

"Hey you," he said, "are you all right?"

Shinoa turned around to face him. She answered in a mischievous tone, clearly enjoying the situation.

"No, I'm not. This guy here just said all sorts of dirty things to me. I think he was trying to abduct me!"

"I knew it!" shouted Mikaela.

Guren glowered at the two before turning on his heel.

"Whatever, just don't forget to deliver my message," he said.

Mikaela spoke up before Shinoa could answer.

"Wait, where do you think you're going? I'm calling the police!"

"You do that, kid."

"If I see you hanging around here again..."

"Geez, kid. I'm going. Just shut up already."

Shinoa cackled in delight. Guren ignored her as he walked away.

After all, if what Shinoa had said was true, it wouldn't help if anyone from the Thousand Nights, or the Hiragi Clan, saw Guren talking to Mahiru's sister.

Of course, Guren still didn't trust her entirely.

"...betraying the Thousand Nights...the end of the world...our destinations are the same..." Guren muttered to himself as he walked away. "This is all starting to sound like some grand romance novel. What are you planning, Mahiru..."

Mahiru. She had been his childhood girlfriend, once upon a time. Guren fell silent as he spoke her name. He sighed, wearily.

It was three days later. Guren was at school.

Rainy season had finally hit. It had been raining off and on all day, since morning.

From his seat next to the window Guren watched the rain fall, turning the dirt in the schoolyard wet and muddy.

Guren's homeroom teacher, Ms. Aiuchi, was standing in front of the blackboard and speaking to the class.

"As you all know, during the attack in April we lost around half of the students in our class—students who were your friends, your comrades, and some of the most elite and promising young cadets in the Order of the Imperial Demons. Let's take a moment of silence now to remember their sacrifice."

The students all closed their eyes to pray.

Guren was the only one who kept his eyes open.

The moment of silence was observed every day. The teachers—who served the Hiragi Clan—obviously believed a simple minute of prayer would cement loyalty among the surviving students.

It was all so obvious and self-serving. Guren smirked as the other students closed their eyes, and turned his absently out the window once more.

When the minute was up, the teacher opened her eyes and resumed speaking.

"Today we have something very important to discuss. The attack also interrupted the qualifying exams, which is of course the most important way in which your skills are assessed here at First Shibuya."

Despite the rain, training was still being carried out in the schoolyard. In fact, the rain offered extra incentive, giving the students a chance to practice using their abilities in muddy terrain.

One of the female students in the yard was sparring with a boy. She was dressed in a sailor-suit school uniform, like all the other girls. She was hit with one of his punches and went hurdling into the mud.

From the front of the class, Ms. Aiuchi continued speaking.

"While this may seem sudden, beginning today exams will pick up from where they left off, so that we can finish your assessments. Only students whose evaluations have not been completed will be tested."

For the first time since she began speaking, Guren turned his eyes toward the teacher.

A murmur of surprise rippled through the class in response to the sudden announcement.

Ms. Aiuchi smiled faintly.

"Don't worry. I know it comes as a surprise, but evaluations for most of the students in this class have actually already been completed. The only students left are Shinya Hiragi, who as we all know will have no difficulty in acquiring a top ranking…"

Guren glanced at Shinya, who was sitting at the desk next to Guren's.

Shinya flashed Guren a grin in reply.

Ms. Aiuchi went on.

"…also, Mito, from the Jujo Clan…and Norito, from the Goshi Clan. Both very talented students…"

The teacher had called out the names of the three most gifted students in the class. Apparently they were holding the exam finals, when the strongest students from the first half of exams faced off against each other to see who was most powerful.

"I wonder if she'll call my name too…" whispered Guren.

"Probably," Shinya whispered back. "After all, you're part of their internal investigation—"

Shinya's whispering was interrupted by the teacher.

"…and last but most clearly least," she said, "the mongrel from the Ichinose Clan. You four have been summoned for exams and should go to the gymnasium at your appointed times. Mito and Norito, your exams are at 8:30. Shinya and Guren, your exams are at 9:00."

Mito turned around in her seat to stare at Guren.

Guren returned her gaze.

"Hmph!"

As their eyes met, Mito turned her head away in a huff. Apparently she was still angry at Guren for what he had said to her the other day. Which suited Guren fine. The only reason he had said those things was to make her angry enough to leave him alone.

Watching Mito give Guren the cold shoulder, Norito flashed him a wry smile.

"Looks like it's more tests for us. Let's give it our best."

Guren ignored him.

The other students began yelling at Guren.

"Hey, Norito is speaking to you!"

"Who do you think you are, ignoring him?!"

Norito waved them off.

"It's fine. That's just the way he is."

"You mean he's a worthless piece of trash?"

"Huh?"

"He should be grateful that you condescended to speak to him. Ichinose dog!"

The students continued heaping abuse on Guren. It was no different than any other day.

Guren just ignored them. He glanced at the clock that hung over the blackboard.

"…Another test, huh?" he muttered to himself. "I wonder if I'll be able to hide my full strength this time, too."

◆

The gymnasium was located on the other side of the schoolyard, across from the main school building.

First Shibuya High School only cared about its students' physical and magical abilities. They weren't evaluated on any other points. As a result, the school didn't have clubs and sports like regular schools did.

Instead of sporting goods, the school's gym was installed with special equipment for practicing spellcasting. Half of the gym was taken up by fighting rings.

Guren pushed open the door. There were barely any students there at the moment. It was nearly deserted.

The time was 9:05.

"You're late, Guren Ichinose."

The voice echoed loudly through the building. It was cold and reproachful.

The voice had come from the center of the gymnasium. Guren turned his attention that way.

Several students were already gathered there.

Guren recognized three of them.

Mito.

Norito.

And of course, Shinya.

Both Mito and Norito were sitting on the floor, with exhausted expressions on their faces. Their evaluations had just ended. Apparently they had fought each other.

As far as Guren could judge, Mito was the slightly stronger of the two. But he didn't really care which of them had won.

"..."

He was more interested in the boy standing in the middle of the gymnasium. His face was cold and expressionless, and he had an intelligent air about him.

Guren had seen him once before, for only a brief minute, standing behind a window.

It was Kureto Hiragi, the student council president.

Kureto had maintained his position as top of his class ever since first entering the school. According to rumors he was one of the strongest of the Hiragis, perhaps even as powerful as Mahiru herself.

He glared at Guren with a piercing stare.

"Sorry," said Guren, making up a story to explain his lateness. "My stomach hurt so I stopped to use the bathroom."

Shinya laughed.

"Get last-minute jitters over the exam? You really are a coward."

"I don't know why a scaredy-cat like you ever came to this school in the first place," jeered Mito.

"Hey, can you blame him?" Norito said. "I nearly shit my pants when I heard I had to fight she-hulk, here."

"Who are you calling she-hulk?!"

"What? All I'm saying is you're strong!"

It seemed that Mito had won their match, just as Guren suspected.

He watched the two bicker a moment before speaking.

"Umm...now that I'm here, what should I do?"

"Step forward," said Kureto.

"O-Of course."

Guren bowed his head and walked toward the center of the gymnasium. He lined up next to Shinya and stood before Kureto.

Kureto's presence was as imposing as Guren had expected.

He had fierce, determined pupils and carefully groomed black hair. A katana was strapped to his waist, and a sash—marking him as student council president—was pinned to his arm.

There was no hint of friendliness about him.

But nor was there any sign of menace.

He simply stared at Guren with his cold and calculating eyes.

"Guren Ichinose..." he said.

"Yes?" answered Guren.

"I have a question for you. Answer truthfully. Have you been selling information to the Brotherhood of a Thousand Nights, the group that attacked us in April?"

Guren hadn't been expecting such a point-blank question.

Both Mito and Norito opened their eyes in shock. They turned to stare at Guren. Shinya also did his best to appear surprised.

Guren tried to appear flustered as he answered.

"I...what? I'm not sure what you're talking about..."

"So you didn't sell information?"

"I...no."

"Are you sure?"

"Of course. I mean, I'm an outsider here anyway, so I'm not even sure what information I would have that's worth selling—"

Kureto cut him off. "That much I believe. The teachers and students at this school may be stupid, but not so stupid that they would leak information to you. Maybe you haven't been selling information. But you have been working with the Thousand Nights. Haven't you?"

"What? No..."

"I don't believe you. You have motive. You bear a grudge against the Hiragi Clan, and would have seen the merit in joining with the Thousand Nights. You've been lying, pretending to be weaker than you are. That's proof enough."

Kureto wasn't holding anything back. And his tone of voice didn't sound like he was interested in having a discussion. Nothing Guren could say would make Kureto believe him. He was simply laying out the facts, as he saw them, before moving on to whatever it was he had planned.

Guren, however, wasn't willing to give up just yet.

"I think you're overestimating me..."

Kureto ignored him.

"If you were as weak as you appear to be, you could never have survived that attack. You're obviously hiding your true strength."

"That can't be," said Mito. "I mean—"

Kureto cut her off. "The only question left is whether or not that strength poses a threat to the Hiragi Clan. That's what we are here to find out. Let's begin."

"What? Just…h-hold on a second," stammered Guren.

Kureto ignored him and turned toward Shinya.

"I want you to kill him," he ordered. "That will tell us everything we need to know."

"Huh? Why do I have to do it?"

"Are you defying a direct order from me? Perhaps you've been collaborating with him?"

Shinya fidgeted uncomfortably before responding, "What? Come on, what have I ever done for you to be suspicious of me?"

Kureto stared at Shinya, stone-faced.

"If you don't want to draw suspicion, then you'll do what I say. That will show us just how strong Guren is."

"Hmph. Fine," said Shinya, turning toward Guren. "Sorry, Guren. Nothing personal, but it's my brother's order."

Shinya raised his hand in a fist. Guren could see that he was using an incantation to accelerate his punch.

"…"

Guren's instinct was to pretend he couldn't see the punch coming.

But if he took the punch full-force…even if it didn't kill him, he would probably wind up in the hospital for a while.

There was only half a year left until the end of the world. Could Guren really afford to get taken out of the action now?

Even if he continued to hide his strength like he had been doing all along, there was no guarantee the day to strike back against the Hiragis would ever arrive.

Nothing was certain. But there was no time left for Guren to think. He needed to predict what might happen, calculate his odds, and decide what to do immediately.

He decided to let the punch strike him.

After all, Shinya was his ally.

Chances are he would try to hit Guren in an area that wouldn't cause too much damage.

With luck, Guren would be out of the hospital within a month.

It would also give him a legitimate excuse to stop attending the school.

"..."

Guren made no attempt to dodge.

Shinya's fist came hurtling toward him.

And just as it was about to make contact with Guren's chest...

It stopped.

Kureto had reached out from the side and seized Shinya's arm before the fist could connect.

"I told you to hit him. Why are you holding back?" said Kureto. He twisted Shinya's arm back, sharply.

"Nggh!"

Shinya's face screwed up in pain. While Shinya was still wincing, Kureto backhanded him, hard, across the face.

Shinya went hurtling backward.

It all happened in the blink of an eye. It was proof of just how powerful Kureto was.

"That's strike one," said Kureto, staring at Shinya where he lay in a heap on the ground. "You've lost my trust. We're going to have to investigate you, as well, to determine whether you've been working with the Thousand Nights."

Shinya didn't get up.

Mito and Norito stood frozen in place. Their mouths were open in shock.

Kureto turned his gaze toward Guren. For the first time since Guren entered the gymnasium, a faint smile appeared on Kureto's face.

"Now then, Guren. It's your turn."

"Hold on..."

"You can drop the act, already. If you're as powerless as you say, then you're going to die in this gymnasium, right here and now. If you've been lying and are stronger than you say, then we're going to inject you with a truth serum and torture you until we find out how you are connected to the Thousand Nights."

As Kureto spoke, he unsheathed the katana at his waist. It seemed he was serious about being ready to kill.

"Just hold on a second," said Guren, still trying to talk his way out of the situation. "If you do this, it will ruin your relationship with the Ichinose Clan..."

"The Ichinose Clan can be easily placated."

Guren clucked his tongue. Kureto had him there. But Guren wasn't going to give up yet.

"I'm telling you, you're overestimating me. I'm powerless..."

A third voice joined the conversation, springing to Guren's defense. It was Mito.

"It's true, Master Kureto! I've tried to provoke Guren into standing up for himself at least a hundred times. He really can't fight at all!"

Kureto glanced toward Mito and narrowed his eyes.

Guren overheard him mutter quietly to himself, "It seems there may be a traitor in the Jujo Clan as well..."

Mito, however, didn't seem to notice. She continued talking.

"I'm telling you—"

Interrupting her, Kureto said, "I've heard enough, Mito Jujo. How does this involve you? What is your relationship with Guren Ichinose? You're not lovers, are you?"

"No...it's not...it's just..." Mito stammered in confusion.

"Explain yourself," said Kureto.

"H-He's just a classmate...and I thought, maybe it wouldn't be right for someone as distinguished as yourself...to come into contact with an Ichinose. S-So..."

Unable to explain herself, Mito's voice slowly trailed off into silence.

To be honest, even Guren was surprised that Mito had chosen that timing to come to his defense. Apparently, Mito's peculiar sense of justice wouldn't allow her to stay quiet under the circumstances.

But what exactly motivated that sense of justice? Was it simply the fact that one of her classmates was about to be killed before her eyes?

Guren really wasn't sure.

Either way, the whole situation was starting to get out of hand.

If things kept going the way they were, Mito was going to get stuck taking the heat for something she didn't even do. Not that that really mattered. But still, nothing about the situation was sitting well with Guren.

"...Maybe I should make a run for it," he muttered.

Guren glanced up at the ceiling, as if in distress.

As he did so, Kureto brandished his sword.

"Enough, everyone be quiet. Guren Ichinose, it's time for you to die."

"Y-You can't!" shouted Mito.

"Come on, man, this sucks," groaned Norito.

It may have only been three months, but the three of them had shared the same classroom, every day, for all that time. It was only natural that Mito and Norito would be upset at the prospect of seeing Guren die.

After all, they were decent people deep down.

And Guren was facing certain death. At least, as far as Mito and Norito knew.

Kureto was a Hiragi. He was beyond human. He was the top student at the school and more accomplished than all of his peers. And he was pointing his sword at Guren, ready to kill.

Guren, on the other hand, was just a mongrel. There was no way he could survive. Not if he was the pathetic loser they all thought he was.

"...Man, what a pain in the ass," muttered Guren.

He turned his eyes from the ceiling back toward Kureto.

Kureto dashed forward.

He was fast. Incredibly fast.

Just what you would expect from the school's top student and president of the student council.

But still...

...*he's nowhere near as fast as Mahiru and her demon.*

Guren drew his own katana from his hip.

It was a new blade. Guren's old blade, Kujakumaru, had been broken in half by Mahiru. Guren had this enchanted blade sent in its place. It was named River's Edge.

Guren raised River's Edge into the air, intercepting Kureto's blade. A metallic clash echoed in the air.

Kureto drew his sword back immediately, following up with a second and a third thrust.

Guren parried each of Kureto's attacks, circling outside and countering with his own slash.

"Ngh!!

Kureto ducked to the side, taking a step back and drawing a *fuda* from inside his jacket. He tossed the *fuda* into the air.

Guren slashed it into pieces before it struck. He slid forward, aiming his blade at Kureto's heart.

Kureto's katana swung upward to block the strike, but Guren carried through with his assault. He took his left hand off his sword's pommel and struck at Kureto's face with the heel of his hand.

Kureto dodged the blow by tipping backward, almost as if falling. He carried the motion through, circling into a kick to Guren's sword arm.

Guren let the kick hit him in the arm, planning to counter with a slash that would cut Kureto's leg clean from his body. Unfortunately he wasn't fast enough.

Kureto shuffled several steps backward, regaining his stance.

Guren took a step back as well, to regain his own stance.

" . . . "

It had all happened in the blink of an eye.

Of the three watching, Shinya was probably the only one capable of catching all of their moves.

Mito and Norito were probably still struggling to understand what had occurred.

Either way, Guren's secret was out in the open.

"Wh-What just happened?" said Mito.

Kureto ignored her.

"…Hmph. It seems the next leader of the Ichinose Clan has finally shown his true colors."

Guren smiled shyly.

"It was never much of a secret," he said. "You've got it wrong. I'm just shy, is all."

"Haha!"

"I mean, I'm not so powerful that I'd be a threat, am I? So I'm a little stronger than I pretended…what does it matter? I was just trying not to draw too much attention from the Hiragi Clan."

Kureto clearly wasn't buying it. He pointed his sword at Guren, staring at him coldly.

"Whether or not you're a threat remains to be determined. We're not finished yet."

"Come on, can't you just give me a break?"

"No. The whole point of this school is to figure out which of us is the strongest."

Guren's face twisted up in annoyance. "You know, you're really starting to be a pain in my fucking ass," he said.

"Ahaha! So that's the real Guren. Do you kiss your mother with that mouth? Still, it isn't often I get the chance to test my strength against a real opponent. Who'd have thought that such talent could be hiding in a lowly branch family? I'm going to enjoy this."

Kureto brandished his sword.

Guren moved in response.

Which of them was stronger?

Guren wanted to know the answer to that question as well. But winning this fight would be pointless. His best move would be to show some talent, but still make it seem like he was no match for Kureto.

They would come to the conclusion that Guren didn't possess the strength to betray the Hiragis—that he had only been hiding his strength to avoid drawing unwanted attention. When all was said and done he would still be just a mongrel, nowhere as powerful as Kureto Hiragi.

It was the best possible outcome for Guren. But...

"...it won't work," he groaned.

He stared up at Kureto's sword, which was still raised in the air. Kureto had said that he wanted to test his strength against Guren.

But Kureto had lied.

As soon as Guren turned his attention toward Kureto, he sensed danger from all angles. It was almost as if they had been waiting for that moment to take him by surprise.

Guren sensed five attackers, spread out through the gym. He was surrounded. Of course, Guren was always surrounded by enemies when he was at the school. That was nothing new.

He could sense the attacks coming but couldn't see anything. The assault was by something small. Spikes? Needles?

Guren spun around blindly, searching for his attackers.

"Shit...!"

He swung his sword in an arc, but it all happened so fast that he was only able to block three of the needles.

The other two struck him, one in his right ankle and one in his back.

They were probably coated in either poison or tranquilizer.

Guren realized it was tranquilizer almost immediately. He was suddenly hit with an overpowering drowsiness.

"...Ngh. You son of a bitch," said Guren, staring at Kureto through drooping eyelids. "Why did you even spout all that stuff about wanting to see who was stronger?"

Kureto stared down at Guren with a slightly contemptuous expression.

"Are you serious? Only a fool would care about something as childish as that."

"..."

"You're no fool either, are you, Guren? You were planning to lose to me."

"..."

"I've already gotten a good idea of how strong you are. You're clearly very capable. We're going to investigate you now to determine whether you've been working with the Thousand Nights. Should our suspicions be cleared, we'll put you to use as a valuable new soldier for the Hiragi Clan."

"..."

"Truth serum and torture will be waiting for you when you wake. Until then, sleep well, Guren Ichinose."

"Dammit..." muttered Guren, as everything faded to black.

Chapter Four

Questions and Answers

Blackness.

And waking.

Blackness.

And waking.

Guren lost count of how many times he had drifted between the two.

"..."

He opened his eyes a crack, having just returned to consciousness once again.

His vision was distorted and wavy.

It was likely due to the truth serum in his blood.

Fortunately, Guren had undergone training to hold up under torture and resist toxins and drugs of this sort.

He took a moment to assess the situation.

The room he was in was small, and extremely bright.

His chair was bolted to the floor.

Guren was tied to the chair. They had been asking him the same questions for what seemed like an eternity.

"Are you working with the Brotherhood of a Thousand Nights?"

The man who questioned him was dressed in a uniform. It belonged to the private army commanded by the Order of the Imperial Demons. Guren couldn't see his face. A bare light bulb hung from the ceiling, burning brightly. The man shoved it into Guren's face. The light was so overpowering it caused Guren's head to throb in pain.

They had been subjecting Guren to this treatment for over three days now. Whenever he lost consciousness he was awakened immediately. By depriving him of sleep, they were steadily weakening his ability to think.

And wearing down his ability to lie.

"Are you working with the Brotherhood of a Thousand Nights?" the man asked again.

Guren figured it was about time to give them an answer.

After all, it was about the point when someone with standard training to resist torture would begin to crack.

Guren had been waiting for that moment to begin spinning his lies.

"A-Ahh…"

"What is it? Is there something you want to say?"

"…w…water…"

"You want water? Answer my questions and you can have water."

"Nn…"

"Are you working with the Brotherhood of a Thousand Nights?"

"…b…brotherhood?"

"The Brotherhood of a Thousand Nights. You're in league with them, aren't you?"

Guren forced his sluggish brain to form an answer to the man's question.

"I…I'm not in league…with them…"

"You're lying. You're one of them."

"No…"

"You're one of the Thousand Nights."

"N-No…b-but I did…get an invitation…from them…"

"An invitation? Then it's true. You joined the Thousand Nights."

"N-No. Our interests didn't coincide…"

"Your interests? What do you mean?" the man asked before continuing, "Hmph. I suppose that question is too complicated for you to answer in your current state. But I understand now. The secret you've been keeping is that you received an invitation from the Brotherhood of a Thousand Nights. Did you know that the attack was coming?"

"N-No..."

"You're lying. You did know."

"..."

Guren remained silent. He was thinking. This moment could be crucial. If he could formulate an answer good enough to satisfy his interrogator, then his torture might end.

But it needed to be an answer that seemed credible. One that was good enough to placate his interrogator...

"You knew, didn't you?" the interrogator said. "You're the one who helped the attackers infiltrate the school."

"No..."

"Admit it."

"I...I...the war..."

"The war?"

"I knew...that a war was coming...but I didn't know..."

"You didn't know when?" asked the man, trying to get Guren to say more.

"They wanted to make us...the Ichinose Clan...their subordinates... They said we were too small to matter. They said it didn't matter either way whether we joined them..."

"I see..."

"That's why...they didn't tell us anything..."

"But you joined with them."

"No..."

"Admit it, you sold out the Hiragi Clan."

Guren threw his head back and began laughing hysterically.

"Ah...hahah... Ahahahaha!"

"What is it? Why are you laughing? Are you ready to admit your guilt?"

"What would be the point of selling out the Hiragis?" answered Guren. "Slaves to the Thousand Nights or the Hiragis' mongrel branch clan...our position would be exactly the same."

"…"

"Enough. Just kill me, already. I'm tired of all this. Why don't you big-shot syndicates fight your own fights?"

"…"

"The Ichinoses are just mongrels, right? So why are the great and powerful Hiragis even wasting their time on us?"

Suddenly, the light was turned down.

The room grew a little darker. It was a few moments before Guren's pupils were able to adjust.

Little by little, Guren's vision faded from white to dark, and he was able to make out the outlines in the room.

The interrogator, who stood next to him, was late middle-aged, with a stern face and a beard.

"That's it…" said the man, turning toward the back wall.

As he did so, a door opened revealing Kureto. He stared down at Guren, who was still tied to his seat.

"That's all you can get?"

"Yes. I believe he may have undergone training to resist questioning. Even with training, you understand, there are limits to what a human can endure. I think we're already come very close to those limits."

"And? Do you believe he's telling you the truth?"

The bearded man nodded.

"Yes. At the very least, I believe he's being sincere about his own motivations."

Kureto stared at Guren with cold, piercing eyes.

"He believes you're being sincere, Guren. But is that really all you know?"

"…"

Guren lifted his head up slightly before he spoke.

"I've been telling you all along, you've overestimated me."

"I'll be very disappointed if that's true."

"Hmph, that's your problem."

Kureto kept his eyes fixed on Guren.

"By the way," he said, "your father came to the compound to make a complaint. He insisted that we let his son go."

"…"

"We took him into custody for questioning. He told us exactly what you did. That the Ichinose Clan had received an invitation from the Brotherhood of a Thousand Nights, but you couldn't come to an agreement. And then this war started while you were still considering your answer."

"…"

"Your father is very weak. He broke down and talked five hours before you did. His heart even gave out, in the end."

"Ah…!"

Kureto smiled faintly.

"That's the first real emotion you've shown, isn't it? That expression of anger? Everything up until now has just been an act, hasn't it? Even under torture, you only shared information you deemed to be safe, didn't you? Incredible. I should commend you. It's not often that someone of such talent is born into such a lowly, minor clan."

"…"

"Don't worry. Your father isn't dead. We revived him and sent him home. You're very strong, Guren. But it's like you said. You're just one person. Being strong doesn't change anything. The Ichinose Clan are nothing but crawling ants in comparison to the Hiragi Clan. You could never be a threat to us. We see that now."

"…"

What Kureto said was true. He went on.

"You've piqued my interest, Guren Ichinose. I'm making you my right-hand man. It will be a chance for you to improve the standing of your lowly clan. Do you understand?"

"…And if I refuse?"

Kureto cocked his head to the side for a moment, as if he was actually pondering the question.

"…I will destroy the entire Ichinose Clan. If my calculations are correct, it would take us a mere five days to massacre every single person in your little Order of the Imperial Moon."

"…"

"Your syndicate, as you call it, would be easy to destroy. That's why the Thousand Nights didn't care whether you joined them or not. The only reason the Hiragi Clan tolerates your organization's continued existence is because you are too weak to matter."

"…"

"You, on the other hand, could prove a very useful resource. Make your choice. Do I kill everyone you know and love? Or…"

"…or will I swear allegiance to you?"

"Precisely."

"That seems pretty high and mighty."

Kureto shrugged, as if he couldn't but agree. "That's what it means to be a Hiragi," he said.

Guren had no choice.

In truth, there was no reason for him not to accept Kureto's proposition. Guren had always intended to act weak and hide his full strength while at the school. But Kureto's backing would actually work in his favor by giving him more cover.

He would swear allegiance to Kureto and do as he was told.

He would show that he understood he was no match for Kureto or the Hiragis. He would be their dog, ready to do their bidding.

And as long as the Hiragis bought his act, life would be easy. The only problem that remained was whether Guren could really gain enough strength to one day bite back at them.

Guren stared up at Kureto as he spoke.

"…Can I have a glass of water, at least?"

Kureto smiled faintly.

"Then you accept?"

"What other choice do I have?"

"It's settled, then. We are now on the same side. Rest easy. I always treat my underlings fairly."

"Your underlings?"

"Do you have a problem with that? Would you prefer I call you my friend?"

"Huh?" said Guren. Kureto ignored him, turning toward the interrogator.

"Untie him," the student council president ordered. "As of today he is one of my retainers…"

Before Kureto had finished speaking, however, Guren dislocated his own arm, drawing it free from the restraints. He could have freed himself all along, if he had wished.

"Ahh…"

The interrogator stared at Guren in shock.

Guren laughed as he met the man's gaze.

"Don't worry, I won't hold a grudge against you. I was in charge of the questioning all along!"

Kureto, however, seemed unsurprised. He tilted his head and peered at Guren, as if appraising his condition.

"You look a little worn out," he said. "Take the rest of today off. I'll have work for you to do starting tomorrow."

"You're already acting like you're my master."

"You still don't get it? I've always been your master. Every day up until now and every day hence. Your children, and your children's children, and so on and so on, will be servants to the Hiragis. Always and forever. That reminds me, I sent your weapon back to the Ichinose compound, along with your father. I'll have a stronger weapon for you tomorrow, something more suited to your abilities."

Having said all he wished to say, Kureto turned around and left the room.

Guren glared at him as he walked away. The interrogator, still standing next to Guren, bowed his head deeply. His attitude had changed drastically.

"My humblest apologies for everything that occurred here, Master Ichinose," he said.

As Kureto's underling, Guren's status had already improved.

When all was said and done, however, nothing had really changed. Things were the same as they had been. Guren sighed.

The Hiragis still held absolute power. And the Ichinoses were still a lowly branch clan.

There had to be something Guren could do to reverse their positions.

The path that Mahiru had chosen was one that was leading her away from her humanity.

It was a path fit for no man. One of death and carnage.

But, what if...

"..."

Guren suddenly remembered what Mahiru had said, in the message she had sent through Shinoa.

Our paths are different, but our destinations are the same...

"...but what is my path?" muttered Guren.

After a moment he stood, and walked free of the torture chamber.

◆

The room had been located in the basement of the school's gymnasium. It had been installed there to train Hiragi-loyal students in torture resistance.

Guren left the gymnasium with a haggard expression on his face.

Overhead, the sky was tinted red.

The sun was just beginning to set.

Classes were probably already over for the day. The schoolyard, however, was still full of students who were using their free time to train.

Guren stared at them out of the corners of his eyes. He was considering whether to head into the school building or return home. He had left his bag inside, but Sayuri or Shigure had probably taken it home for him. His cell phone had already been confiscated. His sword had been sent back to the Ichinose compound.

"I don't know why they bothered..." muttered Guren.

He turned on his heel and set out for home. Before he had gotten very far, however...

"Ichinose!"

Someone suddenly shouted at Guren from across the schoolyard. He recognized the voice immediately.

It was Mito Jujo.

Guren continued walking without turning around.

"Wait!"

"..."

"I said wait!"

Behind him, Guren sensed danger. Mito's anger was about to boil over. He finally stopped and turned around to say, "Could you stop screeching, already? I haven't slept in days." He stared at her through half-lidded eyes.

Mito had distinctive, crimson hair, fierce, slanted eyes, and an attractive face.

She seemed angry. Guren wasn't sure why.

She had already begun chanting a spell. It was Hiragi magic. An invocation spell that would push her strength and physical characteristics to the limit. It was the type of magic Mito excelled in.

Above her head a fiery, three-pointed halo appeared. It burned a bright crimson—even brighter than her hair.

Guren already knew what demon she was calling on for strength. He had seen the spell once before, and investigated it.

It was Vajrayaksa, the Devourer King.

"You're gonna pay for making a fool out of me!" she shouted. She sounded almost like a petulant child.

Mito stomped the ground with her slender leg. A deafening boom filled the air and a crater formed beneath her feet. The force sent Mito's body soaring through the air at incredible speed. She quickly closed the distance between herself and Guren.

244

Mito's movements were fast. Any normal person—even someone who had undergone considerable training—would have been unable to keep up with her.

Mito's power was nearly unmatched.

Guren just stared, looking tired, as she approached and swung her fist, aiming at Guren's face.

"You think you can still hide your true stre—"

Mito's shout broke off in mid-sentence.

Guren stepped back deftly onto one foot. He easily snagged Mito's arm in mid-swing and twisted in into a lock. She tried to dislocate the joint to escape the hold, but Guren anticipated the move.

He used Mito's own momentum to sweep her off her feet.

"Eek...!"

Mito screamed in surprise, tipping head over heels into the air. Guren wasn't finished, however. Still gripping her arm, he yanked her down hard, swinging her body toward the ground. She went tumbling like a stone, just inches from crashing into the ground head-first.

A split-second before she made impact, Guren snagged the collar of her sailor-suit school uniform, saving her from hitting her head.

It all happened so fast that Mito simply lay there for a moment, in shock. She still wasn't sure what had happened.

"What are you doing," said Guren, staring down at her, "tripping over your feet like that?"

Mito finally realized what had happened. She stared at Guren with daggers in her eyes. She seemed angry.

"Q-Quit playing games! If you're so powerful, why have you been hiding it all this time?"

"If people knew how strong I was, they'd only bully me more."

"There's no way, not with that strength..."

"I'm still an Ichinose, Mito."

Mito's eyes widened. It was the first time she got an inkling of the kind of burden Guren might be bearing.

Not that she understand—truly understood—how despised the

Ichinose Clan was. Or how truly omnipotent the Hiragis were. Some things you could never understand as long as you were with the Hiragis, on the inside looking out.

Mito jerked her collar from Guren's grasp and stood up.

"So what? You were powerful all along but you've been hiding it. So every time I showed sympathy, or criticized you, you were really laughing at me? At how gullible I was?"

Guren shook his head.

"Of course not."

"But…but I said so many nasty things to you."

"Did you?"

"Of course I did! And you just took it. You let me pick on you any time I wanted, like it didn't matter! But all along you were laughing at me behind my back. I—"

Guren cut her off.

"I don't care about you enough to bother laughing at you," he said.

"Ah…"

"And I don't have time to waste on something this stupid. Are you done?"

Mito looked like she had just been slapped. Guren thought he could see tears welling up in her eyes. Whether it was because of what he had said, or just because as a Jujo she wasn't used to being talked to that way, Guren wasn't sure.

He really didn't care. After all, he hadn't slept properly in a few days.

Guren turned around and began walking away.

Mito called after him as he left.

"B-But, you saved me!"

" … "

"If you hadn't pushed me out of the way during the attack…I'd be dead!"

" … "

"Why?! If it was so important to hide your strength, wouldn't it have been better if you just let me die? But you saved me. You say you don't care, but you saved me. Tell me why!"

Guren sighed. Why *did* he save Mito and Norito that day?

He had done it without thinking. What else could he say?

People he knew were about to die right before his eyes, so he saved them by instinct. It was a foolish thing to do. It was weakness. And weakness could be fatal.

"…"

Guren continued walking without answering her. He was headed away from the school.

Unfortunately, it was just Guren's luck that Norito was standing by the school gate. He had his arms crossed and was staring in Guren's direction. He had seen the fight between Guren and Kureto with his own two eyes. That meant he knew Guren's secret as well.

"The bull-shitter, himself! So all this time you've really been some kind of boy-wonder."

"…"

"I bet everything comes easy to you, right? Not like us 'normal people'? I bet your mummy and daddy and all your followers think you're such hot shit."

Guren grinned facetiously and replied, "That's right. Every day I get a nice big pat on the head from my daddy!"

"Get serious."

"You're the one who thinks I've got it easy."

"Huh?"

"So I'm actually strong. So what? What difference does strength make when you're born an Ichinose?"

"…"

"You're from the great and mighty Goshi Clan. And that redhead back there is an esteemed Jujo. But what am I? As far as the Hiragis are concerned, I'm just an Ichinose mongrel. No amount of strength can change that."

Norito narrowed his eyes as he peered back at Guren.

"You've got a warped way of looking at things."

"Do I? Maybe you should just keep your distance, then."

"No way, I can't do that. You saved my life!"

"And now you're gonna dedicate the rest of it to me?"

"Quit joking," said Norito, laughing. "I'll be your friend, though."

"How about you don't and we call it even."

"That's cold. I've got to ask the same question as the redhead. Why did you even bother saving me in the first place?"

"I was in the wrong place at the right time," Guren answered without so much as pausing.

"I don't think so," said Norito. "It would have been better, for you, not to save me. Not after all the time you spent pretending to be weak. And yet you did save us. Why?"

"..."

"I think I know the reason..."

Guren wasn't interested in hearing Norito's analysis of his character. He turned on his heel and began walking away.

That didn't stop Norito, though. He shouted after Guren obnoxiously as he walked away.

"The real reason you saved us is you're secretly a nice guy! Or maybe you're just lonely. Either way, you saved my life and I won't forget it. From now on we're friends, you hear me? Friends!"

Guren snorted. He answered Norito without turning around.

"That's the stupidest thing I've ever heard."

"Hahaha!"

Guren could hear Norito's laughter as he walked away. Norito really was a pain in the neck.

But his laughter steadily faded into the distance.

"..."

All that Guren could think about on his way home was what Mito and Norito had said.

Why did I save them?

Weakness like that really could prove fatal. In the days to come, he would need to be strong enough to make sacrifices. Anything necessary to fulfill his desires and achieve his goals. Even the lives of Sayuri and Shigure, if need be.

Because his opponents were the Hiragis.

And the Brotherhood of a Thousand Nights.

Both of those organizations dwarfed the Imperial Moon in size. Guren was planning to build his power, day by day, until finally he could oppose them. He couldn't afford to get distracted by useless sentiment so early on.

"A nice guy...such a nice guy," Guren muttered, his face twisting into a self-loathing sneer.

Guren craned his neck upward. Above him was the high-rise apartment building where he lived.

He wondered if Sayuri and Shigure were home.

Guren pictured their two faces. If it had been them—if Sayuri and Shigure had been the ones in trouble during the attack—could Guren really have sacrificed them so easily? He wondered.

"I know *you're* ready to sacrifice others," Guren murmured. "Aren't you? Mahiru..."

Mahiru, the girl he had once promised to stand by as a child. She was seeking power, and she was clearly in the lead. Speaking her name, Guren had to sigh.

Chapter Five

Guren Plays Hooky

Guren took several days off from school.

He was playing hooky.

"..."

He opened his eyes. He was lying in bed, in his own room. He stared up at the ceiling, and then over at the alarm clock on his nightstand.

The time was 5:00 a.m.

Guren usually woke up at the same time every day. He had woken up at this time for so many years that, even without setting the alarm, his eyes still sprang open. By this point, his mind was just trained to wake up.

He got out of bed. He was dressed comfortably in sweatpants and a sweatshirt. He had ignored Kureto Hiragi's order and taken several days off from school, claiming that he needed to rest to recover from the damage caused by the torture he had undergone. In truth, there was no damage. Since he hadn't been able to move during the questioning, if anything his body was actually over-rested.

He stretched his arms and swiveled his neck around in a circle, checking to see how he felt.

"Everything seems fine..." he muttered, exiting the room.

He was in one of his apartments in the high-rise building. The Ichinose Clan had rented out a few of the upper floors for Guren. The apartment he was in now had five bedrooms. Guren, Shigure, and Sayuri all lived there.

As he left his room, Shigure poked her head out from the living room and bowed toward Guren.

"Good morning, Master Guren. Breakfast will be ready in just a moment."

Sayuri also came rushing out of the kitchen, apparently in a fluster. She had an apron tied around her sailor-suit school uniform.

"We grilled fish for breakfast today, Master Guren. Is that okay?" she said.

"Have I ever complained about anything you've made?"

"No…" said Sayuri.

"Then stop asking."

"I just wish sometimes you'd tell us what you'd really like. Then I could make it for you."

"Curry and rice," said Guren, laughing.

"Arrgh!"

Sayuri laughed back playfully and went back into the kitchen.

Shigure approached Guren.

"Will you be going to school today, Master Guren?" she asked.

"No."

"Aren't you feeling well yet?"

There was a worried expression on her face.

Guren shook his head.

"I feel fine," he said. "I just don't see any reason to go. They've already figured out I'm a slacker anyways."

Guren laughed as he spoke. Shigure didn't laugh with him.

"I'll never forgive those Hiragis. I can't believe they tortured you."

"As torture goes it wasn't all that bad."

"That's beside the point."

"What you should really be angry about is how weak we are. They can torture us and we don't even have the right to get angry about it. They almost killed my father. It's not the Hiragis who are the problem. It's our own lack of power."

"…"

251

Shigure stared at Guren sheepishly. Guren stared back.

"It's not your fault though, Shigure," he said. "It's mine. I'm the one who lacks power."

"No, that's not true..." said Shigure, a look of concern on her face.

That expression—and the fact that Guren could make it appear on one of his followers' faces—was just a reminder of how weak he really was.

Their discussion was interrupted by Sayuri.

"Come and get it!" she called.

Guren nodded, and the three of them sat down to breakfast. Sayuri had also made coffee. It was a breakfast fit for a king. After they finished, Guren switched on the TV and sat down on the couch.

The morning news was on. Since Guren didn't usually watch TV, he wasn't sure who the anchor was.

He stared blankly at the set for a few moments before calling out, "Sayuri, bring me my phone."

"Yes, sir!"

Sayuri brought the phone. Guren took it from her and dialed home. It rang several times before anyone picked up.

"Is that you, Guren?"

The voice belonged to the leader of the Ichinose Clan, Guren's father.

"How are you feeling?" asked Guren.

"More importantly, how are you? I heard that they tortured you."

"I'm fine."

"I see."

"How are you?"

"I'm fine, too."

Guren was pretty sure his father was lying. He had been tortured so badly his heart had stopped. It would take him more than just a few days to recover. His voice sounded tired.

But there were things Guren needed to know.

"How is everything with the clan? No one's questioning your

leadership because of what happened, are they?"

The Hiragis had run roughshod over the leader of their clan. It would only be natural for people to be angry.

If the other members grew disgusted with the weakness of the Ichinose Clan, the Order of the Imperial Moon could begin to show signs of crumbling from within.

But Guren's father, sounding unconcerned, said, "Everyone's already used to it."

"I see…"

"This isn't the first time the Hiragis have treated us this way."

"I know…"

"And others in the Imperial Moon face the same discrimination we do. Even if they wanted to betray us and join the other side, the Hiragis wouldn't accept them."

"…"

"You let me worry about things here. There is something important I need to tell you, though…"

Guren nodded. He was staring at the TV while he listened. It was almost 6:00 a.m.

"During the six o'clock news a story is going to break that the Brotherhood of a Thousand Nights has been squashing," Guren's father told him.

The news started, as if on cue.

"We've just had some breaking news," said the anchor. "It's being reported that all of the animals at Tokyo's Ueno Zoo have been killed by an unknown suspect or suspects. I repeat…"

"Someone killed the animals?" muttered Guren.

His father responded from the other end of the line.

"They're saying that someone spread poison throughout the zoo. Supposedly, the poison might still be there, so they've sealed off everything in a half-mile radius."

Guren pictured a map of Ueno in his head. The zoo was located right next to Ueno Station. That meant the station must be sealed off, too. Ueno Station was a massive hub, with something like 200,000 people passing through it every day. Sealing off the station would cause huge issues for the city.

His father explained, "The trains are still running. But passengers can't get out on the west side. That's where the zoo is located."

"I see. But why is this important?"

"The story actually broke in the middle of last night, around two in the morning. The Thousand Nights has been keeping it under wraps until now."

"And you're sure it was the Thousand Nights who's been squashing it?"

"We are."

"So what in the world really happened?"

"I don't know. We're not even sure if the animals are actually dead. Or if anyone has spread poison in the zoo. All we know for sure is that the area's been sealed off."

"And you want me to figure out why?"

"That's up to you," said Guren's father. "I'm just letting you know what the Imperial Moon uncovered. I figured this was something you might be interested in."

Something Guren might be interested in. In other words, something a foolish child on a wild goose chase to destroy the Hiragi Clan and the Brotherhood of a Thousand Nights might be interested in.

Guren nodded.

"Of course. Thank you."

Guren's father was silent for a moment.

"Guren?" he said.

"Yeah?"

"Don't do anything too risky. It won't do anyone any good if you go and get yourself killed."

"I know."

"Power and influence are all meaningless if you're dead."

"Okay."

"Anyway, I'm sure you'll be fine. You're smarter than your old man, after all."

"If I was so smart I wouldn't care about being powerful," said Guren, chuckling.

"Haha."

"Anyway, I've got to go, dad. I've got something to do."

"Understood."

"I'll visit soon."

"Don't worry about us. You just do your thing."

"Got it. See you."

"Goodbye."

Guren hung up. The Ueno incident was turning into a major story on the news. That made sense. Sealing off the area around Ueno Station was a big deal.

"Some people are so cruel," said Sayuri, watching the news.

Guren turned to her.

"Bring me my clothes," he said.

"Your school uniform?" asked Shigure.

Guren shook his head.

"No, everyday clothes. I'm heading to Ueno…"

Just then, Guren's phone rang.

"Huh?"

He glanced at it. A number Guren didn't recognize was flashing on the screen. He pressed the answer button and put the phone to his ear.

"Who is this?"

"It's me," said the person on the other side.

The voice belonged to Kureto Hiragi.

"What do you want?" asked Guren, narrowing his eyes.

"I heard you've been skipping school," said Kureto.

"I must be scared you'll bully me if I show up."

"I'm sure you can manage a little bullying."

"I'm actually very delicate."

"Haha. I don't think I've ever heard a guy describe himself as delicate before."

"Anyway, what do you want?"

"I'm calling to tell you to come to school today."

"And if I say no?"

"You don't have the right to say no. This is an order. I have something I want you to do for me."

"What is it?"

"I'll tell you when you get here. Be at the student council's office at nine o'clock."

The line clicked dead. Kureto had hung up as soon as he said everything he wanted to say.

Guren grimaced and turned his eyes back to the TV set. There was a professor on the screen now who was supposed to be an expert of some kind in poisons. His face looked grave as he commented on the incident.

Sayuri called out from behind Guren, "Master! Which would you rather wear today, your parka or a jacket—"

"Change of plans," Guren interrupted her. "Bring me my school uniform."

He stood up from the couch. It was time for him to get ready.

◆

Guren was walking along his usual route to school.

But today was different.

The other students just stared, surrounding him from afar. They were whispering in hushed voices to one another. Usually someone would have started messing with him by now. Maybe even thrown a bottle of cola or two at his head.

Sayuri cocked her head in confusion.

"What in the heck is going on?" she said.

A wary expression appeared on Shigure's face.

"Do you think those Hiragi punks are planning something?"

It soon became clear, however, why everyone was acting differently. One of the boys who usually picked on Guren, and who had thrown a cola bottle at him before, came running over.

"H-Hey, Guren..." His voice trembled as he spoke, and his face was almost white with fear. "I-I-I'm sorry that I threw a cola bottle at you b-before. I had no idea you were one of Kureto's retainers..."

Now Guren understood. The other students in the school had already heard that he was working for Kureto. He ignored the boy and continued walking. The boy, however, called after him from behind.

"I'm really, really sorry! I know maybe you won't forgive me...b-but..."

The boy sounded like he was ready to cry.

Guren shrugged his shoulders and sighed.

"I forgive you. Now shut up."

"R-Really?!"

"Whatever, just shut up, okay?"

"Th-Thank you!" the boy said. He still sounded like he was ready to cry.

Shigure peered up into Guren's face.

"What he just said..."

Guren nodded.

"It's true. I guess I forgot to tell you."

"So after they tortured you, Kureto ordered you to serve him?"

"Yes and no. After all, nothing's actually changed, has it? The Hiragis were always in charge of us, remember?"

"In other words...you're just pretending to follow Kureto...but then someday—"

"Shigure," Sayuri cut her off before she could finish speaking. There was a scolding tone in Sayuri's voice, which was unusual for her.

"What?"

"Guren just said that nothing's changed, didn't he? I think that tells us everything we need to know."

Shigure's eyes widened slightly. She nodded.

"O-Of course," she said.

Apparently, Sayuri and Shigure had worked it out for themselves. Shigure looked apologetic.

"I'm sorry I got confused," she said. "Ever since you were taken, I keep thinking about what you must have gone through while I wasn't around. I can't sleep when I think about it."

Guren laughed.

"Heh. I'm the one who got tortured, but you're the one losing sleep."

"My apologies, Master Guren..."

"I understand that you feel disappointed, Shigure. But there's nothing we can do about it. Kureto still has the upper hand."

Individual strength was one thing. But the Hiragis also had their syndicate's power and size on their side.

Guren and the others were gathering intelligence to look for a way to take advantage of the war between the Imperial Demons and the Thousand Nights. They were hoping to amass more power, and then to join the battle when the two organizations were at their weakest to take them out. It was the obvious course of action. But it was also easier said than done.

Shigure spoke up again, this time flustered.

"I-I didn't mean to say that I'm disappointed..."

"It's fine if you are. As long as you stick with me. That's all that matters."

Shigure fell silent. She blushed slightly, pleased.

"What about me?" Sayuri butted in. "You can rely on me too, can't you, Master Guren?!"

"You're annoying."

"Augh...!!"

Sayuri threw both her hands up and rushed to Shigure's side with a look of shock on her face.

"No fair," she said, pouting. "Why do you get Master Guren all to yourself?!"

Shigure smiled faintly and said, "I'm sure Master Guren likes you too, Sayuri."

"You think so?"

"Of course I do. You're always cheerful, you're an excellent cook, and you're much better at..."

Shigure stopped talking mid-sentence.

Sayuri also grew silent.

Neither of them could see the look on Guren's face, but they both knew he hated stupid conversations.

Guren sighed and turned his eyes back toward the school.

As he did so, he spotted a boy standing in front of the gate. There was a group of lackeys surrounding him.

He had brown hair, narrow, serpentine eyes, and a piercing through his lip.

It was Seishiro Hiragi.

Seishiro was the one who had beaten the stuffing out of Sayuri during the qualifying exams.

This time, it seemed Seishiro was looking to pick a fight with Guren. He glared at Guren with a nasty glint in his eyes.

Shigure and Sayuri tensed up, ready to act. They each took a step forward to protect Guren.

"Master Guren, get back—"

Guren cut them off. "You don't have to protect me. I don't need to hide my strength anymore."

"What?!!" the two shouted in unison.

The look of delight on their faces was almost comical.

"S-So, that means, you can finally use your full strength against those Hiragi thugs?" said Sayuri.

Shigure could barely contain her happiness. "H-Heehee... Those fools are in for such a surprise. Just wait till they find out who they've been dealing with."

Seishiro suddenly shouted at them.

"Hey, Ichinose mongrel!"

Guren raised his head up in response.

"Yeah? What the hell do you want?"

Seishiro snickered.

"Oi, now that you're Kureto's little pet you think you can mouth off whenever you feel like it? Just because Kureto took a liking to you doesn't make you tough."

Seishiro's lackeys all laughed along with him. They probably weren't scared of Kureto like the other students. Seishiro was also a Hiragi. As long as they kept kissing his ass, they were safe.

"This is between you and me, not Kureto," said Seishiro. "I'm my own man, I do what I want."

Now Guren understood. Seishiro had a complex over Kureto. They were both Hiragis, but Kureto was the student council president. Kureto was on a whole different level from Seishiro, both in terms of what people thought of them and their actual strengths.

"Don't think you'll be getting off easy," said Seishiro. "I don't know what my brother was thinking, making some Ichinose mongrel one of his followers. It's not right."

Seishiro turned to the students around him.

"You all know what I'm saying, don't you?"

They laughed.

But not all of them. Only Seishiro's lackeys. The others were all too afraid of Kureto. They were waiting to see what happened, and would side with whoever was stronger.

In the end…

"…anyone who isn't a Hiragi is in the same position as me," muttered Guren.

The other students were all trying to read the situation. All they wanted to do was to keep their heads down and to avoid getting caught in a crossfire between those in power.

"What's wrong with you all?" shouted Seishiro, angrily. "Laugh!"

But none of the other students were willing to side with him just yet.

"Dammit!" he shouted, growing angrier.

Guren appraised the scene.

"…"

I can use this, he thought to himself.

Seishiro was a Hiragi. He wanted power, but his abilities were nowhere near as impressive as Kureto's. He knew he was no match for his brother, but he was too conceited to admit it. Guren could use that.

He began walking forward.

"Hey, asshole, where do you think you're going?" said Seishiro.

"…"

"Don't you ignore me!"

"…"

"Hey!"

Just as Guren was about to walk past, Seishiro reached his hand out to shove Guren back.

Guren caught Seishiro's hand mid-push.

Seishiro reacted immediately. His eyes widened and he knocked Guren's hand away. His movements were extremely fast. He was clearly a Hiragi. He was probably stronger than Mito or Norito.

Seishiro flashed a grin and closed his hand in a fist, swinging at Guren.

"Think you can make a fool of me?" he said. "I'll put you back in your pl—"

Before Seishiro could finish speaking, Guren slapped a *fuda*—a paper charm for casting spells—onto his neck. All Guren had to do was mutter the command word and the *fuda* would explode, turning Seishiro's neck into mincemeat. His head would probably come flying clean from his shoulders, spine and all.

Realizing immediately what Guren had done, Seishiro sputtered in shock.

Guren was clearly much more powerful than him. He had struck with the *fuda* in the blink of an eye. Seishiro's eyes widened and his fist stopped in mid-air. Guren, however, grabbed Seishiro's arm and dragged it closer until Seishiro's fist was right next to his face.

"Ngh!"

Even though Guren hadn't really been hit, he groaned and tumbled backward.

As he fell, he swept Seishiro's feet and yanked him forward by the arm.

"Ahh!"

Seishiro was knocked off balance, falling over on top of Guren.

"N-No way…how did you do that…" he said.

Guren whispered quietly in Seishiro's ear.

"Please keep your voice down, Master Seishiro. I'm on a secret mission right now, from Lord Tenri."

"…"

Seishiro tensed up at the mention of Tenri's name.

Tenri Hiragi was the leader of the Hiragi Clan.

He was Kureto, Seishiro, and Mahiru's father.

His position was unrivaled across the clans. He was the most important person in the entire Order of the Imperial Demons.

Seishiro stared at Guren.

"You're on a mission from my father? You're serious?"

Of course it was a lie.

"I can't tell you the details just now," whispered Guren, "but Lord Tenri believes that during the attack by the Brotherhood of a Thousand Nights in April we may have been betrayed by someone in a position of power."

"…Okay."

"So far, the investigation has already proven you completely innocent, Master Seishiro."

"O-Of course I'm innocent," said Seishiro, indignantly. "I'm a Hiragi by birth, one of the elite!"

Guren resisted the urge to laugh out loud when Seishiro referred to himself as elite.

"There is someone, however, who seems to be covering his trail.

Someone who refuses to show his true colors."

Seishiro's face scrunched up in thought.

"Do you mean Shinya? I've always thought he was suspicious. He's not even a real Hiragi, you know. He's adopted—"

Guren cut Seishiro off. "No, I'm talking about Master Kureto."

"What?!"

"It's possible that Master Kureto helped organize the attack to get rid of Lady Mahiru, so that he'd have less competition to become the next leader of the clan. At least..."

"...that's what my father thinks?"

Guren made a conspiratorial face, giving Seishiro the impression that he had already said too much.

"But Master Seishiro, you have to keep this to yourself. This mission is absolutely secret. If Lord Tenri found out that I leaked information to anybody else..."

Seishiro nodded.

"Obviously. We can't just go around accusing Kureto of being a traitor. But why are you telling me?"

Guren hesitated, as if he was too embarrassed to say.

"It's just..."

"What is it?"

"I'd rather not say..."

"Tell me. That's an order."

"It's just...it seems to me that Lord Tenri has high expectations for you. Everyone else thinks Kureto will be the next leader of the clan, but I don't think Lord Tenri really trusts him."

The glee on Seishiro's face was almost palpable.

"So you see," said Guren, "as the Hiragi with a future..."

"You want to get on my good side while you can?"

Guren made an embarrassed expression and nodded.

Judging by Seishiro's face, he seemed to buy Guren's explanation.

"I see. You did good in coming to me."

"But please, don't tell Lord Tenri about this..."

"Don't worry, you can rest easy. So then…the reason you became one of Kureto's followers…"

Guren nodded. "Your father's orders. I don't know how Master Kureto feels about it, but Lord Tenri ordered him to 'take charge of the Ichinose mongrel.' In reality…"

"You're spying on him?"

"Exactly."

"I understand. I'll do whatever I can to help. But what about right now? How do we end this fight? Should I make a big show of forgiving you? Or…"

"Keep acting like you've always acted, Master Seishiro. We don't want anybody to figure out there's something going on."

Seishiro nodded emphatically. He was so excited he could barely contain himself. The prospect of setting a trap to bring down Kureto was too much for him.

"Got it," he said. "I'm gonna punch you now, one more time."

"I'm ready."

"Don't worry, I'll make sure it doesn't hurt."

Seishiro cocked his fist and swung at Guren's cheek. Seishiro was true to his word. The blow didn't hurt. He was very good at faking it. It looked like he had swung with full force. In truth, his fist had stopped just a hair's breadth from Guren's face.

"Do you see who's boss now, you Ichinose mongrel?" shouted Seishiro. "I hope you've learned your lesson, and you better not try and test me again!"

"Forgive me, Master Seishiro," said Guren, still sprawled on the ground.

"That's better," said Seishiro, standing back up. "Come on, you guys, let's go."

Seishiro and the other students dispersed. Guren could hear the lackeys' laughter.

Guren nearly burst out laughing, himself. Seishiro had stepped into quicksand and didn't even realize it. He had been snared by Guren's lie. One misapprehension would lead to another, and he would begin acting more and more suspicious with each passing day. It wouldn't be long before people began to wonder if Seishiro hadn't in fact been the traitor working with the Thousand Nights.

Even if Seishiro realized he was in a trap, there would be no easy way for him to extricate himself. After all, being taken in by such a simple lie would itself be seen as unforgivable weakness.

Seishiro harbored a powerful inferiority complex when it came to his more accomplished brother. He wouldn't want anyone to know that the Ichinose mongrel had made a fool of him with some half-baked lie. Kureto and Tenri were probably the last people he would ever confess the truth to.

Now that he had fallen into Guren's trap, there was no climbing back out.

Guren raised himself up into a sitting position on the ground.

Shigure and Sayuri came rushing over.

"Master Guren?" said Shigure.

"Yeah?"

"What happened? I thought for sure you were going to tear that jerk apart."

A faint smile played across Guren's lips as he answered, "After what he did to Sayuri, that would be letting him off too easy."

"Huh…?" Sayuri wondered out loud.

Guren stood up.

"How much were the two of you able to see? Did you notice when I pulled out the *fuda*?"

The two shook their heads in surprise. Apparently they hadn't seen anything that Guren had done. That was a good sign. If the two of them hadn't been able to spot it from where they were standing, then probably no one else had, either.

Still…

"You two need to train harder," chided Guren.

"What exactly did you do, Master Guren?" asked Sayuri.

"If you didn't see, then I'm not going to tell you."

"What?!"

"That punch looked pretty hard, but I don't see a bruise," said Shigure. "Which means you weren't really punched at all, were you? And it seemed like you and Seishiro were talking about something... As one of your followers, I really wish you'd tell me what's going on."

"As one of my followers, it's possible you could be drugged or tortured," answered Guren. "It's better if I only tell you what's necessary."

"You don't need to worry about that," said Sayuri. "We've both been trained to kill ourselves before an enemy can get any information out of us—"

Guren cut her off. "That's exactly the problem. If I shared any sensitive information with you, you two would probably up and kill yourself before I could count to ten. It's better how things are now. But once the situation develops a little further, I might need your help..."

Guren suspected that he may have set everything in motion with what he had just done.

He didn't think Seishiro would ever spill the beans. But if Guren was really going to take advantage of the war between the Thousand Nights and the Imperial Demons by playing the two organizations against each other, this was a much-needed step in that direction.

If Guren didn't begin taking initiative, Mahiru's lead would only grow larger and larger.

Decisive action was needed.

Guren didn't know how much time was left. But what he did know was that, according to Mahiru, the world was going to end at Christmas. He still wasn't exactly sure what that meant, but a big change was clearly coming.

Guren had to fortify their position before that happened.

It was still June.

That left half a year.

"We might not be at this school much longer," he said. "We're probably going to get mixed up in the war that's coming. A lot of people will die if that happens, and they won't be killing themselves. If worse comes to worse, we might all get killed. We should try to enjoy a little carefree student life while we can. After all, this is probably the last time in our lives the three of us will get the chance to wear school uniforms."

Guren glanced at Sayuri and Shigure and smiled. They both looked good in their sailor-suit school uniforms.

Chapter Six

The Squad

It was 9:00 a.m.

On his way to the student council office Guren ran into Shinya Hiragi in the hallway.

"Long time no see," said Shinya. "I thought you dropped out."

Shinya grinned impishly.

Guren glanced at him before answering, "I've always hated school."

"Heheh. I believe you. With a personality like yours, it must be hard to make friends."

"Huh?"

"I was talking to Norito and Mito. They were telling me how you're really just misunderstood and lonely."

"You gotta be kidding me."

"Haha. Anyway, I'm glad you're here. I thought maybe you made a run for it after Kureto had you tortured and made you swear allegiance to him."

"I tried to," said Guren.

"Hmph. Well, what did you tell them when they tortured you?"

"Nothing at all."

"Did you tell them about Mahiru?"

"No."

Guren hadn't even told his own family about Mahiru. It was why his father didn't spill that information, either. He didn't know in the first place.

"In that case, you're not really loyal to Kureto after all," said Shinya.

"No, I swore my allegiance like a good boy. I'm no match for the great and powerful Master Kureto."

"Haha. You never stop joking."

"What are you doing here, anyways? This hallway leads to the student council office. Did Kureto summon you, too?"

Shinya nodded.

"Yeah. I'm starting to get worried. Apparently he's got some sort of mission for me."

"A mission…"

Come to think of it, Kureto had said something similar to Guren on the phone earlier.

"He told me he had something for me to do, too," Guren said.

As the two turned the corner, the student council office came into sight. Sayuri, Shigure, Norito, and Mito were all standing in front of the closed door.

Sayuri's and Shigure's eyes lit up when they saw Guren walking toward them.

Mito glanced at Guren out of the corners of her eyes with a half-angry, half-embarrassed expression on her face.

Norito just waved his hand and shouted, "Hey!"

Apparently, Kureto had also called Shigure, Sayuri, Shinya, Norito, and Mito to his office along with Guren.

The five of them were among the few at the school who were actually willing to speak to Guren.

"Hey, Guren?" said Shinya.

"Yeah?"

"Maybe we should be on our guard, here. It's possible that Kureto suspects all of us of being traitors. What do you think?"

Guren nodded.

"It's definitely possible."

The two cast watchful eyes over their shoulders. They wanted to be sure there were no assassins creeping up from behind. Kureto was cunning when it came to these things. Even though he was strong, he would never risk a one-on-one fight. He didn't see the point in doing so. He almost certainly had several very capable operatives under his command. His ability to organize others was second to none.

Guren didn't sense any enemies behind them, however. Nor did he detect danger coming from anywhere else.

He remained on his guard, just in case.

"Shinya," he said.

"What is it?"

"If an attack comes, I'll take Shigure and Sayuri and head back in the direction we came. You take Norito and Mito and go down the hallway in the other direction."

"Do you think splitting up will divide their forces?"

"At least it will raise the odds of some of us surviving, won't it?"

Shinya laughed.

"I doubt it. These are the Hiragis we're talking about. If they do decide to come for us, we're through."

"…"

"They could wipe out the entire Ichinose Clan in a matter of days."

"…"

"We'll just have to wait and see how things turn out. If we die here, then I guess that was our fate all along."

Guren supposed it was natural that Shinya felt that way. Since he was just a foster child, the Hiragis could eliminate him if he no longer proved useful.

If we die here, then I guess that was our fate all along…

As philosophies go…

"…it's not all that bad," muttered Guren.

"What?" said Shinya.

"Nothing, never mind."

The two finally arrived at the office door.

"I'm sorry, Master Guren," said Sayuri. "They called us here so suddenly that we didn't have time to report to you first."

"It's fine. More importantly…"

Guren leaned in close and whispered into his followers' ears.

"...be on your guards. They may be planning to kill us."

The two instantly tensed up.

"What are you whispering about over there," said Mito, glaring at him. "More secrets, I bet."

"..."

Guren ignored her.

"Hey!"

"Geez, shut up already. Can't you ever leave me alone?"

Mito, however, still had more to say. "I'll shut up when I feel like it. Besides, if we're gonna be forming a team we're gonna have to start acting like teammates."

"A team?"

Apparently Mito already knew why they had been summoned.

Before Guren could ask her to explain, the door to the student council office swung open and a girl's voice interrupted them.

"It seems like you're all here. Please, step inside," she said.

The girl who opened the door was pretty, with blond hair tied into two pony tails.

"Aoi Sangu?" said Mito, looking surprised. "What are you doing here?"

Sangu. Guren was familiar with that name. It was one of the great houses that served the Hiragis, like the Goshi or Jujo Clan.

There was supposed to be a girl from the Sangu Clan in Guren's class, but so far she had barely ever shown up to class.

Either way, it seemed the blond girl who had opened the door was from that clan.

The girl, Aoi, stared at them through blue eyes. She didn't answer Mito's question.

"Please, come this way," she said.

Guren peeked into the room. It was smaller than he expected.

There were two sofas and a table near the door, for visitors. Kureto was inside, sitting behind a modern office desk placed toward the back of the room.

The room looked like it was designed to resemble a principal's office.

"Come on. Playing principal?" said Guren.

Kureto raised his head and stared at them coldly. He turned his eyes toward the clock hanging on the wall.

The time was 9:02.

"You're late," he said.

"And?"

"The next time you're late you will be punished."

"Is that so? And what will my punishment be?"

"I will kill one of your followers."

Kureto said it very matter-of-factly. Guren had a feeling he would actually do it.

Guren glared at Kureto.

"Understood."

"I'm glad that's settled. Be careful next time. Now, about what you said a moment ago…"

"Huh?"

"You asked if I was playing principal. You should understand that my decisions hold more weight at this school than the principal's. The principal of this school would march to his own death, if I so ordered it. The same applies to you, Guren Ichinose. You and the principal are in the same position at this school. I am the master, and you are my followers. Understood?"

Guren stared at Kureto. It didn't seem like he was interested in a discussion.

"I take it that pecking order is final?"

"You are correct."

"Got it. So why did you call me here?"

For the first time since they entered the office, a smile appeared on Kureto's face.

"Capable people always get straight to the point. That's what I like about them. Sit. Aoi, bring tea for everyone."

Aoi nodded, stepping back into the office before leaving through another door into an adjoining room. It sounded like there were several people in that room—probably the other members of the student council.

"There are six other members on the council," said Shinya, standing next to Guren. "Three juniors and three seniors, all the most elite of the elite. Nerve-wracking, isn't it?"

Shinya grinned broadly. It was hard to tell from his tone whether he was being serious or not.

Mito and Norito, however, seemed genuinely nervous. Guren didn't blame them. Kureto's power over the school was absolute. They were stepping into the lion's den.

"Please, have a seat," the president of the student council said.

Norito, Mito, and Shinya all sat down.

Guren remained standing.

If anything happened he didn't want to be caught off guard.

"What's wrong?" asked Kureto.

"We're not here for a tea party," answered Guren. "If you've got something to say to us, hurry up and spit it out."

"Guren, no!" said Mito. "Lord Kureto asked you to sit—"

Kureto cut her off. "It's fine, Ms. Jujo. I prefer this attitude."

"You do?" Mito turned her head toward Kureto.

He continued speaking. "Someone competent, who isn't interested in wasting time on unnecessary pleasantries. Most people waste too much time. They complain, or make excuses, or want someone to hold their hand. In the end it's all very tedious. Isn't that right, Guren?"

A faint smile played across Guren's lips.

"What's with all the small talk? If you ask me, you seem to waste a lot of time on your own," he said.

"Haha!"

Just then, Aoi returned from the other room. She held in her hands a tray with seven cups.

"Will you be having tea as well, Master Kureto?" she asked.

Kureto nodded.

"Yes, please."

Aoi placed Kureto's cup before him before serving anyone else.

Shinya smirked.

"You serve yourself before your guests, big brother? That doesn't seem like very good manners."

"Guren! Shinya! Stop it already!" Norito shouted in a panic. "How can you act like that? Don't you know where we are?"

Kureto tilted his cup toward Shinya as he replied, "You six aren't here as my guests."

"Hmm? So when you do have guests, you treat them with absolute courtesy?"

Kureto tilted his head, as if considering the question.

"You know, I'm not sure. In this world there are only those on the top and those on the bottom. But when my followers are obedient, I treat them with respect. Hence the tea."

Shinya raised his cup to Guren, in salute.

"Hear that, Guren? This is respect!"

"Hmph. Pretty cheap respect, if you ask me."

Mito and Norito were already past the point of surprise. Their jaws hung open in utter shock, and the color began to slowly drain from their faces.

Kureto just laughed.

"You two are very entertaining. Is there something you would prefer to tea? Care to be showered with bundles of cash?"

Guren turned toward Kureto.

"Stop wasting my time. I don't need your 'respect.' Just say whatever it is you brought us here to say."

Kureto nodded.

"I forgot, you don't like small talk. Aoi? Bring the documents."

"Sir!"

Aoi quickly began passing out several pages of paper to everyone at the table. She then handed the same packet to Guren and his two followers, who were still standing.

Guren glanced over the documents.

Included in the packet was what appeared to be an aerial photograph of Ueno. The date on the photograph was today's. It was the same area that had been sealed off because, according to the news, someone had sprayed poison and killed the animals.

The photograph showed a huge, uneven crater smack-dab in the middle of the zoo's east area. It looked as if an explosion had occurred, or even as if a meteor had struck the area.

"This was on the news this morning…" said Mito.

Kureto nodded.

"It was. Did you all see it?"

Everyone nodded.

"Everything that was said on the news was a lie," declared Kureto. "The Imperial Demons' intelligence bureau has determined that the entire Ueno district was being used as the site of an experiment by the Brotherhood of a Thousand Nights. It seems as if some sort of accident has occurred. Right now, the Thousand Nights is using all of their resources to try to cover up whatever happened."

"What was the experiment?" asked Guren.

"Who knows. We've been aware for some time now that Ueno was being used in this way. But since we never expected a war with the Thousand Nights we didn't investigate further. I'm sure we could have uncovered something if we had looked, but the Imperial Demons have their own secrets and we didn't want them investigating us in turn."

"But things are different now…"

"That's correct. The Thousand Nights has already broken our non-aggression pact. We are at war."

"I'm guessing you've already dispatched a squad to investigate?"

Kureto nodded.

"We've sent seventeen units since last night," said Kureto. "Every single one was destroyed. That's why I called for you."

"I see…"

Guren narrowed his eyes.

Essentially, Kureto was ordering them onto the front lines of a secret war raging beneath the surface of Japan.

Mito and Norito made eye contact with each other.

"S-So…you're ordering us to sacrifice ourselves?"

"The opposite, actually," Kureto said. "I've decided this mission is too difficult for any regular, bumbling troops. That's why I've put together this special team, composed of some of our best assets."

"…"

Mito and Norito could only fall silent in response. They were probably too happy to speak. For Mito and Norito, a compliment like that from a Hiragi was one of the greatest honors they could hope for.

"Man, it seems like you're asking us to go through an awful lot of trouble," said Shinya, "all for just one cup of tea…"

Kureto laughed.

"Would a refill be more worth your trouble? You're welcome to have as many cups as you please."

"I'll pass," said Shinya.

"When is the mission?" asked Guren. "Are we leaving immediately?"

"Yes. In two hours' time we will send four squads into the zoo from the northeast quadrant. They are only a diversion, however. I want your group to slip in while the enemy is distracted."

Guren looked at the packet one more time. He scanned the photo, which took up several pages, before setting the papers down on the table.

"You can take that with you," said Kureto. "When you're done studying it, of course, I'll need you to destroy it."

"It's fine," said Guren. "I've already memorized it."

Mito and Norito jerked their heads toward Guren in surprise. He ignored them.

"Two hours, huh? Judging from the photograph, their defenses are probably weakest from the south. By the way, which of us will be leading the team?"

"I'll leave that to you all to decide," said Kureto, staring in their direction. "As long as you produce results, I don't care how you get things done."

Guren glanced over at Shinya.

"What do you think?"

"You should do it. Your two followers won't listen to anybody else, anyways. Norito, Mito, you guys don't have a problem with that, do you?"

"If that's what you think is best, Lord Shinya."

"It's fine by me, too."

It was decided.

Guren would command the team.

"All right then. We'll meet in fifteen minutes to discuss strategy—"

Interrupting him, Kureto said, "You can use meeting room 302 on the third floor. If you come back alive, that room will be more or less yours in the future. Oh, and Guren?"

"Yeah?"

"I believe I promised you something."

Kureto reached under his desk and drew out a katana, which he tossed to Guren.

Guren caught the sword in mid-air.

"Its name is Hoarfrost. It's an enchanted sword. Someone of your caliber should be able to use it."

Guren glanced at the sword in his hand.

Hoarfrost. Guren had heard tales of the blade before. There were many fanciful stories told about it. According to one, it had cut down over a thousand demons in a row without ever suffering a single nick.

Guren drew the sword from its sheath. The blade vibrated with magic, and a high-pitched ringing filled the air. Guren felt a desire for bloodshed and slaughter well up inside himself.

"Yes, it's definitely enchanted," he said.

Aoi was still standing next to Kureto. She eyed Guren warily, narrowing her blue eyes.

"Calm yourself, Aoi," ordered Kureto. "Guren is too strong for you, even if you do mean to fight him."

"But..."

"Besides, Guren is no longer a threat. He swore total allegiance. Didn't you, Guren? Your sword is already drawn, while I am completely unarmed. If you wanted to kill me, now would be your chance."

"..."

"And yet you don't. Why is that? It's because you know your place in the order of things. Deep down you think you harbor ambition. But that ambition is just a façade. You need it to sustain yourself. In reality, however, you know, more than anyone else, that those ambitions will never come to be realized. The difference in power between the Ichinose Clan and the Hiragi Clan is just too great. That's the truth, isn't it, Guren?"

Guren returned the katana to its sheath.

"Would it make you that happy to hear me say yes?"

"It would," Kureto said.

"Fine then, yes. Glad I could make your day."

"You should be happy as well, Guren. I did give you that weapon, after all."

"Hmph. Just another chance for you to show off how 'respectful' you are."

"Haha! You really are an interesting guy."

Guren ignored him and turned around, exiting the room.

"The rest of you can go as well," said Kureto. "I've given my orders. Bring me results."

Their meeting with Kureto Hiragi was officially at an end.

◆

Meeting room 302 looked pretty much the same as any other

classroom.

It was large, and deserted at the moment but for five students: Shigure, Mito, Norito, Shinya, and Guren. Sayuri had gone down to the cafeteria to buy drinks for everyone.

Mito was out on the balcony at the moment, calling home.

They could just barely overhear her conversation.

"Mm... Yes... Mm-hmm... A direct order from Lord Kureto, but the mission is secret... Yes... It might be dangerous... Mm... I'll do my best to make everybody proud..."

Norito stared at her through the window for a moment before turning toward Guren.

"Man, I don't know how we got wrapped up in this," he said. "The last seventeen squads are all dead. We pretty much just got ordered to go get ourselves killed."

Guren chuckled.

"Aren't you going to call home too?" he asked.

"Heh. Nah, I don't get along with my family all that well. I've got a little brother. He's a grade lower than me, but he's good at everything..."

"So they're always comparing you to him?"

"Yeah, more or less. Anyway, even if I died, I don't think they'd be too broken up about it. I'm sure they'd say all sorts of nice things, though, if they heard I was on a direct mission from Lord Kureto."

Norito glanced toward Mito one more time.

"That won't mean much, though, if we all bite the big one..." he said.

Guren wasn't sure why Norito and Mito were so preoccupied with the prospect of dying. Kureto's mission really had them spooked.

"I'm back!" cried Sayuri.

She had bought paper cups, a bottle of oolong tea, and a handful of different snack foods.

Norito broke into a smile as she entered.

"You're an angel, Sayuri! How did you know I like potato chips?"

Sayuri ignored him, turning to Guren instead.

"Which would you like, Master Guren?"

"I'm fine," said Guren.

"Oh…"

Mito hung up her phone and came back in. She smiled at Sayuri.

"Thank you, Sayuri. Sorry to have made you go for all of us."

"It's no problem."

"By the way, Shigure, my father asked me to give you his regards. I know I mentioned it before, but ever since I told my father about how strong you are, he's been very interested in meeting you… Couldn't you visit our compound at least once?"

"I'm not interested," Shigure flatly turned her down.

For once, Mito simply nodded.

"I guess that makes sense. After all, you already have a stronger master than me…"

Mito glared at Guren.

"Even if he is a jerk," she added.

Guren didn't have time to deal with any nonsense right now. He ignored her and launched directly into the briefing instead.

"Okay, let's discuss the mission," he said. "Not that there's very much to discuss. We know very little. The mission site is Ueno Zoo, and the Brotherhood of a Thousand Nights is hiding something there. We're going in to investigate. The Imperial Demons already dispatched seventeen squads to the area, all of which were destroyed. That means there are enemies on the ground. Of course, the Hiragi army is a pack of fools. It's possible the area's been poisoned and they all just marched in to their deaths without noticing. If that's the case, then there may not be enemies on the ground after all."

Shinya laughed.

"I doubt that," he said. "I'm sure they at least checked for poison."

"It does seem likely. So we should assume there will be enemies. Ones who are completely determined to hide the Thousand Nights' secret. We're going to find something when we get in there."

What was it, though, that they were so desperate to hide? Was there some sort of research material they were trying to keep from getting stolen?

Whatever it was, it could prove very powerful if Guren could get his hands on it. The Thousand Nights was doing its best to keep whatever it was away from the Imperial Demons. There was no telling how valuable it could be.

"You're pretty good at throwing your weight around, Guren," Mito butted in, "but have you ever actually commanded a mission—"

Shigure cut her off before she could finish. "Please don't interrupt. Master Guren has been through danger countless times, ever since he was a young—"

"Be quiet, Shigure. Don't you know what they say? Barking dogs seldom bite."

"Ah…"

Shigure grew quiet.

Guren turned back toward Mito and Norito.

"Like I said, there really isn't much information for us to discuss. But there is something I need to ascertain."

"Something you need to ascertain?" asked Mito.

"Before we leave for the mission, I want to get a better sense of your abilities. For a start, I want to check your reflexes by seeing how well you can both respond to my attack."

As he spoke, Guren drew the sword from his hip.

Mito's eyes opened wide. Norito also flinched, but it took him a beat longer.

That was all they had time to do. Guren had already swung his sword toward Mito's neck. He stopped with the point of the blade resting against her neck.

"A-Ah…"

Mito stared at Guren with an embarrassed look on her face.

"Th-That wasn't fair, attacking with no warning like that. What kind of a coward—"

Guren cut her off. "Are you stupid? Do you think the enemy is going to ask to shake your hand before they attack you on the battlefield?"

"Ahh…"

"In any case, I think I have a pretty good sense of your reaction times now. I'll make sure they're reflected in my orders."

It seemed like Norito was also about to say something. Guren could sense that he was manipulating the atmosphere in the room.

Guren, however, spoke first.

"That's enough, Norito. I already know that your strengths lie more in illusion magic than physical acumen. I saw that during the qualifying exams."

Norito broke off the illusion spell he had begun casting.

"You mean you saw through my spell?"

"It was very well done. It may even help us slip into the zoo. Mito, when we do head in, I want you to use magic to power yourself up. And keep those spells up throughout the entire mission. Without your magic up you're no good. You could be killed immediately."

"Hey, what about me?" said Shinya, seated behind Guren. "Don't you wanna test out my strength?"

"If you die, I'll just laugh that despite all that boasting, the high and mighty Hiragi was the first to eat dirt."

"Real nice," said Shinya.

Guren ignored him. He glanced toward the clock mounted on the meeting room wall.

The time was 9:40 a.m.

"To get to Ueno it will take us…"

Just then the door opened and Aoi Sangu walked in.

"We'll send you in a helicopter from the school. You don't need to worry about the time," she said. "I've also brought Imperial Demon special forces combat uniforms. They've been reinforced to better resist all forms of magic and are equipped with a full range of spellcasting gear. Please use them wisely."

Aoi was holding six uniforms against her chest. She set them down by the door.

She was about to leave without saying anything more, but Guren called out, "Wait."

"What is it?"

Aoi turned around.

"A helicopter for a secret mission? Are you people crazy? We'll go by car. But bring us six pairs of street clothes. We'll change into the combat uniforms once we've arrived."

Aoi narrowed her eyes but still nodded.

"Of course. I'll prepare them right away. Where will you be departing from?"

"Have the cars waiting by the school gate. Two cars."

Aoi nodded. "I'll arrange for a driver, and vehicles camouflaged to resemble travel buses. We'll also arrange to take care of traffic. How much time prior to the start of your mission do you want to arrive?"

"Fifteen minutes, and I want the vehicles to stop a mile away from the site."

"Understood. I will see that it gets done. Please come outside in five minutes."

Aoi left.

Guren turned to the others.

"Is that everything?"

They all nodded, wordlessly.

Guren nodded in reply.

"Then it's time to go to war."

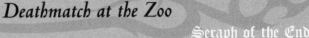

Chapter Seven

Deathmatch at the Zoo

Ueno.

Ueno was the de facto gateway bridging central Tokyo with areas to the north. Usually, hundreds of thousands of people would be thronging the area at that hour.

Guren and his squad were in what was normally a busy shopping district, south of the train station.

The massive Ueno Park was located to the west. It included museums, art galleries, and of course, the zoo.

At the moment, however, not a single soul was in sight.

Guren stared up at the line of trees towering over the park. So much greenery in one place was rare for a city.

"I can't hear any birds…" muttered Guren, listening to the sound of leaves rustling in the wind. "Did they flee? Or are they all dead?"

He remembered what the news had said about poison. It was supposedly the reason the park was sealed off. In the end they had canceled all stops to Ueno Station, only letting the trains pass through on their way to the next station.

Guren's thoughts were interrupted by someone shouting, "If any of you look this way I'll kill you, got it?!"

It was Mito.

Guren turned around. The girls were all hiding behind a large tree, just inside the park, while they changed into the combat uniforms the Hiragis had provided.

"What's taking them so long?" muttered Guren.

He was already in his uniform. He double-checked the pockets to make sure everything was in order.

It resembled the kind of uniforms once worn by the Japanese army. The cloth was supposedly woven from a special thread designed to ward off hostile spells. A variety of magical *fuda* were tucked into the lining, and there was a brace of throwing needles attached to the back of the belt.

"The Hiragis do make nice duds, I'll give them that…" muttered Guren.

"You know, it's kinda scary seeing this place with no one around," said Norito, approaching Guren from behind.

Guren turned around. Norito and Shinya were both standing there. They had already changed into their combat uniforms.

"You've been here before?" asked Shinya.

"Of course. You mean you've lived in Tokyo all this time and you've never been to Ueno?" replied Norito, surprised.

"I'm just not very interested in seeing the pandas, I guess."

"You know they've got lions, too."

"Haha. Tell you what, if we survive today, maybe I'll come back another time."

Guren ignored their ridiculous conversation and scanned their surroundings.

He had also scouted out the area before they began changing, to make sure there were no surveillance cameras or barriers set up nearby.

"Tsk. I can't believe the girls are taking so long to change. I should have just told them to stay in their regular clothes—"

"We're ready, we're ready!" said Mito, stepping out from behind the tree. "It was only a few minutes. Do you have to be so impatient? You'll never get a girlfriend acting like that."

Mito had finally changed into the Hiragi combat uniform.

Sayuri and Shigure, now dressed in their uniforms, also stepped out from behind the trees.

"I apologize for keeping you waiting, Master Guren," Shigure said.

"You don't need to apologize," Guren excused her. "You're an assassin. You need time to make preparations. It's those two fools I'm upset with."

Guren glanced toward Mito and Sayuri.

Sayuri was staring back at him with an expectant look on her face. She wanted to show off her new clothes.

"Th-These Hiragi uniforms are pretty cute, aren't they, Master Guren? D-Do you think it suits me?" she said.

"I don't have time for this."

"I know…but you look really good in your combat uniform, Master Guren! I can't stop staring. Doesn't he look good, Shigure?"

Shigure nodded in frank agreement.

Meanwhile, Mito had taken offense.

"H-Hold on a second, who are you calling fools?!" she shouted.

Guren wondered if they had all forgotten the danger they were walking in to. He was almost tempted to ask them.

"All right," said Guren, "according to our information, the first squads supposedly made it to around this point before they were destroyed."

Mito surveyed the area with a grim expression on her face.

"Something's not right, is it? It's not just people. There don't seem to be any signs of life at all."

"Come to think of it," said Shinya, "according to the aerial photograph, that huge crater…"

"Is farther northeast," said Guren. "I've got a hunch that several barriers may have been set up along the way to protect the area. Once we pass through those, the enemy will likely launch a full-scale attack."

"Are we powerful enough to detect the barriers?" asked Sayuri.

Norito pulled something from his inside pocket. It resembled a matchstick, but with incantations written along it.

He said, "I'm not just good at illusion spells, I also do detection magic—"

Guren held up his hand to stop Norito.

"We won't need it. Once we advance we're going to be detected either way. And since we can't leave until we've discovered what it is that the Thousand Nights is hiding, we might as well just go in a rush."

"So basically there's no plan," said Shinya, exasperated.

"The longer we stall things, the bigger our chance of losing the initiative," answered Guren. "We have to tap ground zero and be gone before the enemy has time to react."

"That seems like a stupid strategy," said Mito.

"You think so?"

"Yep."

"And what do you propose we should do? With so little information, any in-depth strategy will just trip us up. We can spend all the time we like talking about what we think might happen and how everything should play out. But we can't get wrapped up in some foolish plan based on wishful thinking. What we need to do is kill any enemy that shows up. And if we can't kill them, we need to at least try to make it back out alive."

Done speaking, Guren turned his eyes back toward the park and over the line of trees.

That was the direction of the zoo.

"Guren?" said Mito, taking a step closer to him.

She looked uneasy.

"…"

"Have you ever been on a mission like this before? You seem so used to this…"

A smile played across Guren's face. Of course he seemed used to it.

Since the first day he had entered the Hiragis' school, death had been a constant possibility. He was on the front lines every day, never sure what might happen next.

There was no point in telling Mito all of that right now, though.

Instead Guren ignored her question, slapping his hand on the sword strapped to his waist. Next he pulled out the pocket watch from one of his uniform pockets and flicked it open. The watch was bullet, shock, magnet, and even spell resistant.

The squad had synchronized their watches right down to the second before leaving school.

Guren stared at the second hand as it ticked forward.

11:29 and twenty seconds…

…thirty seconds…

…forty seconds…

"It's almost time. The Hiragi squads should begin their diversion to the northeast soon. As soon as the diversion starts, we make our move."

The others grew tense.

Guren continued, "As squad leader I only have one order for you. Drill this into your heads. I don't want you to think of anything else. Nothing else is important, do you understand?"

…fifty seconds…

"The order is…don't die. No matter what else happens, do not die."

…fifty-five seconds…

"Ready…"

Just then, an explosion rang through the air.

It came from the sky to the northeast.

It was the sound of a helicopter being shot down.

Guren didn't bother looking.

"The mission has begun," he said.

His voice was just loud enough for his squad to hear.

Guren broke into a run.

◆

The zoo wasn't far.

Guren wasn't certain whether they had tripped any barriers on their way. It was possible the enemy had already been alerted to their presence.

His squad just kept moving.

They dashed up to the wall surrounding the zoo and climbed over it quickly.

There were no signs of life inside the zoo either. Just as they had expected.

They were met with an eerie silence. A foul stench stung at their noses.

"What is that smell?" said Mito, retching.

Shinya answered her in a low voice.

"Blood."

They were standing before a row of cages where the monkeys were usually housed. Not a single monkey was inside. Instead, the cages were splattered crimson red with blood. The floors of the cages were awash in the stuff. The bars had been twisted open from the outside and were no longer capable of keeping any monkeys caged.

That is, if any of the monkeys were left to cage.

"What in all hell happened here?" said Norito.

Obviously there was no way of knowing yet. That was what they were there to find out.

Guren said nothing. He was considering the best route to take to the crater they had seen in the aerial photograph. The crater—ground zero—was located in the center of the zoo's east area.

From their current position, they could either circle around toward the north—past the cages where the animals were usually exhibited— or go around the other direction from the south.

Alternatively, they could just go in a straight line. Nothing was stopping them from just climbing up and over the animal cages.

"..."

The question barely merited consideration.

They would take the shortest, most direct route.

"Let's go," said Guren, breaking into a run again.

They ran past the blood-splattered monkey cages and into the elephant pens. After that was the bear pens, and then their destination.

There were no animals in any of the pens.

There was only blood.

Massive, massive pools of blood.

No bodies either, only blood.

Nowhere they passed held any signs of life.

It was all quiet. Far too quiet for a zoo in the middle of the day.

The diversion to the northeast should have still been going on. After the first explosion, however, they hadn't heard any sounds of fighting.

Either the other squads had already been wiped out, or a barrier had been set up to prevent sound from traveling between the zoo and its exterior.

Either way, they probably didn't have much time.

Guren and the others finally passed through the bear enclosure and arrived at ground zero.

It was an area between the stork pens and the lion and tiger enclosures.

A huge crater had been gouged into the area. It was big enough to be visible from the sky. It was impossible, however, to tell what had caused the crater.

Guren peered toward the crater's center.

There he spotted a living creature for the first time since they'd entered the park.

It was a single tiger.

Sayuri approached Guren from behind.

"It's a tiger," she said, stating the obvious.

The tiger was huge.

Ordinary people would run screaming in terror if they ever ran into an animal like that outside of its pen.

But Guren and the others were no ordinary people.

The tiger turned its head upward and stared at them. Its muzzle and large fangs were stained with blood.

"Do you think it ate all the other animals?" Norito said.

Impossible, thought Guren. They hadn't come across a single animal until now. In just the pens they had passed through, there should have been a few dozen monkeys, several elephants and cranes, and even a few huge lions and bears. There was no way a single tiger could have killed and eaten them all.

For starters, it simply wasn't large enough to fit them all inside its stomach.

"Well, what should we do now?" asked Shinya. He sounded calm.

The tiger suddenly let out a thunderous roar. The roar was so loud that they could feel its vibrations in their bones.

None of them paid the tiger any mind.

"If this area is being used for experiments by the Thousand Nights, there should be some sort of research facility," said Shigure. "We should search for it."

"Gwarrggh!!"

The tiger roared again, more threateningly. The presence of Guren and the others seemed to have spooked it.

Guren stared the tiger in the eye.

"What are your orders, Guren?" said Shinya. "You're the squad leader, aren't you?"

Guren didn't answer.

He was still staring at the tiger, which was glaring back at him in turn.

"I...don't think that tiger is alive."

"What?!"

Shinya stepped up to the rim of the crater, next to Guren, to get a closer look.

The tiger's eyes looked strangely white and clouded.

Just then...

"Gwarrggh!!"

The tiger roared again, and its tongue came darting out from its mouth. No, Guren realized a moment later, not its tongue. What looked like a tongue at first was actually some sort of blade, white and pointed at the tip.

By the time Guren realized what was happening, the tongue-blade was already hurtling straight toward Mito's neck.

"I don't think so!" Guren shouted, quickly unsheathing his sword.

He swung the sword upward, parrying the creature's tongue. A high-pitched clanging noise filled the air, like metal striking metal. Guren wasn't able to parry the blow clean, though. While he managed to turn it off course, the blow hit his sword with enough force to make his arm go numb.

That was enough for Guren to know that the tiger—or whatever was inside the tiger—was a dangerous opponent. Probably the only other one in the squad able to react to an attack like that was…

"Shinya, did you see that?"

"I think so…"

"All right then, you're up front with me."

"Hold on, what about us?" said Mito.

"You support us from the back. Sayuri, Shigure!"

"Understood!" Guren's two followers shouted.

Guren dashed forward.

He ran along the side of the tongue-blade, which was still extended from the tiger's mouth. He was planning to intercept it from the side and sever it with a blow from his sword. Before he could do so, however, the blade whooshed backward, retreating into the tiger's mouth.

The tiger's eyes turned on Guren. They were clouded and milky. They looked dead, indeed. A *kunai* came flying past Guren from behind, aimed straight at one of the tiger's dead eyes.

The *kunai* was one of Shigure's weapons, an assassin's dirk.

If the tiger moved to dodge the *kunai*, Guren might have a chance to chop its head clean off its shoulders.

The tiger, however, didn't budge. The *kunai* hit the creature right in its milky eye, sinking into the flesh. There was no blood. It didn't seem to even feel it. Guren had half suspected that it wouldn't.

"I don't care what you are," shouted Guren, swinging his sword toward the creature, "I'm about to chop your head off!"

"Gwarrggh!!"

The tiger wheeled on Guren and swiped at him with its front paws.

Guren didn't dodge.

He didn't have to. Shinya had thrown a *fuda,* which stuck to the tiger's paws.

"Explode!"

Shinya shouted the *fuda's* command word from behind. It exploded in a fiery burst, completely obliterating the tiger's paws.

Guren leapt forward at the same moment, bringing his sword in a downward thrust. The blade of the katana sunk into the tiger's neck. Halfway in it struck something solid but Guren persevered, carrying through with his attack. Fortunately, the enchanted sword that Guren had received from Kureto was preternaturally sharp.

The tiger's head went flying from its body.

There was still no blood.

In place of blood, something much stranger came bursting from the headless tiger's body.

It was some sort of monster, covered in a white, synthetic skin like plastic. It stood on a gaggle of skittering legs, each of which ended in a blade-like tip.

It was clearly much larger than the tiger. At least five times as large. It was hard to understand how it had ever fit inside the tiger in the first place.

The creature struck at Guren with one of its blade-like legs. It all happened in the blink of an eye, just moments after Guren had decapitated the tiger.

"Ngh!"

Guren reversed his blade, blocking the strike. The force of the blow slammed him into the ground.

The monster was following up with a second attack. Another leg came crashing down toward Guren while he was still off balance. He lunged to the side, just in time to stop the blade from striking his heart. Instead, it pierced him through the shoulder.

"Nghh!"

The monster raised another leg into the air. There was no way for

Guren to dodge the incoming blow.

He stared at the creature's leg as it descended toward him.

"Shit, I guess this is it…"

But just then…

"This way!"

It was Mito. She latched onto Guren from behind and yanked him backward with supernatural force. Guren's body was tossed into the air, flipping over twice before it landed safely away from the monster.

Shinya and Mito quickly retreated along with Guren. Mito stared at the monster in disbelief.

"Wh-What in hell is that?"

"Who knows," said Shinya. "But we're clearly no match for it. If it had been me back there instead of Guren, I'd be dead."

Guren's shoulder throbbed painfully. Blood came gushing out. There was no way he could continue to fight without patching it up first. But they were hardly in a position to treat his wound.

"Master Guren!" shouted Sayuri.

She tossed a handful of *fuda* into the air between their group and the monster. The *fuda* exploded, creating a smokescreen that blocked them from sight.

In the same instant Norito began working an illusion. He lit several of his matches. They gave off intoxicating fumes that mingled with Sayuri's smokescreen. Hopefully, the smoke would ensnare the monster in a deceptive illusion.

Matches in hand, he came rushing toward the others.

"Hey, do you think an illusion will work on that thing?!" he threw out to his squadmates.

"Who knows?!" shouted Mito. "We gotta try something. Just do it!"

"I already am!"

Snap. Snap. Snap. Norito clicked his fingers three times. It was discordance magic, a simple but very compelling form of illusion.

It seemed to do the trick. The monster began fighting with some unseen assailant on the other side of the smokescreen. It was no longer attempting to attack Guren or the others. At the speed it was moving, however, they didn't dare get any closer to it, either.

Shigure, meanwhile, had crouched down next to Guren and was taking a look at the wound on his shoulder. She screwed her face up in a grimace.

"M-Master Guren…we need to do something about your wound…"

"Burn it. That will stop the bleeding. We don't have time to treat it properly."

Guren drew out several *fuda* from his inside pocket as he spoke. Ignoring his wound, he skewered the *fuda* onto his sword and began soaking them in the blood pouring from his shoulder.

"Whoa, whoa, whoa. Hold on," said Shinya, watching him work. "You're not planning to use bloodbane magic, are you? In your current state…"

Shinya was right to worry.

Bloodbane magic was a forbidden art that could consume a person if anything went wrong. And the possibility of something going wrong was extremely high.

During a bloodbane spell, Guren would turn his blood into poison. Afterward, he'd have five minutes to strike the target nine times and to chant the appropriate incantation. The poison would then be transferred from him to his opponent, causing certain death.

However, if he failed to kill his opponent within the time limit, the spell would rebound on him. All of the blood would erupt from his body, and he would die an agonizing death.

Bloodbane magic was a double-edged sword, and not very useful to begin with. After all, under normal circumstances, if you could strike your opponent nine times you could probably kill them. There just wasn't very much reason to expose yourself to the spell's risks.

Supposedly, it had been invented as a way to kill special enemies who couldn't be felled by sword strikes alone.

"You're gonna get yourself killed," warned Shinya. "That spell was created to kill vampires, right? But no one's actually ever tried using it. After all, vampires are so much faster and stronger than humans that it's hard to imagine anyone getting nine hits off on them in the first place."

"..."

"The same applies here, Guren. How are you gonna get nine hits off on that creature? It's time to retreat. If we stay here, we'll all be killed."

Guren looked up into Shinya's face.

He was right.

If they valued their lives—if they didn't want to throw them away pointlessly—they needed to run.

But...

"You five, run for it... While you go, I can buy you some—"

Just then, Shigure slapped a *fuda* onto Guren's shoulder. It burst into flame for a moment, cauterizing Guren's wound and halting the bleeding. Guren gritted his teeth, swallowing an involuntary moan of pain.

Sayuri came rushing up to his side.

"Master Guren," she said, "let's run. We've seen the enemy. If we bring this information back with us, I'm sure the Hiragis will understand."

Sayuri was probably right. After all, none of the other squads had even managed to make it back alive.

Any information they brought back with them would be enough to preserve their honor.

"..."

But for what?

The Hiragis would obtain another piece of information.

The Thousand Nights' research would continue uninterrupted.

And the Ichinoses?

If Guren let the monster go without learning anything more about whatever experiment it was the Thousand Nights was carrying out, when would the Ichinoses ever have another chance to rise to the top?

The smokescreen was beginning to fade. Guren stared at it as he considered his options.

It was time to decide.

His hunger for power, a hunger he'd harbored ever since he was little—was it real or had it all just been a game?

"..."

Guren readied his sword.

"Geez, Guren, come on! Enough joking!" exclaimed Shinya.

Guren ignored him.

He was going to kill the monster.

And then bring it back to the Ichinose Clan.

That way, the Ichinoses would get their hands on whatever information it was the Thousand Nights had been so desperate to protect.

If Guren was serious about wanting power...

"If I'm serious..."

...then he could do it.

He'd kill the monster, and then kill the two witnesses to the event—Mito and Norito. He could make it look like the whole squad had been destroyed, and simply disappear off the Hiragis' radar.

No one would suspect a thing.

After all, none of the other squads had made it back alive, either. How hard would it be to believe that Guren's squad had also fallen?

"..."

If he was going to act, he had to do it now.

Kill the monster.

Kill Mito.

Kill Norito.

It was his chance to claim real power.

"What are you thinking, Guren?" urged Mito. "It'd be stupid to face that creature the way you're wounded! Let's go. We can make it out of here together!"

"Listen to her," said Norito. "My illusion is going to run out soon. The monster will know we're here. We have to run while there's still time."

Guren turned his eyes toward the two.

Mito's expression softened. She seemed to think that Guren was finally willing to listen to reason.

"Come on then, let's go," she said, reaching out her hand. "This time, let me be the one to save you."

Guren stared at her.

"..."

He gripped the hilt of his sword. Killing them would be easy. Just one hard swing with his sword. They wouldn't have time to dodge. They wouldn't even be able to react. They were both fools in the first place, for placing so much trust in someone from the Ichinose Clan.

Shinya realized something was amiss. He turned his eyes toward Guren and stared coldly at his hand where it gripped the sword.

"Ahh, I guess that's one way this could play out," he said, sounding disappointed.

Apparently, he'd guessed what Guren was thinking.

Shinya wouldn't stop him, however. He couldn't even if he tried.

If Guren let this chance slip by, he might never get another one to knock the Hiragi Clan down to size.

If Guren was serious...

If I'm serious, if it's real power I'm after...

"I..."

Mito suddenly reached her hand out and touched Guren gently on the arm. The arm he was gripping his sword with.

"Please, Guren, put your sword away..."

He brushed her hand away.

"Don't touch me," he said. "Fine, I get it. We'll retreat. For now."

Guren canceled his spell, leaving the bloodbane curse unfinished.

Shinya smiled faintly.

Mito also smiled, relieved.

"Finally! Come on, we have to hurry."

Guren nodded. But just then...

"Hmm, I'm disappointed. You're not really planning to retreat now, are you?"

A girl's voice interrupted them.

Mito was struck from behind before any of them could react. She fell unconscious. In a matter of moments Norito, Sayuri, and Shigure were all taken by surprise as well. They were knocked unconscious before they could even see their attacker.

Only Shinya's reflexes were fast enough.

"Dammit, what the—"

That was all he was able to say before he was cut off.

Slender fingers, belonging to a girl's hands, gripped him around the neck from behind. Shinya desperately began trying to pry the fingers from his neck.

"M-Mahiru…why are you….doing this? Wh-What are you trying…to accomplish…?"

The hands belonged to Mahiru.

Mahiru Hiragi.

Her long, mysterious ashen hair. Her wide eyes. Her beautiful face. Her confident smile.

Even though she had turned her back on the Hiragis, she was still dressed in her First Shibuya High School sailor-suit uniform. There was a katana strapped to her waist.

"Don't try to resist, Shinya," she said. "You wouldn't want me to slip and accidentally kill you."

"Ghh…j-just…tell me what's going on… I can…h-help you…"

"Unfortunately," said Mahiru, smiling, "you really, really can't. Go to sleep now, Shinya."

Mahiru squeezed her hands once, tightly, and Shinya lost consciousness. His body went limp, and he fell to the ground.

Guren glanced down at Shinya, then back up at Mahiru.

"Hmph. I thought you said we weren't going to meet again until the world comes to an end."

"Aren't you happy to see me?" said Mahiru, laughing.

"Not really."

"Ha! I'm very happy to see you, Guren… But that's not why I'm here."

"So why are you here?"

"You came to me, this time, Guren. I've got business here."

Guren glanced at their surroundings. Even though Norito had been knocked unconscious, his illusion was still running. The monster continued to fight with an imaginary assailant on the other side of Sayuri's smokescreen. The illusion, however, would probably wear off soon. Spells generally didn't last long once their caster was knocked unconscious.

Guren stared at the monster's shadow through the smokescreen.

"I guess you do. You're in league with the Thousand Nights, after all. Are you here to clean up after their failed experiment?"

Mahiru made a puzzled expression.

"You still think I'm in league with the Thousand Nights?"

She stared at Guren.

"Huh, I could have sworn I sent you a message," she said.

"You mean from Shinoa?"

Shinoa was the name of Mahiru's younger sister.

"Exactly. Did she give you the message?"

"You mean that you're also planning to betray the Thousand Nights?"

"Yes."

"If that's true, then where *do* your loyalties lie?"

Mahiru just raised an eyebrow.

"What are you trying to accomplish?"

Mahiru laughed. It seemed like she was enjoying herself. Her laugh was charming, almost bewitching. She reached out toward Guren's chest with a delicate hand. She stroked his neck, and then ran the hand soothingly along the cauterized wound on his shoulder.

"My loyalties lie in the same place as yours do, Guren. Wherever there is power. Enough power that no one can ever interfere again.

Enough power so that no one can keep us from the people we love, so that no one can take our freedoms away from us again."

"Where is that power?" said Guren, staring into Mahiru's face.

"Right here."

"Where?"

Mahiru dug her fingers into Guren's wound in response. Fierce pain went darting through his body, but Guren didn't react. Next, Mahiru pressed a hand against her own chest.

"My loyalties lie deep in the heart, where madness and depravity live. As do yours. Don't they, Guren?"

"…"

"But it's not enough. You need to sink to the same depths as I have."

Mahiru pressed harder, digging her fingers deeper into Guren's wound.

"Why didn't you kill that girl from the Jujo Clan a moment ago? Or that fool from the Goji Clan? It's what you should have done."

Mahiru twisted her hand into a claw, raking her nails into Guren's open wound.

"You need more hate, more madness. Let it rush through your body, Guren, let it consume you. Demons thrive on the hopes of man. In order for a demon to choose you—"

Guren grabbed Mahiru's hand with his own.

"Ahh…"

Her face suddenly convulsed with joy at Guren's touch.

He ignored her reaction.

"My path," he said, "and your path—"

"Are the same, Guren," she said, interrupting him. "Everyone's path is the same. In the end, we all die. Humans are weak. 'What is the point of living?' 'Are we here for a reason?' Time passes before we know it. Too fast for us to waste it asking such foolish questions. So, how do we live during that brief span? What path do we choose? We're going to die either way. Do you really think taking the long way there changes anything? Ha."

Mahiru suddenly drew the katana from her waist.

Its blade was black and ominous. It was so dark it seemed to distort the very space around it.

The sword had been created through research into cursed gear—a type of magic, previously thought impossible, that involved binding and sealing demonic entities into a weapon.

Mahiru thrust the sword into the earth at their feet.

In mere moments the ground turned inky black, its darkness spreading from the sword in a radius of a dozen feet. It was the sword's curse, spilling free and corrupting the earth. The curse began to seep into Guren's feet. As soon as it did, he could feel it trying to infect his body and to invade his thoughts.

"..."

Guren began chanting an incantation in his mind to resist the curse.

"Ah, I should probably tell you," said Mahiru, "the fortitude charm you're casting right now won't be enough to ward off the sword when it touches you."

Guren glared at Mahiru.

"Why are you doing this?"

"You said you wanted power, didn't you?"

"I won't be your puppet, Mahiru. I'm not interested in dancing on anyone's palm..."

"You've got it wrong. I'm not trying to pull your strings, Guren. The decision is yours to make. But you won't resist it. You thirst for power. You need it. You're just like me. You've already fallen. You've fallen deep, and there's no climbing back out."

Just then...

"Grawwrrrr!"

...a roar shattered the air.

It was the monster. Norito's illusion spell had finally worn off.

Mahiru turned her eyes toward the creature.

"Ahaha! In the end, it looks like you really don't have a choice. That creature is a chimera. It's been altered using the genetic material of the

Four Horsemen of the Apocalypse. If you don't draw the black sword from the ground, you'll never be able to defeat it. You'll die. And all your little friends, lying unconscious on the ground here, will die along with you."

Mahiru leapt backward. Her feet skimmed effortlessly over the ground as she went. She smiled at Guren.

"I'll be here watching, Guren, to see what choice you make. Are you serious about wanting power? Or was all your ambition just a child's game?"

"..."

"The truth is I already know what's going to happen. You're going to fall, just like I did. Power is everything. You're just like me. It's why I love you, Guren. Ahaha!"

The chimera suddenly turned its attention toward Guren. Mahiru said that the creature contained the genetic material of the Four Horsemen of the Apocalypse, whatever that meant.

Guren had a feeling he wouldn't be able to defeat it on his own. He didn't know its anatomy, what magic would work against it, or any of its weak points. In fact, he didn't know anything about it. The moment the creature had shown its true form, it was already clear that there was no way Guren could defeat it.

If Guren died, he wouldn't be able to save the others, either.

Sayuri, Shigure, Norito, Mito, and Shinya.

They had all been caught off guard and knocked out. They would die without ever waking back up.

"Without power..." Guren muttered.

He stared down at the sword, its black blade thrust into the ground. He reached out toward the hilt.

"That's it," Mahiru said from behind him. "Take the power that's offered to you. Give up your humani... S-Stop, Guren, don't! If you do it, you'll never be able to return... Shut up! SHUT UP! He almost did it. You... I... Shut up!"

Thwack! Mahiru beat her chest once with her fist.

The outburst seemed to stop.

It was almost like there were two people inside Mahiru who were at odds with each other. Come to think of it, she'd had a similar outbreak during the attack on the school in April.

"Tell me, which one of you is the real Mahiru?"

Mahiru laughed, seductively.

"Does that really have anything to do with what choice you make?"

A grin flashed across Guren's face.

"I guess it doesn't," he said.

Guren reached out and grasped the sword.

The moment he did so...

He felt an unbelievable strength surge through his body. It was more power than the sword could possibly contain. But Guren knew, instinctively, that it was a power he shouldn't let in.

Kill.

Ravage.

Destroy.

Annihilate.

Guren's mind was overcome with fantasies of death and destruction.

Rage and hope.

Joy and despair.

All were swept away. In their place only blackness remained. The whole universe was floating in a sea of blackness.

What Mahiru said was true. There was no time for Guren to cast a fortitude charm or any other incantation that might strengthen his spirit against this dark magic.

In the most precious part of what made Guren himself—the very deepest depths of his soul—a hatred began to fester and swell. And like a flower in the center of that hate, a single demon sprouted.

Although it was a demon, it looked entirely human in appearance. Like an exquisitely beautiful, androgynous doll.

Guren couldn't even tell if it was male or female.

But he was certain it was a demon. One belonging to the class of demons known as Bodhisattvas.

The demon smiled sorrowfully as it spoke.

Humans are such sad creatures, always seeking power.

"..."

You chose incorrectly, Guren Ichinose. You shouldn't have come to this place.

"..."

For my own sake, though, I am happy that you are here. As your desire, your lust for power turns to madness, it will sustain me. I feed on such emotions...

"..."

Do you crave power?

"I do," answered Guren.

Even if you must sacrifice something else to gain it?

"Yes."

You'll be alone. There's no other way. This path is one of madness and carnage. Do you see? Sayuri... Shigure... You're going to kill them. Your first step is to kill them. Embrace your madness.

"...Yes."

Good... Let it go. Let the madness flow from your soul, Guren Ichinose. And I will grant you power!

For a moment, everything grew quiet.

And then Guren's consciousness returned to reality.

The chimera was standing before him. Three of its deadly legs were hurtling straight for him. Moments ago, they would have spelled certain doom for Guren.

But now...

"Choke on this!" Guren shouted.

He swung Mahiru's demon sword in a broad arc.

With one swing it was over. Guren's strike split the creature completely in two. For a moment, it seemed like even the space behind the chimera was ripped asunder.

"Ha! Amazing, just as I expected!" shouted Mahiru ecstatically. She was still standing behind Guren.

Guren wheeled around, turning his attention on her.

Mahiru just laughed.

"Ah...hahaha... I bet you want to kill me too. You can't control it, can you, the impulse to destroy?"

"..."

"You want to kill your friends here too, don't you? You want to string the boys up by their innards, don't you? Rape the girls and then twist their heads off their shoulders? That's the one problem with that sword... The demon ends up possessing the wielder, turning his soul murderous and dark."

Guren raised the sword into the air. He looked down at his feet. Sayuri and Shigure were there. He was about to kill them both.

"Don't worry, Guren," said Mahiru. "Killing these five should temporarily quench the sword's thirst for blood. Afterward, we can search for a way to control the cursed gear together. If we work together, I'm sure the two of us will be able to perfect this power. No one will be able to stand against us. No one will ever get in our way again."

Mahiru let that sink in for a moment before going on.

"For now, all you have to worry about is killing them. Take the next step forward, Guren. Claim your power."

Guren's grip on the sword tightened.

Kill Shigure.

Kill Sayuri.

Kill Mito.

Kill Norito.

Kill Shinya.

Guren knew killing them would fill him with indescribable pleasure. His whole world would change. Everything that had been holding him back—convention, sympathy, love—would crumble away. He would be free. Only the simple desire for power would remain.

"Now I see," muttered Guren. "So this is power..."

"Yes, Guren, power," said Mahiru. "This is what you and I have been searching for."

Guren turned to face her. Mahiru. The urge to ravage and slaughter her rose in him. But first his bodyguards. They would be so much easier to kill, like lambs to the slaughter. The two had been by his side for nearly as long as he could remember.

The demon spoke from deep within his soul.

Cross that line, it said. *Cross it now.*

A line…

But what did it represent, Guren wondered in a daze. Was it his own humanity? Once he crossed that line, would he cease to be human and live a life of carnage instead?

Perhaps that was what was necessary.

In order to destroy the Hiragis.

In order to gain power, to gain freedom.

But all that would come in time. First…

Destroy them all.

Guren swung the sword downward, at the demon's command. He would kill Sayuri first. His strike was aimed toward her neck.

His left hand suddenly twitched, raising Hoarfrost into the air.

Hoarfrost was the enchanted sword Guren had received from Kureto. Compared to Mahiru's demon sword, it barely deserved to be called enchanted.

There was no way Hoarfrost could stop the demon blade. It didn't have to, though. Instead, Guren intercepted his own right arm with Hoarfrost's edge. It struck near the joint.

The blade was incredibly sharp.

There was no sound. Not even pain. But Guren's arm was sliced cleanly off.

"Ahh?!"

Mahiru screamed in surprise from behind Guren.

"Stop it, what are you doing?!"

Guren's severed right arm sailed through the air, the cursed sword

still tight in its grasp. Guren pressed his left hand to the wound, trying to stem the fountain of blood that spurted from his arm.

"N-Ngh... Dammit," groaned Guren. "I can finally think clearly again..."

He fell to one knee. He was losing too much blood. Far, far too much blood.

He shouted at his followers.

"Shigure, Sayuri... Dammit, open your eyes! We have to run away!"

They didn't open their eyes.

Mahiru ran toward Guren in a panic. She picked up his severed arm and pressed it stupidly against his spurting wound.

"W-We have to be quick... If the demon's regenerative ability is still inside you, the arm might reattach..."

Mahiru squeezed the arm together. Just as she had said, the two severed ends began to writhe against each other grotesquely. It was monstrous and inhuman, but the arm seemed to be regenerating.

"No, no, why isn't it attaching yet? At least the nerves...please..."

She seemed ready to burst into tears. She turned on Guren suddenly, angrily.

"What were you thinking?!" she shouted.

Tears welled up in her eyes and began to spill down her cheek. Mahiru had lost nearly every last trace of humanity, but still she cried for Guren.

Guren stared into her face. It was only inches from his own.

"Mahiru..."

"..."

"You've got to stop this research into cursed gear. It's no good."

"..."

"This is the kind of power that will make fools of us. It will control us."

"...You're wrong."

"No, I'm not. We'll think of another way. There's got to be something else, another path..."

"There isn't!"

Tears were still spilling down her face as she shouted.

She was angry that Guren was rejecting the path she had chosen. But in her heart, Guren suspected, a part of her knew he was right.

Guren peered into her face.

"There must be a way," he said. "I'll find it."

"You're lying. You can't do anything, you're powerless."

"That will change."

"You're lying! You're lying! It's all lies, don't try to make me feel better…"

Guren reached his left hand out toward Mahiru's heaving shoulder. He gripped her tight.

"This time, I'll protect you," he said. "Come with me, Mahiru."

Mahiru lifted her face up to stare at Guren. She was still crying. Her eyes trembled with a mix of fear and hope.

"If you want to protect me… If you really want to protect me… then come with me, Guren. Kill your followers, kill your friends, and come with—"

Guren cut her off. "Enough," he said. "You're coming with me."

Mahiru laughed, shyly. Her tears finally stopped.

"Heh… You always were dashing, Guren."

"…"

"I wish I was the kind of girl who could be swept off her feet like that. I wish I really could just go with you. I know I'd be so happy if I did."

"Then do it, Mahiru."

Mahiru shook her head and stood up.

"I can't, Guren. You know that. That's just child's play, a silly dream. This is reality."

Mahiru stepped backward. It was just half a step. In her hand she held the demonic sword. The one Guren had cut his own arm off to be rid of.

"I'm trying to make it so that those dreams can come true," Guren persisted.

"That's why your progress has been so slow, Guren. You're still playing a child's game."

"Hmph. Haven't you ever heard of 'The Tortoise and the Hare'? If you keep rushing forward at this pace you're going to destroy yourself."

Mahiru smiled dismissively. Destruction was old news to her.

"You'll just have to save me first, won't you, Guren?"

"I can save you now. Throw away the sword and come with me."

"Ha! Pretty words. But are words all you've got to persuade me? What about strength? Why don't you just knock the sword out of my hands, grab me in your arms, and make me listen to you?"

"..."

"That's right. Because you can't yet, can you? I'm so much stronger than you that it's almost heartbreaking. I guess that's what makes me the hare. Hurtling headlong toward destruction. I'm still waiting for my tortoise prince, Guren. Try and save me if you like, before it's too late."

She laughed, gripping Guren's right hand tightly in her own. Guren could feel her hand.

But it was the arm he had cut off only moments before.

"Wha?!"

Guren stared down at the arm in shock. It really had reattached itself. The wound where the arm had been severed writhed in an eerie black pattern. The torn skin was attempting to knit itself back together.

"It worked," said Mahiru, "but be more careful in the future. The arm only reattached itself because traces of the demon's power remained in you. Don't expect it to happen again. Of course, if you were to wield the sword one more time..."

"That sword isn't meant for human hands."

Mahiru laughed seductively again.

"No, no it isn't," she gloated. "But you're not really human anymore. Could a human arm reattach itself after it had been sliced off? The demon has already tainted a piece of your soul."

"..."

"In the end, you'll fall. Your heart will grow black and twisted, just like mine. Do you see, Guren? We just can't stay apart. We'll keep each other company on the road to hell."

As she spoke, Mahiru stepped further away from Guren. Her eyes shone with happiness and affection as she stared at him.

"For now, though, I have to say goodbye. I wish I could kiss you before I go, but there are other things I need to do."

With that, Mahiru broke into a dash.

She swooped up one half of the chimera that Guren had cut in two, planning to take the creature's body away with her.

Guren suddenly realized that someone else was already there, picking up the other half of the chimera.

"..."

No, not someone else. Something else.

At first glance he looked human, but he was clearly anything but.

He had skin as white as alabaster and a perfectly chiseled face. He was dressed in ostentatious clothing that was embellished all over with ornaments. The clothes looked like something a noble might wear.

He also had long silver hair and blood-red eyes.

"A vampire?!" shouted Guren.

In a flash, Mahiru drew the sword at her waist.

The silver-haired vampire drew his own sword in response. The sword's blade was strange. It almost looked as if it were made of glass.

The two struck, and the glass sword and Mahiru's demon katana crashed against each other.

As the blades touched, a dark miasma erupted from Mahiru's blade, sweeping over the vampire.

The vampire, however, easily withstood the assault. He grinned in amusement.

"Heh... I didn't know human demonology had come so far. You're much stronger than you look, aren't you?"

Mahiru glared back at the vampire.

"The way you're dressed... Are you a vampire noble?"

"Oh, it seems you know something about vampire society as well. Indeed. Ferid Bathory, Progenitor of the Seventh Rank. Though I doubt a mere human can appreciate the importance of that title."

The vampire, who was named Ferid, drew back his sword as he spoke.

He struck suddenly.

"Ngh!"

Mahiru moved in response, and their swords clashed.

Guren was able to follow their first five strikes, but after that he was lost.

Their movements were too fast.

Mahiru suddenly changed tactics, attempting to retreat backward.

"Aww, running away already?" said Ferid.

As he spoke, Ferid flicked his leg out effortlessly. The kick connected with the side of Mahiru's head. There was so much force behind it that for a moment Guren thought Mahiru's head would be ripped clean off her shoulders. Instead, tossed off her feet, she flipped over once in the air and fell.

"Game over!" cried Ferid in a sing-song voice.

He raised his sword over his head.

Guren dashed forward. He leapt in front of Mahiru, brandishing the enchanted sword he had received from Kureto. He still couldn't move his right arm very well, so he gripped it in his left hand and used his right to hold the hilt steady.

Ferid laughed.

"Farewell, humans," he said, swinging his sword downward.

Ferid's strike hit Hoarfrost with incredible force. Guren leapt backward as the blow struck, but even so he was unable to fully parry the blow.

The bones in Guren's left hand—the one which held Hoarfrost—shattered in several places on impact. The sword itself was knocked backward, and the flat of the blade struck against his chest, breaking several more bones. Guren's body collided with Mahiru as she struggled to her feet behind him. The two were thrown like ragdolls, only landing a couple of dozen feet away.

"Ngh…"

Guren collapsed in the dirt, unable to stand back up. He could barely move. The damage was too severe.

"Guren… Are you alive…?"

It was Mahiru. Guren raised his head to see her staring down at him. She looked worried.

"Forget about me," Guren told her. "Just keep your eyes on the fight. I won't be able to block another of his strikes."

Mahiru's face twisted up in embarrassment.

"It looks like he's already lost interest in us," she said.

Guren turned his eyes toward Ferid. It was true. The vampire wasn't even looking their way.

Guren shouldn't have been surprised. All vampires were like that. They saw people as no more than livestock and rarely ever interfered in human affairs. The humans on the surface and their petty squabbles over power meant little to vampires. They had their own eternity to mind, deep underground.

And yet…

"…what are you doing here?!" Mahiru shouted at the vampire.

Ferid raised his head up from what he was doing.

"Huh? You're still alive? That's amazing. Are you sure you two are really humans?"

"Answer me. What did you come here to do?"

"I heard that you humans have been poking your nose into research beyond your ken," he said. "I came to investigate."

Ferid looked down.

One half of the chimera's body lay at his feet. He gave it a kick, tossing it into the air. It flew up and up before coming back down and landing on his shoulder with a thud.

"This is frightening stuff, you know," he said. "I have no idea what you humans were thinking, meddling in this sort of thing. If you keep playing with forbidden magic like this you'll bring the whole world crashing down on our heads."

Ferid turned his eyes back toward Mahiru.

"That sword of yours is a kind of madness all on its own. The way you humans crave power is disgusting."

Mahiru brandished her sword in response. She smiled grimly at the vampire.

"So you're here to punish us greedy humans?" she said.

Ferid just laughed.

"I've got no interest in what you humans do. Tear each other apart for all I care. What does it matter to me if the pigs start feeding on each other? Assuming you two really are human. Seeing how you survived a blow from my sword, I'm not so sure. I suppose it doesn't really matter either way, though."

"…"

Ferid turned his back on them with a shrug. The difference in strength between them was so great that he didn't need to worry about what they might do.

Mahiru made no move. Even with a surprise attack from behind, the chance of her defeating him was…slim. Mahiru was just as aware of that as Ferid was.

"Dammit…if I could only perfect the cursed gear…" she muttered bitterly.

She returned her sword to her waist.

Guren glanced down at the sheathed sword. Apparently, it still hadn't been perfected. Obviously, the fact that its power couldn't be controlled completely was a problem. But Guren suspected Mahiru was referring to something else.

"Are you saying the cursed gear can be even more powerful than it is now?" he asked.

Mahiru smiled faintly.

"I'm afraid there's not enough time left for me to explain…" she said. "But remember what I said before. In the end, you'll choose the same path that I have. The demon is already inside you."

Mahiru ran over to the remaining half of the chimera's body, picking it up in her arms.

The sound of a helicopter suddenly intruded from overhead.

Mahiru glanced up at the sky.

"The Brotherhood of a Thousand Nights is coming, Guren. They've realized the chimera is dead... You should run before it's too—"

Mahiru broke off, mid-sentence. Looking down, she realized that several dozen *fuda* had been placed on the ground. They formed a barrier around her.

"My, my... When did you wake up, Shinya?" she asked.

Guren sensed someone behind him. He didn't need to look. He knew it was Shinya.

Shinya grinned at Mahiru as he answered.

"I could hardly sleep while my fiancée is getting chummy with her ex-boyfriend, could I?"

"In other words, you were awake the entire time?"

"That's right."

"So you were just pretending to be knocked out?"

"I had no choice. If you thought I was awake, would you have been willing to reveal your true intentions?"

"You're useless to me, Shinya."

"Hey, I do what I can. You can't fault a guy for trying, can you?"

Shinya crept up next to Guren. The smile was still plastered across his face.

"Guren," he whispered.

"What?"

"Let's work together. We have to stop her from leaving."

"..."

"If we let her go now, she'll destroy herself. You can see that, can't you?"

Of course he could. What Mahiru was doing was beyond dangerous. It was leading her straight to ruin. It was even possible that they were already too late.

Guren touched his own right arm where it had reattached itself.

The arm had regenerated. They were dealing with a power beyond the realm of humanity.

"Hey, Shinya?" Guren said, leaning in close and staring at Mahiru as he spoke.

"Yeah?"

"Are you really that in love with Mahiru?"

Shinya laughed.

"Who knows? Maybe I am. After all, I was raised as a puppet, all for her sake… But what about you?"

"I forgot about her a long time ago."

"Ha. You could have fooled me."

"I am interested in that sword, though. And in what she knows about the chimera experiments…"

Guren stood up. He gripped Hoarfrost in his right hand, whose strength had already returned. Whether that was due to the demon's curse or not, Guren didn't know.

The fingers of his left hand and the bones in his chest, however, had been broken afterward by the vampire. They still hadn't recovered. Apparently, the power of the cursed gear had already left his body by that point.

As a result, Guren held Hoarfrost with only one hand.

"You're not leaving, Mahiru," he said.

Mahiru stared back at him. She laughed in amusement.

"You know you can't stop me," she said.

"…"

"The difference in strength between us is still too—"

Guren suddenly dashed forward.

"Enough talk!" he shouted, swinging the sword with his right hand in a surprise attack.

As he did so, the *fuda* that Shinya had scattered on the ground shot upward and twined around Mahiru's legs, holding her fast.

It was only for a moment, though. The difference in strength between Shinya and Mahiru was too great for him to restrain her.

Mahiru smiled dryly.

"Hopefully you two are stronger the next time we meet," she said. "It could be fun."

Mahiru began to move backward, stepping through Shinya's barrier as if it were nothing.

But Guren's real target had never been Mahiru. He already knew that he couldn't defeat her in a swordfight.

He had something else in mind.

His real target was the half of the chimera corpse that Mahiru held in her hands. Guren's blade easily pierced its flesh. He carried through with the slash, slicing off a chunk. It went flying into the air behind them.

"Ahh!" gasped Mahiru.

She had been caught off guard by Guren's move.

"So that's what you wanted," she said. "You know I can't let the Hiragis get their hands on that."

"Don't worry," said Guren. "I won't give it to them."

"In that case, it's all yours... It doesn't really matter to me now, since I'm betraying both sides."

"Mahiru."

"What is it?"

"Enjoy this while you can. I'm going to catch up to you before too long."

Mahiru smiled. She seemed pleased.

"I'll be waiting," she said.

With that, she spun around and dashed off. She took her half of the chimera's body with her.

Guren stared at her back as she ran away. When he finally turned around, Shinya was already leaning over the piece of the chimera that Guren had sliced off. He picked it up.

"Hand that over, or else..." said Guren, brandishing his sword again.

If it turned out that Shinya was actually an ally of the Hiragis, and was planning on giving them the piece of the chimera, then Guren would have to fight one more battle before the day was over.

He would have to kill Shinya Hiragi...

Shinya turned toward him and smiled.

"Don't tell me you still want to fight? You look like you've just been through a meat grinder."

"Against you, that would just make for an even fight."

"Don't be so quick to underestimate me."

Suddenly, Shinya disappeared from sight. It was an illusion. Shinya's physical abilities weren't amazing, but he was able to use almost every school of magic with unparalleled skill.

Guren closed his eyes and searched for Shinya's presence with his mind.

Suddenly he sensed Shinya behind him. Guren brandished his sword in that direction before Shinya could move any closer.

However, Guren stopped in mid-swing. It wasn't Shinya behind him. It was just the piece of the chimera.

Shinya had tossed it his way.

The illusion dissipated. The real Shinya was already running in the other direction, toward the others who lay unconscious on the ground. He began trying to revive them.

The piece of the chimera Guren had cut off was the tip of one of its bladelike claws. Guren picked it up off the ground.

The issue was settled.

By tossing Guren the sample, Shinya was admitting Guren's claim to it. In other words, he had agreed that the Ichinose Clan should investigate and research the chimera.

The others—Norito, Mito, Sayuri, and Shigure—finally began to come to. When Guren's two guards saw his broken arm and the wounds all over his body, they rushed toward him in shock.

Mito and Norito approached next, eager to flee with everyone else.

While they spoke, Guren deliberated.

"…"

He was trying to decide whether or not to kill Mito and Norito.

If he killed them both he could disappear without a trace. It would be some time before the Hiragis picked up on his trail. It might even buy the Ichinoses enough time to research the chimera's claw.

Killing them was the smart thing to do. Was it not?

Guren gripped Hoarfrost tighter in his right hand.

As he did so, Mito reached hers out gently and touched Guren's chest, staring at his wounds.

"You…you saved us again, didn't you?"

No, thought Guren. *I almost killed you.*

"Man, I can't believe you saved us again," said Norito, joining them. "I don't know where we'd be without you."

What's wrong with these idiots? thought Guren. *Can't they figure out what really happened?*

"Next time," said Mito, oblivious to Guren's discomfort, "it'll be me risking my life to protect yours. I swear it."

Shinya leaned in and whispered into Guren's ear.

"You could never be like Mahiru, Guren…"

"…"

"But I don't think that's a weakness. After all, if you were willing to make the same choice that she made, we wouldn't be trying to save her in the first place. Would we now?"

"…"

"You know I'm right, don't you, Guren?"

Guren gave an exasperated sigh.

"All I know is that I'm tired…" he said.

Guren released his grip on Hoarfrost. The sword sank blade-first into the ground.

As soon as he let the sword go, Guren felt the strength drain from his body. Apparently, he had suffered a lot more damage than he'd realized. Maybe it was all the blood loss from cutting his arm off, maybe it was the blow from the vampire.

Pain suddenly flared up in his right arm where it had fused together. The pain was almost blinding.

Guren glanced down at his arm. He thought he could see an inky black shadow seeping from where the cut had been. He could feel darkness creeping into his arteries and coursing through his veins.

He collapsed onto one knee.

Sayuri and Shigure rushed toward him in shock.

"Master Guren!" they shouted. But their voices already seemed far away.

Deep in the heart of enemy territory, Guren finally passed out.

◆◆◆

I dreamt.

It was a strange dream.

In my dream, something was standing in the middle of a deep shadow.

The something spoke.

Tell me the truth, Guren. You wanted to kill them, didn't you?

I heard glee in its voice.

It stared at me hungrily as it spoke.

Norito, Mito, Shinya, Sayuri, and Shigure. You wanted to cut them up into little pieces, didn't you?

The shadows seemed to leap and tremble with the voice.

Don't worry, you'll get your chance soon enough. Before long you won't think twice about taking a human life. Not even the lives of your precious friends.

I listened to the voice.

I stared into the shadows and listened.

"Who are you?" I asked.

I am you, the thing answered.

"Who are you?"

You are me.

"Who are—"

Enough! I am a demon. A thing of ambition and revenge. A demon, just like you.

"..."

I am already a part of you. Listen to my voice. Every time your heart beats, we grow more entwined.

"..."

Listen to me, listen to my voice. You've entered a new world, just like Mahiru. Welcome, Guren. Welcome to the abyss. I've been waiting for a human just like you, someone strong and full of desire.

"..."

Wake up, now. But don't forget, you are no longer human. You are not human. Desire and hatred. Love and sorrow. Overwhelming ambition. Together, we can crush this vile world!

So screamed the demon's voice…my own voice.

"Master Guren…?"

It was a girl's voice.

Guren's eyes fluttered open.

"Master Guren? Master Guren…?"

She kept calling Guren's name. He recognized the voice.

It was Sayuri.

Guren turned his eyes in the direction of the voice, finally realizing where he was.

He wasn't in Shibuya, where the school was located.

And he wasn't in Ueno, where he had lost consciousness.

He was in a secluded village—crouched in the mountains of Aichi Prefecture—where only members of the Ichinose Clan or the Order of the Imperial Moon lived. Guren was lying in one of the bedrooms in a compound located at the village's center.

Sayuri stood on the other side of the sliding paper doors leading into the room. Just like she once had many years ago. Any time Guren was badly injured during training growing up, Sayuri and Shigure had taken turns watching over him as he recovered.

Sayuri opened the door just a crack.

Guren turned his eyes toward the door and attempted to sit up.

Sayuri's eyes opened wide.

"You…You're awake!" she cried, overjoyed.

She rushed into the room. Unable to contain herself, she ran over to Guren and hugged him tightly.

She nearly smothered him in the process.

Guren felt a sharp pain in his chest where Sayuri's weight pressed down on him. His ribs were broken. His left arm felt heavy, too. The whole arm, not just the hand, was covered in a plaster cast.

"You wouldn't open your eyes, I was so worried!" cried Sayuri, nearly in tears. "It's been a month... You've been in a coma for a whole month, Master Guren. Everyone said you'd probably never wake up... but...but...I never believed them!"

So he'd been out for a whole month...

The tears in Sayuri's eyes began to spill over and her face twisted up in sobs. She couldn't hold back any longer. She buried her face in Guren's chest, trying to hide her tears...

"Waahhhh!"

...but as soon as she hid her face, the crying began in earnest.

Guren stared at the top of her head as she cried.

"..."

A month, he thought. *A whole month.*

That meant it was already July.

A month was a long time. A long time to be out of the game. With the way things were unfolding lately, a month was too much time to lose.

Guren hoisted himself into a sitting position. Sayuri's head was still pressed against his chest.

He wanted to know what time it was, but there was no clock in the room. Judging from the light coming through the half-open door, it was still the middle of the night.

"What day is it?" Guren asked.

"Waa...ahhh..."

Sayuri continued to sob against Guren's chest.

Guren grimaced. He stroked Sayuri's long hair, trying to soothe her, before asking again.

"Sayuri, what day is it?"

She finally pulled her head away. For some reason, the expression on her face seemed angry.

"What does it matter anymore, what day it is?"

"Huh?"

"Please, you can't put yourself in danger anymore, Master Guren! I can't take it. I've already worried enough for at least two lifetimes!"

"..."

"Can't you just stay here?" she said. "You can live the rest of your life in peace. A quiet life, just like your father's, away from all power. What's wrong with that?"

A peaceful, quiet life...

Sayuri was right, that was also an option. He could bow his head to the Hiragis. He could tremble in fear like a slave. The choice was his to make.

But he just couldn't do it. Guren had never been able to think in that way, not even when he was little.

"I know it's dangerous sometimes, being by my side," Guren said. "If you don't like being with me, I could release you from my service—"

"I didn't say that!" Sayuri interrupted him. She was clearly angry this time.

"Huh?"

"That's not what I meant at all!"

She seemed ready to cry again. She glared at Guren, but her cheeks blushed bright red.

"Master Guren, do you..."

Sayuri trailed off, mid-sentence.

"Do I what?" Guren said.

Sayuri remained silent.

"What is it? Tell me what you were going to say."

Her face twisted up uncomfortably. She seemed to be having trouble getting the words out.

"Master Guren, do you still..."

"Yeah?"

"...love Mahiru Hiragi?"

The moment Sayuri said it, tears began spilling down her face again. It was as if all the tears she had stored up so far were finally bursting free.

"Is that why you're trying to get stronger? So you can get Mahiru Hiragi back one day?"

Her voice shook as she said it.

So that's what Sayuri thought. Guren stared at her.

She buried her head in Guren's chest once more, apparently embarrassed to have him stare at her.

"I-I'm sorry..." she said. "I shouldn't have said that...or cried like that..."

Guren shook his head.

"Don't apologize."

"B-But..."

"You're right to complain. If I made you think I've been doing everything for selfish reasons—"

"That's not it, either!" Sayuri cut him off again.

"It's...not?"

"No...it isn't. I wasn't accusing you of anything."

"So what are you saying?"

Sayuri buried her head in Guren's chest and sobbed again. This time it sounded almost like she was groaning. She made the noise several more times before speaking.

"I-It's just..."

"Yeah?"

"I'm jealous... If you're still so in love with Mahiru Hiragi then... then how can I..."

"..."

"...how can I ever hope to compete?"

"Huh?"

Guren sighed.

"So that's what all this is about?" he said in an exasperated tone.

Sayuri jerked her head up in surprise.

"Augh! Wh-What do you mean, 'all this'? It took me a lot of courage to say that…"

Guren frowned.

"Maybe you forgot, but I just woke up from a coma. Maybe you could save all this nonsense for another time?"

"'N-Nonsense'! I-I-I mean, I know this isn't the best time for this, but…"

Sayuri suddenly froze. She stared at Guren and her face turned beet red.

"Aughh, what did I just do?!" she shouted. "I think I just confessed to being in love. Noooooooo!"

Even in the middle of the night, Sayuri knew how to be a bother.

Guren nearly burst into laughter. Instead, he just chuckled quietly. Even that hurt his ribs.

Sayuri noticed him wince.

"Ahh, Master Guren! Are you in pain?" she said.

Guren shook his head.

"It's nothing."

"M-Master Guren?"

"What is it this time?"

Sayuri stared straight into Guren's eyes as she spoke.

"Do you think…I could ever be enough to fill the hole in your heart?"

Guren was caught off-guard by her question. What she'd said earlier had been crazy talk. But now Sayuri's expression was serious.

Guren got the impression that Sayuri had resolved in advance on asking him that question when he woke up.

Her face was still beet red with embarrassment, but Guren could see that she was being earnest.

"I'm saying that I love you very much, Master Guren," she said.

Guren stared back at her. Bathed in the moonlight from the half-open door, she looked very beautiful.

If she hadn't been assigned as Guren's bodyguard, she'd probably be living an ordinary life as a high school girl. She was stylish, she was intelligent, and to top it off she was also attractive.

She could be doing much better for herself than a life of violence and bloodshed.

Guren, on the other hand, could find himself dead at any given moment. He couldn't understand why she should fall for someone like him in the first place.

"You really are a fool," he said.

Sayuri laughed.

"I don't know. It's occurred to me that loving you might be foolish. But in all the time we've been together, that thought has only occurred to me…let's see…maybe two times?"

"Haha. Is that so?"

"It is."

"I can't give you what you want, Sayuri," said Guren.

Sayuri's face collapsed instantly.

"I-I see… Is it because I'm too…"

"No. It's not that I dislike you, Sayuri."

"Huh?!"

"But I don't have the time for a relationship. I'm already too busy following my own ambitions. You know, the ones you wish I didn't have? You should give up on me."

"Ahh…th-then, that means, I still have a chance?"

"No, I'm telling you to give up…"

"But you don't dislike me, right?"

"No…"

"And that's pretty much the same as saying you do like me, right?"

"Hold on a second!"

"I've got an idea. For now, why don't you just stroke my head a little bit longer?!"

Sayuri leaned in to hug Guren tight.

"Stop right there, Sayuri!"

The sliding door suddenly banged open and Shigure came stomping in. She gave Sayuri a swift kick straight to her backside.

"Eek!"

Sayuri went flying off of Guren and rolled onto the floor. Shigure narrowed her eyes and stared at her.

"Keeping him all to yourself?" she said in a low voice.

"Aughh…"

"As your friend, I was willing to keep watch while you confessed your love to Guren. But this is just going too far now, isn't it?"

"B-B-But, Shigure, I just wanted Master Guren to stroke my head one more time."

"But nothing! Master Guren has been in a coma for a whole month, remember? Show a little more care."

"Ah…o-of course."

Sayuri nodded.

Shigure turned toward Guren.

"How do you feel, Master Guren?"

"I'm fine," Guren answered.

To prove it, he sat up straight and stretched his upper body. He was actually able to move his muscles much better than expected. After a month in a coma he should have been weak. But he felt just fine.

"…"

Guren glanced down at his right arm. It had reattached itself perfectly. He could move it freely—even the fingertips. He made a claw with his hand and clutched at the tatami mat beneath his sheets. His fingers sank easily into the fibers.

Mahiru's words echoed in his head.

But you're not really human anymore. Could a human arm reattach itself after it had been sliced off? The demon…

…already tainted a part of his soul. That's what Mahiru had said.

Guren stared at his right arm once more and stood up. He was dressed in a light gown, like a yukata. He rolled up the right sleeve. There was no sign of scarring where the arm had fused together.

"What happened to my arm?" he asked.

Shigure answered.

"It's broken in several places, but it's been healing at a remarkable pace. They think they'll be able to take the cast off in another two weeks."

Shigure was talking about his left arm. Apparently she was completely unaware of any issues with his right arm. The injury must have disappeared by the time he'd lost consciousness.

It was unusual how quickly his bones were healing, as well. The vampire had damaged his left hand pretty badly. The recovery should have been long and painful. But Shigure had just said that the cast could come off in two weeks. It didn't seem normal for a human to recover so quickly.

"Bring me a phone," said Guren. "A secure one."

Shigure pulled a mobile phone from one of her pockets. It had probably never been used before. She always kept several such phones on hand.

Guren dialed the number for the Imperial Moon Occult Research Laboratory.

"Lord Guren, I'm glad to hear you're awake."

"I hope I didn't worry you. I'm calling because I have a request."

"What might it be?"

"Are we still conducting any research into cursed gear?"

"Cursed gear? Isn't that magic supposed to be infeasible—"

Guren cut off the researcher. "Someone has succeeded. I've come into contact with the gear, and there's a chance I've been infected."

"…"

The man suddenly grew tense.

Guren could sense his nervousness, even over the phone.

"We're going to do a study. Your guinea pig will be me. I want you to analyze the curse so that we can try to develop our own gear."

"…I understand. We'll begin preparations."

"Do it immediately."

"Yes, sir."

Guren hung up. He turned toward Sayuri and Shigure.

"I have a question. What happened to the piece of the chimera I was holding? Did the Hiragis get their hands on it?"

Sayuri and Shigure cocked their heads in confusion.

"A piece of the chimera? I don't remember you holding anything…"

Guren knew immediately who had taken the sample: Shinya.

"Sayuri, do you have Shinya Hiragi's number?"

Sayuri nodded. She gave him the number, and Guren dialed.

"Who is it?"

Guren didn't answer. Instead he hung up.

Shinya called back immediately, but from a different phone number.

"Well, who is it then? And you don't have to be so careful. The first line was already secure."

"Is that because you're not important enough to the Hiragis for them to bother spying on you?"

"Ahh, Guren, is that you? You're finally awake?"

"Yeah."

"We thought you were dead. Mito even cried."

"Ha! That works out well, actually."

"Anyway, I think I know why you're calling. It's about the chimera piece, isn't it?"

"Exactly. Did you take it? Or did the Hiragis steal it?"

"I've kept it hidden."

"I want it back."

"Haha. I figured you were gonna say that. But to be honest, I doubt I can get it all the way to Aichi Prefecture without either the Hiragis or the Brotherhood of a Thousand Nights catching on. You're gonna have to come back to Tokyo, Guren. You won't find any answers while you're hiding away in the country."

"…"

"By the way, the Thousand Nights contacted me. Mahiru betrayed them, and they wanted to know if I had any information. I think they're willing to share some of what they know about cursed gear and the chimerae."

"…"

"Come on, Guren, this is our chance to take down the Hiragis from in—"

"You talk too much, you fool," said Guren, hanging up the phone.

◆

Another ten days passed.

It was already mid-July.

It was almost time for summer vacation to begin.

Guren was finally returning to First Shibuya High School. He was late. Very late. It was 8:15.

Morning homeroom had already begun for Guren's class. The teacher, Saia Aiuchi, was speaking with her back to the blackboard.

Guren opened the door and stepped inside.

Ms. Aiuchi and the students all turned toward Guren and stared.

Mito and Norito, of course, were also in the class.

Mito's eyes widened in surprise. She looked like she wasn't sure whether to laugh out loud or burst into tears.

A huge grin spread across Norito's face.

Guren ignored them. He walked to the back of the classroom and sat down at his desk.

Shinya was sitting at the desk next to his.

"Welcome back," he said.

"Get bent."

"It sure took you long enough."

"I had things to do."

"I bet you did. I've got some pretty interesting things to fill you in on."

"When are you gonna learn not to talk so much?"

"I don't know. When are you gonna learn some manners?"

"Ugh."

"Heh. Anyway, while you were busy getting your beauty sleep a war's been brewing. We've got a lot of work to do…"

Guren let his eyes roam over the classroom before turning his attention out the window.

Outside, the sky was clear and blue and reassuring.

The temperature that day was high. It seemed like summer was already underway.

But if what Mahiru said was true…

If the world was really going to come to an end at Christmas, this summer would be the last peaceful one Guren would ever see.

Guren gazed at the scorching sunshine as it poured through the window panes.

"The war began for me when I was just a little kid," he said.

"What's that?" asked Shinya.

But Guren didn't elaborate.

Instead, he just continued to peer out the window at the lazy summer sky.

"I hate the heat," Guren Ichinose moaned.

Meanwhile, time continued to slip past.

Closer to the end.

To a new kingdom of blood.

No one hoped for that day to come.

No one even imagined that it was in store.

Yet the world continued to hurtle, inexorably, toward the end.

Later, some would say that mankind had been too proud, or too complacent.

Others would say that humanity's sin had been too great and that perdition was inevitable.

This, however, is the true story of that end.

A story of those last days, before the demise of mankind. A story of their final pains and struggles, before the trumpets of the apocalypse sounded, and the hammer of fate came crashing down upon the world.

Thank you for reading book two of the *Seraph of the End* novels!

What did you think?

The manga shows the world after it has already come to an end, while the novels show the time leading up to the end—but since we already know from the manga that the world ends at Christmas, the story barrels along pretty mercilessly, doesn't it?

But how the world comes to an end is still obscure.

Why does it end?

Who was responsible?

What happened afterward?

The complex web of relationships will slowly grow clearer. A lot of characters from the manga have also made fleeting appearances. Keep reading to find out what happens next. I hope you find the story as exciting as I do!

There's one more thing about writing a story where we already know the world is going to come to an end: it means my schedule also comes to an end! You might have noticed that my bio is the same as it was last time…which means it isn't an update at all!

Here's a funny conversation I had with my editor:

Editor: Hello, Mr. Kagami? We're still waiting for your bio…

Me: Uhhhhhh, oh. I guess you need that. I'm sorry, I'm sorry, I know.

Editor: No, don't worry, it can be the same as last time. In fact, we don't have much time left, so why don't we just go with that? Just this once, okay?

Me: Uhhhhhhh…

Editor: Then it's settled! Everything's fine. And then you can talk about how they're the same in your afterword. That kills two birds with one stone!

Me: GREAT IDEA!

And so that's why the bio is the same for both books. It's definitely not because I'm lazy. I just thought it would be a great idea if I could tie it in with the afterword…okay, you got me. I actually just ran out of time. Sorry!

By the way, I recently got to write a one-off *Seraph of the End* special for Weekly Shonen Jump magazine.

It feels a little weird to write about Shueisha/Jump in the afterword to a title being published by Kodansha. But I figure with stuff coming out from different companies, we can all work together to support each other. So if you haven't yet, check it out!

Until next time, keep reading, friends!

Takaya Kagami
Website:
"Healthy Living with Takaya Kagami"
http://www.kagamitakaya.com

TAKAYA KAGAMI

Self-intro. I'm the author of *The Legend of the Legendary Heroes* and *A Dark Rabbit Has Seven Lives*. I love to—I want to say "play the guitar," but I haven't done much of that lately. I want to say "go for a drive," but I haven't done much of that lately. I hate deadlines. Please treat me well!

YAMATO YAMAMOTO

Mangaka and illustrator. The comics series is being published as well. Please check it out, too.